OPEN SEASON

FOR

MURDER

A MAC FARADAY MYSTERY

BY

LAUREN CARR

OPEN SEASON FOR MURDER

For information call: 304-995-1295
or Email: writerlaurencarr@gmail.com

Designed by Acorn Book Services

Publication Managed by Acorn Book Services
www.acornbookservices.com
acornbookservices@gmail.com
304-995-1295

Cover designed by Todd Aune
Spokane, Washington
www.projetoonline.com

ISBN-13: 978-0692437520
ISBN-10: 0692437525

Published in the United States of America

To Everyone Who Has a Past

OPEN SEASON

FOR

MURDER

A MAC FARADAY MYSTERY

Cast of Characters

(in order of appearance)

Ashton Piedmont: Last seen five years ago, swimming naked in the dark chilly waters of Deep Creek Lake.

Carlisle Green: Billionaire heiress. She was the last one to see Ashton Piedmont alive. Unfortunately, she has no memory of that night—including whether or not she had killed her.

Gloria Lander: Carlisle Green's "difficult" neighbor.

Parker Lander: Gloria Lander's husband. He tried to keep the peace between his wife and their party girl neighbor that night.

Mac Faraday: Retired homicide detective. On the day his divorce became final, he inherited $270 million and an estate on Deep Creek Lake from his birth mother, Robin Spencer.

Archie Monday: Former editor and research assistant to world-famous mystery author Robin Spencer. She is now Mac Faraday's wife.

Gnarly: Mac Faraday's German shepherd. Another part of his inheritance from Robin Spencer. Gnarly used to belong to the United States Army, who refuses to talk about him.

Robin Spencer: Mac Faraday's late birth mother and world-famous mystery author. As an unwed teenager, she gave him up for adoption. After becoming America's queen of mystery, she found her son and made him her heir. Her ancestors founded Spencer, Maryland, located along the shores of Deep Creek Lake, a resort area in Western Maryland.

Police Chief Patrick O'Callaghan: David's late father. Spencer's legendary police chief. The love of Robin Spencer's life and Mac Faraday's birth father.

Lindsey York: Billionaire heiress—until her father Randolph York disowned her. Now she has to find other ways to keep herself in the lifestyle to which she has become accustomed.

Kassandra Van Dyke: Last year's Playmate of the Year. Her father is grooming her for reality stardom.

David O'Callaghan: Spencer police chief. Son of the late police chief, Patrick O'Callaghan. Mac Faraday's best friend and half-brother.

Tonya: Spencer Police Department Desk Sergeant. She runs things at the police station.

Vincent Van Dyke: One time sex symbol and television star. He's come to Spencer to produce a pilot for a reality television show starring his daughter. He'll do anything for a comeback.

Jeff Ingles: Manager of the Spencer Inn, the five-star resort owned by Mac Faraday, who likes to keep Ingles' life interesting.

Brian Gallagher: Summer intern at the Spencer Inn. The poor college student doesn't have a penny to his name. He's also got a secret.

Ben Fleming: Garrett County Prosecuting Attorney. His wife is Senator Catherine Fleming.

Rudy Crowe: Works in public relations at the Spencer Inn. Mac has trouble remembering his name.

Riva Sinclair: She's tracked her runaway husband Rock Sinclair and his mistress to the Spencer Inn.

Rock Sinclair: Television producer of investigative news shows. Claims he's not having an affair with his lovely protege Jasmine Simpson. Riva Sinclair's estranged husband.

Jasmine Simpson: Rock Sinclair's lovely protege. She wants to be an investigative news producer and television journalist. Claims she was best friends with Ashton Piedmont.

Samuel Nash: Director for Jasmine and Rock's in-depth investigative report.

Catherine Fleming: Ben Fleming's wife and Archie Monday's friend. She is assisting Archie Monday in coordinating the Diablo Ball. She's also a United States Senator from Maryland.

Chelsea Adams: Paralegal for Ben Fleming. David O'Callaghan's girlfriend. Suffering from epilepsy, she has Molly, a service dog trained to sense and warn of seizures.

Dr. Elizabeth Breckenridge: Chair of the medical school at the University of Maryland. She has been considered a pioneer in medicine publishing her research on 3D printing technology for transplant surgery.

A.J. Wagner: Ashton's boyfriend. They went to pre-med together. They grew close after his father, president of the University of Maryland, passed away shortly after her grandfather died.

Corey Haim: A.J. Wagner's best friend. He's very loyal and protective of his friend. How loyal and protective? You're going to find out.

Rachel Breckenridge: Elizabeth's daughter. She grew up with Ashton Piedmont.

Deputy Chief Arthur Bogart (Bogie): Spencer's Deputy Police Chief. David's godfather. Don't let his gray hair and weathered face fool you.

Dr. Dora Washington: Garrett County Medical Examiner.

Hector Langford: Chief of Security at the Spencer Inn. A lean, gray-haired Australian, Hector has been with the Inn for over twenty-five years.

Officers Fletcher, Brewster, and **Zigler:** Officers with the Spencer Police Department. They serve under Police Chief David O'Callaghan.

Gopher: Camera Operator assigned to follow Lindsey York and capture everything on camera.

Betty Cosgrove: Registration desk manager at the Spencer Inn. She may be a grandmother in her forties, but Ben claims her legs are what draws in most of the Spencer Inn's male guests—particularly Randolph York.

Savannah Cosgrove: Young server at the Spencer Inn. A single mother, she is Betty's daughter.

Randolph York: Lindsey York's billionaire father. He is the sole owner of SuperMart, a discount department store chain with stores across the globe. He plays golf with Mac and Ben when he summers in Spencer and spends a lot of time checking out Betty's legs.

The past cannot be changed. The future is yet in your power.

Mary Pickford, film actress

PROLOGUE

Spencer, Maryland - Five Years Ago

The sun's touch on Carlisle Green's face felt like the jab of a sharp knife through her red eyes to the back of her head and down to the base of her skull.

Covering her eyes with an arm, she sat up on the chaise at the end of the boat dock and cursed the sun chastising her as it rose up from behind the ridge on the other side of Deep Creek Lake. Growling at anything and everything, she grabbed her head with both hands. *Another day, another hangover.* She turned around on the deck chair to place her bare feet on the dock.

Voices from the next dock over caught her attention. Twenty yards down the Deep Creek Lake shoreline, she saw two teenage boys staring at her with wide eyes.

"What are you looking at?"

They almost knocked each other into the water to run up the dock and disappear behind the privacy fence next door.

Carlisle didn't get the answer to her question until she pulled herself upright to realize that she was naked. Her clothes were strewn around the dock. It took a minimal amount of rationalization to turn her shame to amusement. *Like they've never seen a naked woman before? What are they? Puritans?*

An empty tequila bottle lay on its side next to the chaise. A foot away rested an empty wine bottle. Shiraz. Carlisle recognized the turquoise blue dress and matching sandals neatly folded and placed on the deck chair.

Ashton.

A vague memory came to her mind—a late night swim off the dock with her best friend.

"Ashton!" Carlisle called out while picking up her own panties and stepping into them.

"Ms. Green!" a shrill voice yelled from the next dock.

Bracing for a fight, Carlisle turned around to face Gloria Lander, the mother of the two boys. Carlisle made no attempt to cover her naked breasts. "What do you want, bitch?"

"It's bad enough my having to keep my sons inside at night because I don't know what you and your idiot friends are doing out here, but last night was the last straw!"

"Last—"

"I just about called the police!" Her voice went up an octave higher. "It was only because Parker, bless his heart, insisted that we be good neighbors—even if you don't know the meaning of the word—that we didn't."

"What the hell are you talking about?"

"Your cat fight after midnight!" Gloria's hands went to her hips. "Don't you remember, lush?"

"Now look here, bitch!"

"When Parker came over to break it up before someone got hurt, you attacked him! I came this close—" she held up her fingers to show her a tiny amount "to calling the police to have you locked up for assault, but Parker wouldn't let—"

"Gloria, that's enough!" Carlisle heard Parker Lander scream from behind the fence. "Let it go!"

"I'm not—" Gloria turned her attention to her husband.

"Stop screaming like a banshee and get inside!"

Gloria's face screwed up. She pointed a finger at Carlisle. "If I hear about you walking around out here without your clothes again, I'm calling the police! I don't care if you are young kids. You're over eighteen and that's old enough to know how to be civilized!" With that, she stormed back inside.

"Bitch!" Carlisle replied. *At least I got the last word in.*

In rebellion, Carlisle didn't bother picking up her clothes. Leaving them and the empty bottles on the deck until she cooled off enough to clean up, she staggered up the dock and into the luxurious round home that had been passed down from generation to generation for over fifty years. *That'll teach them.*

"Ashton!" She assumed her childhood friend had come inside during the night to sleep in the guest room because she was too drunk to navigate the path through the woods to the rustic home that she had inherited from her grandfather.

The guest room was empty.

Guess she went home. Carlisle picked up her cell phone from the coffee table and hit the speed dial number for Ashton Piedmont.

Seconds later, Carlisle heard the cell phone ringing from outside. Pulling herself up off the sofa, she went to the window to place the ring of the phone. It was coming from the chaise where Ashton had placed her clothes.

Funny. Ashton is never without her cell phone. Guess she was so plastered that she forgot to take it home with her. She'll get it later when she comes to and remembers where she had left it.

Tossing the cell phone back onto the table, Carlisle dropped back onto the sofa and closed her eyes. Her head was pounding.

Cat fight? Attacked Parker Lander?

Carlisle checked her hands. They were bruised and dirty with splinters embedded in her fingertips. Clutching her knees, she found them bruised and bloody.

Oh, man! Why would I attack Parker? What was I fighting with Ashton about?

Having known the big—and dorky—man for years, Carlisle could not imagine him striking her back if she had attacked him. *If he had a backbone, he would have killed that witch of a wife years ago and buried her in their back yard. I know I would have. Anyone who knew her could claim temporary insanity and a jury would believe them.*

Carlisle pushed through the cobwebs of her mind to search the foggy events of the night before. All that she could dredge up were flashes of faces and words.

"You're going down, hell bitch!"

Who said that? Did Ashton say that to me? Why? Or did I say that to her? What did she do to get me mad?

Slowly, Carlisle sat up. She remembered a scream. A loud blood-curdling scream. Hearing it again from deep in her memory, Carlisle tried in vain to stand, but her legs buckled under her. She dropped to her knees, sending a shock wave from the bruises up to her aching head.

"Ash … Ashton!" Raising from the floor, Carlisle staggered out the back door and down the path along the lake to the Piedmont home. In her haste, she didn't bother clothing herself. She grabbed the doorknob to find it locked. Without regard for tidiness, she overturned a potted plant to get the house key, unlocked the door, and rushed inside—triggering the home security system.

The vacant mansion was quiet. The silence echoed in Carlisle's foggy head. The vastness of the estate made the silence even more frightening.

There was no one around, but Carlisle heard the answer murmured inside her head. Even if she did not remember what had happened, in the dark shadows of her mind, she knew. She felt her friend's fate in the pit of her stomach.

Ashton Piedmont was dead.

CHAPTER   MONDAY

CHAPTER ONE

Spencer Manor, Spencer, Maryland: Present Day

Mac was up to his eyeballs in a shootout. He wasn't wearing a bullet-proof vest and his gun was tucked away in the top drawer of the nightstand on his side of the bed, but his heart was still pounding. Anxious to see how Mickey Forsythe and his faithful canine partner Diablo were going to get out of this one, he hit the forward arrow on his e-reader to take him to the next page.

The bathroom door swung open.

He sensed rather than saw his lovely bride, Archie Monday, step into the doorway to strike a pose with her arm up above her head on the doorframe. She hitched her slender hip to the side. "Notice something different?" she asked in a sultry tone.

With effort, Mac tore his eyes from the e-reader to evaluate the situation. He did not want to give the wrong answer.

She was clad in the rose-colored negligee that he had given her for Valentine's Day. It was see-through. Underneath, she wore a rose-colored lacy bra and thong.

Mac swallowed. "Your nose has stopped running?"

With a wicked grin, she nodded her head. Her emerald eyes twinkled. "Mom's chicken soup really helped." To further illustrate her recovery from the nasty spring cold, she raced across the room and jumped onto the bed.

Forgetting about Mickey and Diablo, Mac tossed the e-reader aside.

Straddling him, she pinned him down onto the bed. Before he could object, which was the last thing he wanted to do, she covered his mouth with hers.

"Remind me to send her a thank-you note," he gasped out when she let him up for air. He rolled her over and clasped her face in his hands. "We have a whole week of celibacy to make up for."

Giggling, she tore at the waistband of his lounging pants. "I'm up for it if you are, big boy."

He kissed her hard and passionately.

The sound of a loud whine came to their ears.

They stopped.

The German shepherd uttered a sound that resembled the clearing of his throat. Mac and Archie looked over at Gnarly, who was sitting at the foot of the bed. He seemed to almost arch an eyebrow at them.

"Seriously?" Mac asked him. "We're married. Go lay down."

Without moving, Gnarly glanced over at the clock on the night stand. His message: It was past his bedtime. He wanted to turn in for the night and his den was under their bed. If they continued, they were going to keep him awake.

"You don't need to go to bed at ten o'clock every night," Mac argued. "Go watch television or let yourself out and find your own date. Leave us alone."

Gnarly narrowed his eyes. After a long stare down, Mac won. Gnarly stood up, turned around, and strolled out the bedroom door.

With a sigh, Mac turned back to Archie who was giggling.

"Poor Gnarly," she said.

"Poor Gnarly? Poor me." He stroked her short blonde locks and peered into her green eyes. He was so blessed to be married to such a woman. "Oh, man, I love you so much," he breathed before kissing her with all of the pent up passion he had bottled during her week-long headache.

"I love you more." She wrapped her arms around his waist and thrust his pants down beneath his hips.

Mac slipped his hands up under the overwrap of her negligee.

The cell phone on the night table rang.

Their hands, filled with clothing, froze. They stared at each other to wordlessly ask if it was their imagination.

The phone rang a second time.

In the hallway, Gnarly barked as if to answer their question. *Someone answer that, will you?*

"No," Archie said with a plea in her tone. "Don't answer that."

The phone rang again.

Gnarly raced into the bedroom and jumped up onto the bed. Using his nose for a plow, he wedged them apart.

"It might be David with a case." With an apology in his voice, Mac reached for the phone. The caller ID read "private number." "It's not David," he sighed with relief while pressing the button to accept the call.

Gnarly plopped down between them.

Mac groaned when he said, "Hello…"

"Robin?" a timid female voice came from the speaker.

It took a moment for Mac to piece together who Robin was.

Robin Spencer. The American Queen of mystery novels until her death four years before, at which time she had left her vast fortune to the underpaid homicide detective she had given up for adoption when she was an unwed teenager.

"No," Mac replied to her query, "Mac. I'm—"

"It's Ashton," she interrupted. "Robin, it's me, Ashton."
Click!

Puzzled, Mac looked at the phone in his hand.

"Who was that?" Archie asked.

"Ashton."

"Who's Ashton?" She rose up onto her elbows to ask him over Gnarly's body.

"Don't know," he said. "She asked for Robin."

"Obviously a wrong number." She shooed Gnarly up and down to the foot of the bed.

"Obviously." After tossing the phone onto the night stand, Mac rolled over to take her into his arms. "Now, where were we?"

With a whine, Gnarly pawed at his leg.

"I wasn't talking to you." He shoved the dog off the bed. With a "humph" Gnarly went back out into the hallway.

"We were discussing who loves who more." Archie stroked his bare chest.

"Well, let's just see who's right."

She rolled him over onto his back and straddled him. While massaging his shoulders, she kissed him on the lips and worked her way down his neck to his chest.

Even as Mac felt his heart racing with the touch of her lips, his attention wondered to the phone resting on the night stand. "I wonder where she got my cell phone number. And why is she asking for Robin?"

Archie dropped down onto his chest. She then went to pull cotton pajamas out of the dresser.

❦ ❦ ❦

Next Morning

"That didn't take long," Lindsey York told Kassandra Van Dyke when the black SUV police cruiser fell in behind them and turned on its lights.

Tossing her long red curls into the wind whipping by them as they raced along in the bright red Lamborghini, Lindsey squealed with delight. "This ought to be good."

With a grimace, Kassandra gripped her seat. "You're only going twenty miles over the speed limit and almost ran that Mercedes into the lake."

Lindsey pulled the sports car over to the side of the road. The police cruiser followed suit.

Inside the cruiser, Police Chief David O'Callaghan noticed in his rear view mirror that a white van had also pulled over to the side of road that marked the outline of Deep Creek Lake.

"Tonya, I've got a late model Lamborghini, red, pulled over for speeding and reckless driving," David called into the radio. "Request a ten twenty-eight license plate Maryland number Lincoln Ida Nora David Sam Edward Young."

Out of the corner of his eye, David saw the van doors open and two men jump out. He could see that they were carrying something. Without time to determine what they each carried, he dropped the radio's mike with one hand, grabbed the gun on his hip with the other, and whirled around to aim it out the window at the men approaching the side of his cruiser.

"Hold it right there!" he shouted.

"Holy—" The man coming up on the driver's side dropped the movie camera he was carrying and held up both of his hands. The equipment crashed when it hit the pavement.

Behind him, David could hear a woman in the sports car erupt with a peal of laughter while another shrieked, "He almost shot him!"

The man on the passenger side of the cruiser froze. "Don't shoot! We're just shooting some footage, man!"

"Put down the camera and keep up your hands where I can see them!" David ordered while easing out of the cruiser.

"Ah, this is great!" Lindsey screamed from the front seat of the sports car while the terrified camera operators followed the police officer's instructions to the letter.

"Chief!" Tonya called out from the radio. "What's your status? Do you need assistance?"

David tapped the button on the radio on his shoulder. "Ten-twenty-three, Tonya."

"Roger that, Chief."

After confirming that he was not in danger, he returned his gun to its holster. "Do you realize exactly how stupid it is to sneak up on an armed police officer?"

"We weren't sneaking," the first camera man said. "We were just trying to stay out of the way to catch some candid action." Keeping his focus on David, he slowly knelt down to check the condition of the recorder he had dropped.

An older man climbed out of the van. Unlike his young cohorts, who were dressed in jeans and pull over shirts, he wore a sports jacket in an attempt to conceal his stomach which extended over the waistband of his slacks. His broad chest combined with his tubby midsection gave him a barrel shape. His dark wavy hair had silver streaks through it. He chuckled while sauntering over to David. "Sorry, officer, but you have to excuse my camera operators. You see, it can be hard sometimes to appear unobtrusive while filming a show."

"Show? What show are you talking about?"

He stuck out his hand. "Vincent Van Dyke. You may remember me from *Hawaii Night Watch*. I was the star—"

"No, I don't," David interjected with no attempt to conceal his annoyance. He realized that the car speeding through his jurisdiction was nothing more than a ploy to get some good television footage. Technically, they were obstructing justice with their staged traffic violation. While he was dealing with them, he could be preventing a real crime.

The camera operator whose equipment still worked moved on to the sports car to film the two women. Grumbling, the other operator returned to the van to check the damage to his equipment.

Decades earlier, Vincent Van Dyke's square jaw and muscular build would have been eye candy to the feminine sex. As was so often the case, a lifestyle of excessive booze and drugs extinguished the sparks in his blue eyes. His once firm body gave way to fat. Beneath the surface of Van Dykes' leathering skin, David could make out broken blood vessels that could be evidence of heavy drinking.

Vincent read David's name tag. "O'Callaghan? I knew a Chief O'Callaghan back when my late wife and I used to summer here. We still have a place—is he your father?"

"He's passed away," David said. "Now I'm chief of police and I have work to do. I would appreciate it if you and your crew got out of my way."

He went over to the driver's side of the Lamborghini and spoke to the redhead behind the wheel. "Welcome back to Spencer, Lindsey. It's been a while. I see you still have a lead foot."

Lindsey had her driver's license and registration ready.

Instead of looking at her license, he was observing the lack of focus in her bloodshot blue eyes and the stench of gin. "How many martinis have you had to drink today, Lindsey?"

"I lost count, Davey." She giggled. "Why don't you break out that magic toy you have and tell me?"

With a sigh, David opened the car door. "Step out of the car, Lindsey."

"What are you doing?" Vincent Van Dyke rushed forward to ask.

"Giving her a breathalyzer test and then most likely taking her into the station to book her for DUI." David held her arm to help the young woman, unsteady in her high heels, back to the cruiser.

The blonde in the passenger seat threw open the door and jumped out. "What's happening?"

Her sudden movement caused Davie to whirl around with his hand on his weapon. "Stay in the car!" He had seen and heard of too many routine stops go bad when a seemingly innocent passenger would leap out of the car and blow away the officer focused on the driver.

Startled by his tone, Kassandra dropped back into her seat and slammed the door shut.

"It's okay, baby." Vincent gestured for the camera operators to continue recording David and the driver.

The second camera operator had retrieved a backup recorder to join in capturing the scene.

David opened the rear door to the cruiser and eased Lindsey into the back seat. Instead of being appalled or embarrassed, she was giggling. To her, this arrest was simply one more tick next to the items on her growing list of notorious activities. The seriousness of what harm could come from her driving while drunk or high was completely lost on her.

"Listen," Vincent told him, "we're trying to record a pilot episode for a television show to sell a series." He pointed over at the blonde who was sitting motionless in the front seat of the Lamborghini. "She's my daughter. Kassandra Van Dyke." In search of a sign of recognition to the name, he turned to see David inputting information into the breathalyzer that he was using to measure the redhead's blood alcohol contents. There was no recognition on the police chief's face.

"How much do you weigh now, Lindsey?" he asked the young woman in the back seat of his cruiser.

She sat up straight to show off her body encased in a form fitting pink dress that ended high up on her thighs. "Take a guess."

"One hundred and twenty-five pounds," David said without humor.

"One hundred and ten," she objected.

"No, you put on weight since the last time you blew through town."

"Did not!"

"That was at least five years ago," David said. "You've grown up and filled out. We all do."

"You haven't," she purred. "Hey, that offer I made the first time you grabbed me still stands."

"I'm taken."

"Since when does that have anything to do with it?"

"In your dreams, Lindsey," David replied without looking up from the device he was programming.

Pouting, she dropped back into her seat and crossed her arms.

"Kassandra was Playboy's Playmate of the Year last year," Vincent said.

"You must be a very proud father." There was a note of sarcasm in David's tone. He held out the tube to Lindsey. "Open up."

Like a child, Lindsey opened her mouth and David stuck the tube in. She snapped her lips shut over it.

"Now blow."

Looking the well-built police chief, with his blue eyes and blond hair, up and down, she said in a naughty tone, "maybe when I'm through blowing on this—"

"Give it a rest, Lindsey," David said. "I'm *still* not interested."

"Hugh Hefner said my Kassandra was a natural," Vincent Van Dyke huffed at David's elbow.

"I'm only interested in the drunk driving like a bat out of hell into my town." David took the monitor from Lindsey and studied the reading. "Congratulations, Lindsey. You blew point-one-four."

"If you hadn't have stopped me, I could have blown higher in another hour." She took his hand to help her out of the back of the cruiser.

With no direction from him, she turned her back to him, spread her feet apart, and bent over with her hands behind her back. "I've been dreaming about this moment since I booked my flight back here. Only, Davey, in my fantasy, we were alone ... and naked."

"Welcome back to Spencer, Lindsey." David slapped his cuffs on her.

CHAPTER TWO

"Ashton?" Archie Monday stared into her coffee cup while quietly repeating the name over and over again. Each time she said it her voice became softer to the point of barely audible.

Finally, she declared in a clear tone, "Nope. I have no idea who Ashton could be." She stood up to carry the plate, which had been home to her cinnamon roll, from the back deck into the kitchen on the other side of the French doors. "Seriously, Mac; it had to have been a wrong number."

In spite of his one hundred pounds of muscle, fur, and teeth, Gnarly pranced at Archie's heels with the grace of a butterfly in hopes of snatching a crumb.

Archie Monday had held the coveted job of editor and assistant to best-selling mystery writer Robin Spencer for over a decade before the writer's sudden death from a brain aneurism.

Thanks to a trust fund left to the author's Girl Friday, Mac Faraday was blessed by the companionship of the green-eyed blonde living in the cozy guest cottage at the end of his back deck overlooking an inlet on Deep Creek Lake. He thanked his late birth mother every time he saw the charming emerald-eyed blonde sunning herself on his deck. He especially thanked her when Archie married him.

They were still newlyweds.

It had been two years since Mac's half-brother, Police Chief David O'Callaghan moved into the guest cottage while renovating his childhood home to sell.

Spencer Manor was one of the most expensive pieces of real estate on Deep Creek Lake. It rested at the tip of a boulder-lined peninsula that was home to half a dozen luxury homes. Boasting of lakefront views on three sides, the log and stone home was the largest on Spencer Point.

The late author's love for gardens contributed to a wide array of floral majesty, which the mistress of the manor now tended. Archie insisted that it was a loving touch, not a special fertilizer, that made the gardens one of the most splendid along the shores of Deep Creek Lake. Vacationers snapping pictures from the lake of Robin Spencer's birthplace and legendary gardens was not an uncommon occurrence.

Another inheritance from his mother, Gnarly ran out onto the deck with a treat-filled bone clenched in his teeth. He took the goodie down from one level of the deck to another until he came to a sunny spot on the dock next to the jet skis. There, he plopped down to chew on the bone as if to show it off to the flock of ducklings that Archie had fed before breakfast.

"She asked for Robin," Mac told Archie when she returned. She leaned down to kiss him softly on the lips before refilling his mug of coffee from a carafe that she had brought out from the kitchen.

Wondering if his waistline could stand a second one, he reached out to the plate of fresh cinnamon rolls she had also brought with her. They were still warm from the oven. Archie had risen early to make them from scratch. At his last physical, he was informed he had gained close to twenty pounds since his inheritance. He had visions of becoming one of those old, fat, rich guys he used to go up against when he had been a homicide detective. Not liking what his life of leisure was doing to his body, he withdrew from the cinnamon roll.

The warmth of the sun and scent of the flowers sprouting in the gardens reminded him that Memorial Day was less than a month away.

"Your birth mother was not the only Robin in the world." Archie pointed out while slipping into the chair next to his.

"The caller called my cell, at a phone number that I didn't have back before I moved out here, and asked for Robin."

"Which I believe goes to prove her asking for Robin was just a coincidence. This Ashton did not mean Robin Spencer." She shot him a smile. "You're putting too much thought into this. Why don't you help me with the menu for the Diablo Ball? That will take your mind off this *mysterious*—" She held up her fingers in quotation marks, "Ashton."

The Diablo Ball was Archie's first major social event since officially entering high society by marrying Robin Spencer's son.

Every May, Robin Spencer had kicked off the summer season by hosting the Diablo Ball at the Spencer Inn. Named after the four-legged sidekick in her Mickey Forsythe mystery series, the formal charity event had been to benefit the Humane Society of America. Attendance was by invitation only to the two thousand dollar a plate dinner and dance the last Saturday in May. The annual event had ceased with Robin Spencer's death. This year, Robin Spencer's daughter-in-law was resurrecting it.

What had started out as an exciting, massive social event had turned into a headache for Mac. While he had heard about the Diablo Ball since his inheritance and move to Spencer, he had never realized the social importance attached to receiving a gold-engraved invitation to the event. Suddenly, he and Archie were on the receiving end of pleas from socially-conscious friends and acquaintances begging not to be forgotten. Those pleas were not as shocking as the calls and emails from famous socialites whom he had never met or spoken to, not asking but insisting, some even demanding, an invitation.

To not be invited was on par with being marked as a social outcast.

The whole event was leaving a bad taste in Mac's mouth.

"You'll be happy to know that the invitations are going out today. Catherine is sending out the printed and email copies."

"Now we can get the calls and emails from the insecure and broken hearted," Mac groaned.

Archie agreed. "I have been getting daily emails from Vincent Van Dyke begging for an invitation for him and his daughter, Kassandra."

"I'm sorry," he said. "Call me a social misfit but, if it's so important to this guy and his daughter, and the purpose of the party is to collect money for charity, then why not let them come and write us a big check to protect the Robin's Pets?"

Gnarly had picked that time to gallop up onto the deck, climb into the chair, and wipe his mouth on Mac's chest. As if to bring home his point, Mac wrapped his arms around the shepherd's big head in a hug. The two of them looked imploringly at Archie.

Fighting the grin working its way to her lips, Archie explained, "I had the same attitude when I first started working with Robin on this. Believe me, she'd sworn that she did not originally set out for the Diablo Ball to be some snooty, hoity-toity, fancy dress ball. *They* made it that way. Not her."

"They being who?" Mac released Gnarly, who refused to remove the front half of his body from his master's lap.

"The High-And-Mighty." Archie took a sip of her coffee. "Robin had this bright idea after her second or third book had come out. She'd throw a fancy, formal party at her daddy's Inn on top of Spencer Mountain to benefit the local Humane Society, which was about ready to close due to lack of funds. Of course, in order to make it worthwhile, the well-heeled guests had to write big checks for Robin's Pets. Poor people can't write very big checks. So she'd invited all of her rich friends, both those who lived in Spencer, and the literary crowd that she had come to know. It worked and word got out about the big shindig. So, then, the next year, Robin had invited more rich friends, many being from the movie crowd since she had sold her first book to Hollywood. Richer friends. Then the year after that she'd won the Pulitzer and those folks came out. Since they would get all dressed up, she called it the Diablo Ball. Diablo, after Mickey Forsythe's sidekick, the ass-kicking German shepherd. To her, it was almost a joke. Before she knew it, the rich folks Robin had invited were saying among themselves that only the cream of the social crop would be invited to the Diablo Ball. *They* had declared that if you hadn't received an invite that you had been dropped from the A-list. Robin realized that since they were paying big money for this exclusive event, if anyone deemed less-than-worthy got invited then it threatened the exclusivity of the event. If these snooty folks, who had made this event a success, sensed that just anyone could come, then it would directly impact the success of her cause."

Mac shook his head. From what he had read and learned about his birth mother, snobbery had not been one of her traits. She had a lot of close friends who were not blue bloods.

Archie sensed the source of his head shaking. The corner of her lips curled. "But if you're really lucky, you make the I-list."

"I-list?"

"It stands for 'icky.' Those were the people who were of no social use to Robin except for personal enjoyment. People on the A-list would not be caught dead shaking hands with those on the I-List. The I-list folks don't have to pay. They are invited both to the ball and the exclusive party at the Spencer Manor beforehand. That is the short list. David and Chelsea, Deputy Police Chief Art Bogart, aka Bogie, and Doc, Tonya and the whole Spencer Police Department, and Sheriff Chris Turow and his son."

"Were the Van Dykes on either of these lists?"

"No," Archie said. "Of course, I'm not a Vincent Van Dyke fan. He was a little before my time."

"Ouch," Mac cringed. "Now I remember where I know the name. He was a sex symbol back in my day. Flashy clothes. Hot car. Gun blazing on television every Friday night. Then, I graduated from the police academy and found out the hard way what real police work was all about. I didn't get the hot car and flashy clothes until I retired."

Archie paused to look Mac's tennis whites up and down. His golden tan stood out against the bright white. "Well, their persistent e-mails caused me to look up where Vincent Van Dyke is now. After walking out on his hit cop show to become a movie star, Vincent's fans had scattered to the four winds. After a couple of forgettable movies, he went back to television, which didn't seem to want him either. Lucky for him, Delia Kaye did."

"Delia Kaye of Kaye Cosmetics?"

"Sole heir to the Kaye fortune," Archie said. "He retired to marry her. They had Kassandra and lived fat and happy with the blue bloods until Delia passed away a few years ago. He took his daughter back to Hollywood and he tried to make a comeback, but failed. So, he's turned his attention to his lovely daughter's career." She lowered her voice to a hiss. "He actually managed to make her Playboy's Playmate of the Year last year. Now, he's trying to use that as a taking off point to make her a reality star with her has-been daddy and her Hollywood lifestyle."

"I guess once you get a taste of fame and fortune," Mac said, "you get so hooked on it that it's hard to give it up."

❧ ❧ ❧

"Do you have any questions, Mr. Faraday?" Jeff Ingle startled Mac out of his daydream of being outside on the tennis court instead of in the Spencer Inn manager's office looking out.

Gnarly seemed to share Mac's fantasy. He sat at the window with his nose pressed against the glass.

In contrast to Jeff's tailored suit and tie, which he wore like a uniform for running the Spencer Inn, one of the country's most luxurious mountaintop resorts, Mac was still dressed in tennis whites and had his athletic bag resting next to his chair. He planned to hit the court right after blessing the hiring of a summer intern. As the Inn's owner, Mac didn't feel he was needed except to rubber stamp Jeff's new assistant.

Dressed as properly as the Inn's manager, Brian Gallagher sat up straight in his chair. Having completed his junior year of college, the intern applicant had driven in from Chicago the day before.

Mac could see that he was clean. He struck Mac as a little on the thin side. His red hair was short and neatly combed. A splattering of freckles across his nose and both cheeks gave him a boyish appearance. Still, he looked older than most college students. Mac learned during the interview that he had started college late—after spending two years tending to his dying mother.

"Where are you going to stay this summer, Brian?" Mac asked.

"A friend of mine is lending me his condo right here next to the Inn," the young man responded. "It's within walking distance."

"Good friend." Jeff looked questioningly at Mac for his seal of approval. "I was planning to have Brian assist the event coordinator with the Diablo Ball."

"Archie is handling that on our end," Mac said. "She used to help my mother with it. I guess they had a system. Senator Catherine Fleming is helping Archie."

"Senator Fleming?" Brian uttered a gasp before getting hold of himself.

"The Flemings have been lifelong members of the Spencer Inn's club," Jeff explained. "County Prosecutor Ben Fleming uses the sporting facilities almost daily."

"Catherine was good friends with my late mother and is my wife's best friend," Mac explained. "She's a compassionate and lovely person. You have no reason to be afraid of her."

"Well, Brian will be the Inn's liaison with Archie and Senator Fleming," Jeff told him. "Speaking of the ball, we have been inundated with calls from people asking for invitations." He referred to a list on his desk.

"Archie assured me that the invitations are going out today," Mac said with a shake of his head. "Why anyone would want to be invited to a party where you have to pay thousands of dollars a plate to get in is beyond me."

"It's a matter of social status," Jeff explained. "For many people who live here in Spencer, it would be a slap in the face if they weren't invited. Those on the boundary of the A-list get very nervous about finding out if they get in or not." He chuckled. "Based on the calls and emails I've been getting, I think some folks would kill to get an invitation to the Diablo Ball."

❧ ❧ ❧

"Mac!" Garrett Country Prosecutor Ben Fleming called to Mac from across the Inn's lobby.

Seemingly at the same time, the clerk behind the registration desk called out, "Mr. Faraday, someone left an envelope for you."

Torn in two directions, Mac decided to go for the envelope while Gnarly went to Ben. As Mac had hoped, the county prosecutor followed him with Gnarly at his side. The clerk handed the inn owner a square crisp white envelope with Mac's name printed in blood-red ink on the front.

"Ah," Ben said when he saw it, "It appears you're on the A-List."

"I'm sure it's only temporary," Mac said with disgust. "Just wait until I break social protocol by accusing the wrong person of murder."

He tore open the envelope to reveal a greeting card. The front and inside were both printed in the same blood-red ink. "Thinking of You," was the greeting on the front page, while inside it read:

It's the season of
Hide & Seek.
You're It.
Find me if you can.

Ashton

Ben frowned when he saw the puzzled expression on his face. "What is it? A bill?"

"Mr. Faraday ..."

While handing off the card to Ben, Mac heard someone call in a timid voice. Out of the corner of his eye, he saw a young man he recognized as an employee in the Inn's marketing department. Mac wished he could remember his name.

This guy works for me and I don't know his name. How weird is that?

"Who's Ashton?" Ben interrupted Mac's thoughts to ask.

"I have no idea," Mac said. "Last night a woman called me on my cell phone … a phone number I don't give out. She asked for Robin and said her name was Ashton. Archie swore it had to be a wrong number. I was starting to believe her until I got this."

Ben read the front of the envelope. "This is addressed to you."

"I know," Mac said. "Someone is trying to send me a message."

"Mac, when are you going to stop thinking like a cop?"

"It's because I think this way that I became a cop in the first place. Don't you find this suspicious?"

"Yes, I do," Ben replied.

"You knew Robin," Mac said. "What Ashton could this be about?"

"I'll ask Catherine," Ben referred to his wife. "She kept up on everything that Robin Spencer was into. If Robin knew an Ashton, then Catherine will know."

"Excuse me, Mr. Faraday." The slightly built young man in ill-fitting slacks and a sports jacket with the Spencer Inn insignia embroidered on the breast pocket approached them from the corner of the reception desk. Mac had seen him clutching some sheets of paper in his sweaty hands while waiting for a break in the conversation to interrupt. "I wrote a press release for the Diablo Ball. I was wondering if you could approve it before I send it out to the media." He thrust the papers in Mac's direction.

"Sure." With an embarrassed grin, Mac paused in hopes that the young man would offer up his name.

"Rudy, sir." His thin face was pale. A weak chin gave him an almost feminine appearance. "Rudy Crowe." He gestured at the papers in Mac's hands. "I write the resort's press releases. I thought it best to have it approved, either by you or maybe since Mrs. Faraday is chairing the ball, she should approve it before I send it out."

The name reference brought an image of Mac's late adopted mother to his mind. "Mrs?"

With a grin, Ben nudged him. "He means Archie."

"Oh," Mac chuckled before explaining to Rudy, "My wife kept her maiden name. I never hear anyone refer to her as Mrs. Faraday." He folded the press release in half and tucked it into his athletic bag. "I'll have her take a look at this."

Their conversation was cut short by a scream from across the lobby. Mac was startled to see Gnarly running in their direction with a clutch bag in his jaws. A woman wearing large sun glasses that covered most of her face clasped her red sun hat on top of her head while chasing after the dog.

"Gnarly! You thief! I'm going to kill you!" Mac yelled.

In spite of the threat, Gnarly shoved the handbag into Mac's waiting palm before taking cover behind his legs.

"That dog is a purse snatcher!" The woman pointed an accusing finger at Mac.

Ben burst out laughing at the scene.

Mac apologized. "Gnarly gets bored and—"

"He stole my purse!" the guest screamed. "I set it down to fill in my registration and he snatched it right off the counter."

"Here!"

As if in protest, Gnarly barked when Mac held it out to her.

"Shut up!"

"Well, I never!" She slapped Mac across the face. "First, your dog steals my purse. Then, *you* tell *me* to shut up?"

Ben covered his face to conceal his amusement.

Rudy's eyes were as wide and round as humanly possible.

Clutching his cheek still stinging from the attack, Mac explained, "I was talking to the canine kleptomaniac!" Realizing that the handbag was covered in dog droll, he took the bag back before she could take possession of it and wiped it off with a sweat towel from his athletic bag. "I don't think he put any teeth marks in it."

"Can I just please have my purse back?" she ordered rather than asked.

"I am terribly sorry," Mac continued to apologize. "Listen, I'm Mac Faraday. I own the Spencer Inn. If I can make this up to you, I would be glad to offer you a free dinner in the lounge."

"All I want is my purse back!"

"Believe me—" Before Mac could offer any further apologies, his hands felt a familiar shape inside the handbag. It was not the square shape of a wallet, or round like a compact. Or tubular like a lipstick. Rather, his fingers felt a form that sent shockwaves to his brain. "Ma'am?" He held the bag back out of her grasp.

"Do I have to call the police?"

"Do I have to call security?" Mac gauged her to be approaching her mid-thirties. He had a good guess that she was making every effort that money could buy to stop time and put a halt to the aging process. He could see that her large breasts were not natural, as were her face which looked almost like the skin had been stretched across her skull.

"Mac?" Ben asked with a warning tone when he hesitated to hand over the purse.

Before the county prosecutor could stop him, Mac whipped open the bag and reached inside.

"How dare you!" she gasped.

Before Ben could echo her dismay, Mac extracted the handgun from its confines. "This is how I dare." A quick check showed that the safety was off.

The Inn's guests, who moments before had been amused by Inn owner's dog being caught red-pawed in the act of thievery, switched to shock. A cry went up within the lobby.

The lady, who had been indignant, changed her tone to compliant in an instant while begging for understanding. "I'm a woman alone. It's for protection."

After identifying himself as the county prosecutor, Ben asked, "Do you have a permit to carry a concealed weapon?"

After she confessed to no permit, Mac asked, "What's your name?" She didn't need to answer him. He was already reading the name on the California driver's license from her wallet, which he had found in her purse. It read Riva Sinclair. The age was listed as twenty-nine years of age. Mac guessed that she was lying.

"Riva Sinclair," she answered. "My husband, Rock Sinclair, is staying with his mistress in one of your suites."

"You just said you needed this for protection. Who from? Your runaway husband or the woman he ran away with?" Mac studied the gun in his palm. It was a thirty-two caliber semi-automatic. Nothing fancy, but lethal all the same.

"Mr. Faraday?"

Mac turned around at the sound of his name. Startled, Jeff Ingles threw his arms up as if he had encountered a burglar when his eyes fell on the gun in Mac's grasp. Brian Gallagher let out a gasp and stepped back and sideways to hide behind his boss.

"Any problems?" Jeff stuttered out.

"That still has yet to be determined," Mac replied.

Ben asked the guest. "How did you get on the plane with that thing?"

"Do I look stupid to you?" she asked.

"Well, you did just admit that you followed your estranged husband and his mistress here," Mac said, "and you do have a gun hidden in your purse."

"Mac," Jeff whispered, "it is not good customer service to imply that our guests are stupid."

"It's not politically correct," Ben added.

"She's the one who brought a gun into my hotel," Mac said. "Why are you making me out to be the bad guy?"

Jeff said, "Because she's a paying customer and—"

"I only sign your paycheck," Mac said.

"Actually," Jeff said, "it's direct deposit."

"What?" Mac countered.

"I'm paid with direct deposit," Jeff explained. "You don't *sign* anything."

"Can I have my gun back?" Riva Sinclair interrupted to ask.

"No!" Mac and Ben answered in unison.

"Where did you get this?" Mac asked her.

"None of your business," she challenged him.

"Excuse me," Mac replied, "but if the purpose of this gun is to commit murder in my inn, then that makes it my business." He turned to Jeff. "Lock this in the inn's safe until we get this matter straightened out." Carefully, he extracted the clip and placed both the hand gun and clip into the manager's outstretched palm.

"You have no right!" she exclaimed.

Jeff assured her, "We will give you a receipt, ma'am."

Ben countered, "Excuse me, Mrs. Sinclair, but he has every right. The gun is not registered and the Inn has rules about firearms. I am afraid we will need to turn this weapon over to the police who will probably be pressing charges against you for carrying a concealed weapon without a permit. It's a state law."

With a force grin, Jeff said, "But, ma'am, we'll be glad to serve you a drink on the house in the lounge to make up for any inconvenience while you're waiting for the police to come arrest you."

Uttering a growl from her throat that sounded as threatening as Gnarly's, she stomped off in the direction of the hotel lounge.

"We're giving her a drink on the house to make up for the inconvenience of being arrested?" Mac muttered at Jeff.

"Do you think the Spencer Inn's five-star rating just happens?" With that, Jeff spun on his heels to lead Brian back into the hotel's office wing.

Exonerated for his thievery, Gnarly pressed his nose against Mac's leg. With a pat on his head, Mac declared, "Good dog."

CHAPTER THREE

"As police chief of this burg, what do you intend to do about this?"

Police Chief David O'Callaghan and his officers were paid well to protect Spencer's citizens and their high-priced properties from anyone wanting to do harm to either. The down-side of his job was catering to the whims of spoiled, self-indulgent individuals. That was when David felt like an overpaid babysitter.

It had started with a call from Jeff Ingles, manager of the Spencer Inn, to report that one of his guests had tried to check in with a concealed weapon without a permit.

Once he got wind of his gun-toting estranged wife's arrival, the run-away husband wasted no time in ordering an audience with Spencer's police chief. Rock Sinclair had booked a block of rooms at the hotel for him and an entourage, all of whom flowed in and out of the producer's suite.

Young enough to be the gray-haired man's daughter, Jasmine Simpson had shown the police chief into the suite upon his arrival and perched on the arm of the overstuffed chair where Rock Sinclair was seated. She had her long, auburn hair tied back into a ponytail. The still-moist layer of sweat on her arms and midriff told David that she had been to the Inn's athletic club.

During their meeting, a young man with dark hair and a goatee wordlessly worked away at two laptops and a tablet at the kitchenette counter. Occasionally, David would notice him smirk in their direction, like a boy enjoying the sight of another child getting chewed out by the principal.

Seeing David eying the young man, Jasmine announced in a bored tone, "This is Samuel Nash. He's our director."

Clutching his cell phone to his left ear, Samuel sprung off his bar stool to offer his hand to the police chief. "Nice to meet 'cha, Chief." With a wide grin, the director winked at him.

"Isn't there anything you can do about this?" Rock demanded the return of David's attention.

"We have confiscated your wife's gun and charged her with carrying a concealed weapon without a permit," David said.

"What about attempted murder?" Rock demanded to know.

"We have no evidence that she attempted to murder you or that she intended to murder you," David said.

"She could always get another gun," Jasmine pointed out.

"That's true," David said.

Jasmine Simpson said, "It doesn't take a rocket scientist to figure out what she's doing; she flew out here to kill us."

The producer of a variety of news programs, Rock Sinclair may not have been surrounded by stars from the big screen, but his arrogant attitude was no different from other Hollywood types whom David had encountered during his career.

Decades before, soon after Robin Spencer had sold her first book to Hollywood, a movie producer had discovered the rustic jewel of Spencer, Maryland, tucked in the mountains along Deep Creek Lake. Since that discovery, producers, screenwriters, and actors in search of authentic rest would visit the town to commune with nature and recharge their batteries.

The resort town wasn't the place for celebrities wanting to see and be seen. Fame-seekers making that mistake would fly out within an hour after being joined on the back deck by the first black bear of the morning.

"Contrary to Riva's claim, I am not here having an affair," the producer said while stroking Jasmine's thigh.

"I'm his executive assistant." She drained off the last of the water in her bottle and reached for a second one.

"We're partners," Rock went on.

"Partners?" David parroted.

"This is a business trip," Jasmine said. "Not a romantic getaway like that boob thinks."

"I told Riva that," Rock insisted, "but she doesn't believe me."

"Have you given her reason not to believe you?" David sensed he knew the answer. After thirty seconds with Rock Sinclair, the police chief didn't trust him. He didn't know if it was his smirk or the way he stroked his "business partner's" almost naked body while claiming he wasn't cheating on his wife.

"Jasmine and I are working on an investigative news report."

David sensed the producer had something hiding up his sleeve that he was about to reveal to the police chief—something specifically meant for him.

"As a matter of fact, the case we're investigating is a cold case in your own town, Chief O'Callaghan," the producer said. "It's the Ashton Piedmont disappearance."

"Ashton was a very dear friend of mine," Jasmine said with a well-rehearsed choke. "She disappeared five years ago and from what I've seen, your police department has done nothing toward trying to find her."

Rock caressed her hand. "So, when Jasmine came to me with the story of her grief and frustration, I thought it would make an amazing story … our coming back to Spencer, bringing together all of Ashton's friends … and suspects in her disappearance … to find out the truth about what'd happened." There was that smirk again. "I'm sure as a man who has dedicated himself to the pursuit of truth and justice, you'll appreciate our help."

"In exploiting and sensationalizing a horrible accident and death?" David replied. "I don't think so."

"Ashton's body was never found," Jasmine said.

"She was last seen skinny-dipping in Deep Creek Lake late at night after downing more than a bottle of wine," David said.

"Neighbors heard her fighting with Carlisle Green," Jasmine said. "One tried to break the fight up and Carlisle went ape on him and attacked him."

"During which he saw Ashton dive back into the lake," David said. "He saw her alive and swimming naked in the lake—drunk but alive. The case is still open, but it is presumed that she drowned."

"But without a body, you don't know that for a fact. Right, Chief?" Rock asked with that cocky grin.

David bit out. "That's why Lindsey York blew into town today. You're stirring up the case again by bringing together everyone connected to Ashton Piedmont."

"We're shooting some background footage right now," Jasmine announced. "Interviews with the local residents and things around the lake. We'll kick off our investigation with the place where the last week of Ashton's life all started—the beginning of the end—at the Diablo Ball—"

"Diablo Ball?" David seriously doubted if the producers could have received permission to use the Diablo Ball for anything so slimy.

Rock seemed to sense David's doubt. "Of course we don't plan on shooting the Diablo Ball. We plan on filming interviews with all of Ashton's closest friends, who were last seen together at the ball."

Jasmine's cool exterior melted slightly in her excitement. "It seems so fitting. After all, the Diablo Ball has always been considered the kick-off of the summer season on Deep Creek Lake. When we got the invitation we knew that this was the right thing to do. It was like the seal of approval on our project."

David tried to conceal his doubt. "You've been invited to the Diablo Ball?"

Both Rock and Jasmine were insulted by his doubt. "Of course," Rock said. "I may not be Steven Spielberg, but I do have quite a name in Hollywood."

"Of course," David apologized. "May I see your invitation?"

❧ ❧ ❧

"Well, it's plain to see that someone wants me to look into Ashton Piedmont's disappearance," Mac told David after showing him the greeting card that had been left at registration desk and learning the news about Rock Sinclair's invitation to the Diablo Ball.

As David had thought, Archie had only to take a glance at the copy of the gold invitation that Rock and Jasmine had given the police chief to declare it a phony.

"I've never even heard of Rock Sinclair. How can I invite someone I don't know to a party?" She shoved the copy back at David. "Let alone his tootsie, too?"

David said, "I don't think these people are your average party crashers. They came all the way from Hollywood to film this cold case profile, which, while it is technically a cold case, isn't. They've gone to a lot of trouble and expense—"

"They're party crashers."

David tapped the badge on his chest. "They're not fools. They were talking to the chief of police, who they know has resources to determine if they weren't supposed to be here. If they were crashing, they would not be talking so openly about coming to the ball and shooting a whole program around it. I don't think they know this invitation was a phony. That makes me wonder. How many other phony invitations could be out there?"

"They aren't on the list," Archie said. "The fact that they got this before the invitations were even put in the mail proves it's a fake."

"Maybe it's a joke on Rock Sinclair," Mac suggested from where he was sitting on the love seat next to Gnarly, who was sleeping off an upset stomach brought on by a pork chop he had stolen from the garbage.

Before Archie could voice her agreement, her tablet buzzed to indicate she had received an e-mail.

Perturbed that she interrupted their conversation to answer an e-mail, David rolled his eyes and turned back to Mac, who stroked Gnarly's tummy. The German shepherd looked up at David with a dreamy expression in his brown eyes.

"Tell me about Ashton Piedmont," Mac said.

"Nice girl," David said. "Twenty-two years old. I was involved in investigating her disappearance—presumed drowning. It was after Dad had passed and the town council had hired an acting police chief. Her parents were both doctors who had passed away in a small plane crash while flying across the mountains down in South America. She was raised by her grandfather, who was a professor at the medical school at the University of Maryland. He passed away a couple of years before she drowned." With a sad shake of his head, he added, "She had just been accepted to medical school at the university. She was planning to be a doctor like everyone else in her family."

"You say she drowned," Mac said, "but her body was never found."

"Now you sound like Sinclair and his strumpet," David said. "A witness saw her swimming in the lake. He said she and her friend, Carlisle Green, were both drunk and possibly doing other illegal substances. It is assumed she drowned—"

"Why didn't this witness try to save her?"

"He didn't *see* her drown." Exasperated, David sighed and sat down across from Mac. "Do you want me to tell you what happened?"

"That's what I meant when I asked you to tell me about it."

With a growl, Archie tossed her tablet back onto the coffee table. "Give me that invitation!"

"Oh, now you have time for me," David cracked.

Archie whirled around at Mac. "Remember Kassandra Van Dyke?"

Mac told David, "Another social climber trying to get on the A-list."

"She blew into town with Lindsey York this morning," David said.

"Who is Lindsey York?" Mac asked.

"A living example of what happens when you get too much before you're mature enough to handle it," David said. "I arrested Lindsey for DUI. She was in jail a total of seventy-two minutes before she posted bail and got out. Record time."

"According to Kassandra, she's on the list." Archie told David, "She just e-mailed her RSVP to me. Seems she received an email invitation and her housekeeper says she got a printed one at her home. Amazing postal service considering that Catherine only put the invitations in the mail *today*."

Mac tried to object. "But—"

Archie was continuing her rant. "Kassandra is thrilled that her invitation had finally gotten to her and she never should have doubted but that she would have been invited to the Diablo Ball because her good friend *Lindsey York* got her invitation more than a week ago."

"I knew it!" David gasped. "Someone is bringing them all together again."

Mac interjected, "Exactly who is Lindsey York? Could she have killed Ashton Piedmont?"

"Lindsey York is a trouble maker that Robin Spencer had blackballed permanently from the Diablo Ball the year before she passed," Archie answered.

"How did she get an invitation?" David asked while Archie snatched the copy of the phony invitation from his grasp.

Planting her hands on her hips, Archie said with a growl, "Has to be Rock Sinclair for his little news program." Mac's laughter redirected her disgust. "What's so funny?"

With a grin, Mac sat back on the love seat and folded his arms behind his head. "Suddenly, I have a feeling that the Diablo Ball isn't going to be as boring as I had originally thought."

CHAPTER FOUR

"Oh, it was the stuff of bad movies." Catherine Fleming rolled her eyes at the memory.

"A really bad chick flick." Ben was helping Mac to set up the DVD in the home theater, located on the ground floor of the manor, across from what had been Robin Spencer's study where she penned close to a hundred literary masterpieces.

It had been quite some time since Mac and Archie had watched a DVD. For many years, the Diablo Ball had been filmed and DVDs of the event had been given as souvenirs to attendees. As soon as she had learned about the non-invitees, Catherine grabbed her disk of the very last ball. She and her husband rushed as fast as their Mercedes could get them from their estate at the top of Spencer Mountain to the Point at the bottom.

"I still don't know why she came." The prosecutor's wife accepted Archie's offer of a glass of sherry. "The Diablo Ball was in no way the MTV awards. We were made up of the literary set. Writers, publishers, agents, Washington DC politicians who fancy themselves to be educated and highbrow. After Robin's books were made into movies more of the Hollywood set—"

"None of the fast crowd." David handed a bottle of beer to Mac, which he had helped himself to from the kitchen.

51

"I really can't imagine Lindsey even being remotely interested in attending such a boring event." In response to the daggers shot to him from both Catherine and Archie while he took a sip of his beer, he swallowed and then cleared his throat. "Not that *I* think it's boring."

"You've never gone," Archie pointed out, "even though you were invited."

"I've always had to work."

"Volunteered to cover that shift to let other officers attend?" Mac whispered.

"What can I say? I'm a nice guy," David replied.

"Admit it," Archie ordered, "you arranged to be working for an excuse not to go."

"Why would you *not* want to go to the Diablo Ball?" Catherine's tone was wounded.

"You're coming and bringing Chelsea this year, aren't you?" Archie asked. "She knows you're getting an invitation and she's looking forward to it."

"It would be good for her career," Ben said. "One day, I'm going to want to retire and if she knows the right people, she could stand a chance of taking over as county prosecutor."

"Doesn't she have to graduate from law school first?" David asked.

"You have to think about her future," Ben said.

Mac recognized the expression of dread on the police chief's face. "With this group crashing, I don't think it's going to be boring." He invited David to sit next to him in the home theater's reclining seats.

Shaking his head, David dropped down into the chair with a groan. "I hate the thought of spending an evening stuck in a room full of Rock Sinclairs and Lindsey Yorks."

"People like them usually don't make Spencer their party spot," Ben said. "We're too low key for them, which is why it was so odd Lindsey York coming to the ball and causing such a ruckus."

"Between Lindsey and her friends' behavior, that last event ended up being a fiasco." Catherine pointed a finger bearing a long pink fingernail in Archie's direction. "In twenty years of the Diablo Ball, we had never seen anything like it."

"How did she get an invitation?" Mac asked.

"Her father is Randolph York," Ben said. "He owns SuperMart."

"I know him," Mac said. "He has a big estate at the top of the mountain and spends a lot of time at the Spencer Inn. During the summer season, he has lunch there every single day." He noticed Catherine and Archie exchange knowing glances. "What?"

Archie giggled. "Nothing."

Ben reached over to nudge Mac in the arm. "It's common knowledge that it's not the food that brings Randolph York to Spencer and the Spencer Inn every summer."

Mac furrowed his brow.

Chuckling next to him, David said, "For a first class detective, you can miss some very obvious clues."

"What does Randolph York come to Spencer for?"

"Only to admire the greatest pair of gams this side of the Mississippi," Ben said. "Don't you notice that when Randolph York is at the Spencer Inn, he's not very far from Betty, the manager at the registration desk?"

Considering that he had failed to notice that one of the Inn's most important frequent guests was so attracted to one of his employees, Mac didn't want to confess that he had missed noticing what Ben and David considered to be an exceptional pair of legs. To him, Betty Cosgrove was simply a very pretty and extremely nice woman who many guests raved about.

Now that I think about it, most of those guests raving about Betty are male.

"You never noticed," David said with a grin.

"That's because he's so in love with Archie," Catherine said.

"Exactly," Archie said.

"Betty Cosgrove is dating Randolph York?" Mac couldn't envision his dedicated, hardworking employee, a single mother who had put herself through college while working the night shift at the Inn, in a romantic relationship with someone who had to be one of the top five wealthiest men in the country.

"No," Archie said, "not dating. He's clearly attracted to her. Everyone sees it, but as far as I know, he's never taken her out."

"Maybe he thinks she's too low class to be in his league," Catherine said. "Nice to look at, but not good enough to touch."

"No," Mac said with certainty. "Randolph York is very down to earth. If he's attracted to Betty but hasn't acted on it, there's another reason. Maybe he's scared."

"He's a *billionaire*," David laughed.

"Money doesn't erase fear of rejection," Mac said. "The man clearly has some issues. I've known him for years. Played golf with him. Had drinks with him. Never once did he mention a daughter to me."

"As far as Randolph is concerned, he doesn't have a daughter," Ben said. "He disowned her. A couple of summers ago, he asked me for advice about how to insure she didn't get a penny of his money."

"Lindsey's mother was Stephanie Williams, an actress who was heavily into sex, drugs, and rock and roll," Archie said. "She was found drowned in their pool one morning after one of her famous parties down in Cancun. Luckily, Lindsey was with her father at their estate and didn't see it happen. Lindsey is following right in her mother's footsteps."

"He lives right down the road from us," Catherine said. "He'd come to the Diablo Ball every year and make a huge donation."

"He's nothing like his daughter," David agreed with a nod of his head. "Every time Lindsey would get into trouble here and the police were called, Randolph York would send a big gift basket to the police department as an apology for how his daughter treated us."

"At that last ball, Lindsey was going to be her father's date," Catherine recalled. "At the last minute, he got called away to a meeting in New York. So she came and brought her friend Kassandra Van Dyke. Kassandra's father knew Lindsey's mother from their party days in Hollywood."

While handing the DVD player's remote to his wife, Ben laughed. "Picture *Girls Gone Wild* meets Harvard's Book Club."

Holding the remote like a baton, Catherine stood in front of the big screen to set up the scene for the audience. "It was after the cocktail party, before the dinner. Archie and I had spent a full month working on the seating chart. That's not easy. By then, Archie knew most everyone and who got along with whom. We tried to place all of the young people together at the same table."

Archie jumped in. "When Randolph had notified Robin that Lindsey was bringing Kassandra in his place I redid the seating to have them sit with A.J. Wagner and his party. He had just graduated from University of Maryland in pre-med. His father, Dr. Howard Wagner, the university president, had died only the year before. A.J. was with a party of four. His date, Ashton Piedmont. The other two were another couple, his college roommate and Rachel Breckenridge. Her mother is Dr. Elizabeth Breckenridge. She's now the dean of the School of Medicine at the University of Maryland."

She rushed on, "I was originally going to have A.J. Wagner's party sit with Dr. Breckenridge and her date, but then, when I'd found out that Lindsey and Kassandra were coming, I realized I had enough young people to make up one whole table. That worked out well because Dr. Breckenridge's table was full of medical academic types. She had published a book the year before that was on its way to becoming a huge hit."

"Something about using a three-D printer to make body parts," Ben said with a shiver.

"Her book and research has become like a bible at medical schools all across the country," Archie said. "At the time of this last ball, it had only come out the year before and there were a lot of academic and publishing big-wigs begging to be seated with her."

"So Dr. Breckenridge was safe from the big event," Mac clarified. "But her daughter was not. Neither was Ashton Piedmont, who ended up missing and presumed dead."

Ben said, "Ashton was just a witness to all this, Mac, not an active participant."

"Mac is right about one thing, Ben," David said. "A week later, Ashton Piedmont disappeared."

"Am I the only one who finds that suspicious?" Mac asked.

"It was an accidental drowning," Ben said.

"I don't know if Ashton and Wagner had even met Lindsey and Kassandra before that night," Catherine said. "As a matter of fact, Wagner and his party were not banned from the ball."

"Lindsey, Kassandra, and Jasmine Simpson were banned," Archie said. "Robin was specific."

"What do you know about Jasmine Simpson?" David asked. "She's Rock Sinclair's mistress and date this year for the ball. Did she know Ashton before that night? A couple of hours ago, she made it sound like they were BFFs."

After whipping out her tablet to check the information, Archie held up her finger. "Jasmine Simpson got her degree in communications from the University of Maryland three years ago. That is the same university where Ashton Piedmont attended. Both of their families own property here on the lake in Spencer, and they did summer here regularly."

"So they most likely, at least, knew of each other," Mac said. "How was Rock's mistress involved?" He peered at the picture that Catherine had frozen on the big screen television while she set up the scene. It was a large round dining table in what he recognized to be the main banquet room at the Inn, reserved for weddings and special events. Everyone was in formal dress. Three men wore tuxedos, while their dates were dressed in cocktail dresses. The seating was girl-boy-girl-boy.

"Watch," Catherine replied. "I'm just showing you the climax." She pointed the remote and hit the play button. "Dinner was right about to start. Lindsey York was already inebriated when she got there."

Ben said, "A.J. Wagner is the blond haired man with his arm around his date, Ashton Piedmont."

A.J. Wagner was a handsome young man with a chiseled jaw. In his early twenties, he still had schoolboy charm. His date sat at his left, the last in the line of the round table. Ashton was dressed in a pale pink dress that flowed over her slender curves. Her hair was cute in a simple cut to the nape of her neck. She was attractive, but not overtly glamorous.

"Ashton," Mac mouthed with narrowed eyes.

The next man seated at the table contrasted A.J. Wagner's fair features. He had dark hair that was longer and curved around his face.

The woman sitting next to him was dressed in a blue gown. Her long hair flowed down to her shoulders. Catherine reiterated that the other couple was guests of A.J. Wagner.

"What's the name of A.J.'s roommate?" Mac asked.

"Corey Haim," Catherine replied. "He's from West Virginia. I don't know much about him except that he and A.J. are real close buds."

On the opposite side of the table, the next couple was Jasmine Simpson and her date. David noted that Jasmine looked much the same, though the years had made her more sophisticated. In the five year old recording, shot when she was still in college, she had more of a baby-face in her appearance.

When the camera zoomed in for a close-up of the couple, David sprang upright in his seat. "Freeze it right there."

Juggling with the remote, Catherine hit the pause button to freeze the frame on Jasmine Simpson and her date.

David squinted at the young man sitting next to Rock Sinclair's now mistress. In the years since, he had trimmed his hair and grown a goatee and mustache. The cocky smirk and wink he was flashing at the lovely server pouring the champagne was unmistakable.

"I met that man today," David said. "He's Samuel Nash, the director for Rock Sinclair and Jasmine Simpson's film project."

"And now his date from back then is sleeping with another man and they are both his boss?" Ben asked. "Awkward."

"Very." Catherine hit the play button.

Two young women joined the group at the table. One was dressed in a red sequin dress that plunged to reveal her ample bosom. The red in her hair matched the hue of the dress. The other's gown matched the red one, in black. Her platinum mane contrasted the black in her gown.

The redhead staggered to the table. "Hey, there's table thirteen!" Leading her friend, Lindsey left an empty chair between her and Corey before flopping down at the table.

Her companion introduced herself to the group. "I'm Kassandra Van Dyke. This is Lindsey York." She offered an awkward wave of her hand. "This is going to be so much fun. It's such a great cause. I just love Robin's Pets. Don't you?"

"Shut up, Kassandra, and put your ass in the chair," Lindsey said with a sneer. "Have they come to take our drink orders yet?" she asked those at the table.

Glancing around, Ashton asked, "Are you sure you're at the right table?"

"This is thirteen, ain't it?" Lindsey picked up an envelope placed under her napkin in the center of her plate.

Ashton responded to her date's questioning look. "I thought—"

A.J. told her, "There was some last minute seat changes due to cancellations."

Lindsey laughed. "Shit!"

There was a stunned silence at the table.

"Excuse me?" Jasmine Simpson replied.

"Someone thinks they're hot shit because they know my secret." She waved a card like a flag at those at the table and surrounding tables.

A.J. told her, "Listen, Miss York—"

"No, you listen!" She sneered, "You want to talk about screwing around with people's secrets!"

"Calm down, Lindsey," Kassandra pleaded. "People are looking."

Lindsey stuffed the card down her bosom and grabbed her wine glass. "Why should I calm down? So what if some gutless coward knows my secrets? He thinks he can screw around with me over my secrets—" She wagged her head. "Bring it on!"

Ashton blurted out, "Maybe it was just some misunderstanding."

"*Miss* Understanding? Misunderstanding? Yeah! I'm sure it was a misunderstanding!"

"Lots of people have secrets," Corey said.

"Oh, yeah!" Lindsey yelled. "And I know quite a few!"

"Listen, Miss Lindsey," Jasmine said, "I think you better go sober up before you say or do something that you're going to regret."

Lindsey mocked her. "You think I better go sober up before I say or do something that I'm going to regret." She scoffed. "Who are you anyway?"

"Jasmine Simpson," she answered with pride. "My mother was Miss America and my father is the CEO of Simpson Enterprises."

Lindsey laughed. "Do you mean Orson Simpson? Don't you mean he *used to be* CEO?"

"How old are they?" Mac's nose wrinkled with disgust. "Ten?"

"The social hierarchy of rich kids is directly connected to the success of their parents," David said. "The only reason I got through high school alive was because my daddy was chief of police."

Mac shot a grin in David's direction. "Lucky you."

On the television screen, Jasmine's expression toward Lindsey was deadpanned.

"My daddy bought your daddy out." Lindsey doubled over with laughter. When she sat up, she made the shape of the letter L and held it up to her forehead. "Loser!"

Jasmine threw the contents of her wine glass into Lindsey's face.

Before everyone could scatter to safety, Lindsey was up and taking the table—dishes, glasses and all—with her. Wine and water flew, along with trays of food that servers had been delivering at the same time that the table went flying.

A.J. sheltered Ashton.

Leaving his date behind, Samuel Nash ran for the exit. "What a gentleman," David said upon seeing Nash's hasty retreat.

Mac chuckled in spite of Archie and Catherine's continued dismay over the disruption, which they had replayed more than once in the past.

David and Ben seemed to be equally amused. "What is interesting," the prosecutor said, "is that both Lindsey and Kassandra have been asked to come back, via the phony invitations. And so has Jasmine Simpson, who, while provoked, started it with the toss of her wine glass."

Mac said, "The evidence may be circumstantial, but it looks like whoever is behind this is looking for a reunion of some sort." He asked Archie, "What about A.J. Wagner? Is he coming back?"

Archie nodded her head. "Most likely. He's already in town at his family estate on the lake with his best friend Corey. Rachel Breckenridge's in town, too. Their names are on the invite list."

"And Jasmine Simpson is back, too," Mac mused while stroking Gnarly's ears. During the playing of the video, the German shepherd had come in to sit up tall between Mac's legs. "Someone is using the Diablo Ball to engineer a reunion and they're going to lengths to entice me into looking into Ashton's disappearance." He hugged Gnarly, who returned the show of affection with a tongue in Mac's ear. "And it's working."

Pushing Gnarly aside, he sat up. "I want to see where Ashton disappeared." After standing up, he went to the door. "Come on, David, let's go."

"I can't."

Mac turned around. "Why not?"

With a glance in Archie's direction, David said, "I have to go pick Chelsea up at work."

"Chelsea gets off work in a half hour," Ben Fleming confirmed with a nod of his head.

David's girlfriend, Chelsea Adams was Ben Fleming's paralegal. David drove her because she didn't have a driver's license due to her epilepsy. At the mention of Chelsea's name, Gnarly's ears stood up. Chelsea's service dog, a white German shepherd named Molly, was his best pal.

"Well," Mac said, "we'll swing by and pick her up and take her to the crime scene along with us."

"I don't think so." Again, David stole a glance in Archie's direction.

"Why not?" Mac asked.

"Maybe David and Chelsea would like to go get something to eat … without additional company," Archie told Mac with a cock of her head.

"I'm going by the house on the way back," David said. "I want to check out how the new siding came out."

As soon as the winter season had given way to spring, David had hired a building contractor to complete renovations to his childhood home, which had been vacant since he had committed his mother to a nursing home. They hoped that the improvement in the housing market and summer season would bring some nibbles from potential buyers.

"Mac," Archie said in a gentle, yet firm voice, "David will take you to the crime scene *tomorrow.*"

Mac's expression was similar to that of a child being told that he had to wait to go to the circus. "Okay."

David mouthed a thank you in Archie's direction. Passing Mac on the way out the door, he patted him on the shoulder. "It's okay, Mac. The lake where she drowned will still be there in the morning." With a jab to Mac's shoulder, David turned and ran up the stairs. "Wish me luck!"

"I'll be rooting for you, David!" Archie called out.

"What was that about?" Mac asked Archie.

Her face filled with mock innocence, she shrugged her shoulders. "Nothing."

"Yeah, right," Mac replied. "If I believed that, I'd believe Gnarly wasn't the one who stole the Schweitzer grandchildren's Easter eggs."

"That was Gnarly?" With a gasp, Catherine covered her mouth and gazed at the German shepherd eying each of them in turn.

"We found them under the back deck almost two weeks later," Mac said.

"How many eggs did he steal?" Rising out of his seat, Ben stared at the dog with wide eyes.

"Over three dozen. Do you know what three dozen hard boiled eggs that have been outside for two weeks smells like?"

"How did he steal that many and hide them under your deck?" Catherine's tone was filled with doubt.

"Very carefully." Mac shot a glare at Gnarly. "Egg sucking dog."

"We don't *know* that was Gnarly," Archie said.

Laying his ears back flat onto the top of his head, Gnarly uttered a belch.

CHAPTER FIVE

As Spencer's chief of police, David O'Callaghan was part of Spencer, but he was not one of its wealthy residents—nor was his father before him.

Patrick O'Callaghan had made his home on the outskirts of the resort town. As a young police officer, he had managed to secure a small lakeside lot along a quiet, out-of-the-way cove, where he had built a cozy home for his wife and son. While the property was lakeside, it was several feet above the water. A steep set of steps led down to the dock and boat house.

The property had significantly increased in value over the decades. However, the rundown three bedroom, one bath, ranch-style house left much to be desired to potential home buyers when compared to the more luxurious estate homes around the lake. Almost two years after his mother had stabbed him in the chest with a fork during a demented fit, David had yet to return to live in the house in which he had been raised. It was not filled with exclusively happy memories.

Years after Robin Spencer had given in to her parent's order to end their relationship, Patrick married Violet, only to have Robin return to discover that the love of her life—and the father of the baby she had been forced to give up for adoption—had started a family.

Being a loyal and honorable man, Patrick had kept his marriage vows and refused to give in to the temptation of pursuing the love of his life, which Robin Spencer had respected. The couple developed a deep, loving friendship which endured even in the face of rumors.

Alzhiemers and alcohol had acted like gasoline when added to Violet O'Callaghan's jealousy, which simmered long and hard. Her bitterness would erupt into episodes of depression or even suicide attempts.

During her numerous hospitalizations, the busy police chief would send his son to live at Spencer Manor. At one point, David had spent a full year living under the peaceful, calming roof of the world famous author—unaware that she was his secret half-brother's mother.

It seemed only natural, after his mother had been committed to the nursing home, that David would return to Spencer Manor, where Mac offered to let him stay in the guest cottage for as long as he wanted.

After two years, it was time for David to have a home of his own.

"David?" The sound of Chelsea's voice jarred David out of his thoughts.

After pulling his police cruiser into the driveway, David's mind had drifted onto a merry-go-round made up of memories from his childhood. He was staring at the huge oak tree right on the edge of the drop-off down to the lake. A thick, rotten rope hanging from a tall branch was all that was left of the tire swing that David and his friends used to play on. The water was deep enough that they used to swing out and launch themselves off the tire to plunge into the water several feet below.

"David, is everything all right?" Chelsea's worried tone broke through his thoughts again.

Startled, David turned to her to see her light blue eyes filled with concern.

Chelsea Adams' fair complexion gave her an appearance of being almost albino. Combined with her platinum blonde hair that fell in silky waves to her shoulders and exceedingly thin figure, she appeared quite frail. It made David want to protect her from the world's wicked ways.

In the back of the cruiser, Molly, Chelsea's service dog, whimpered.

"I'm fine," David told both of them. He reached over to caress Chelsea's cheek.

"What do you think?" she asked.

"About what?"

Chelsea cocked her head at him. "About the siding. You wanted to stop by to see how the contractor did with the siding. But we've been sitting here for like five minutes and you haven't even turned off the car."

David realized that while he had put the cruiser in park, he had indeed left the engine running. After turning off the motor, he opened the door and slipped out. Aware of Chelsea's puzzled gaze on him, he went around the cruiser to open her door. Molly waited for him to open the rear door to escort her charge.

Clutching Chelsea's hand, David strolled around the house.

"What does the realtor think?" She peered up at the new white siding. Fond memories came to mind of her trying to keep up with David and her older brother while they played on the lake.

Like David, Chelsea was from Spencer, but not of it. Her late mother had been the high school secretary.

"The property value is so high due to the location," David said. "Anyone who could afford to move onto the lake in Spencer would want a bigger house with more perks. A real downer is that this house only has one bathroom. Most have at least two full baths."

"Then she doesn't think she can sell it?"

"Mac has offered to buy it for a vacation rental," David said. "He thinks the location and small size would be perfect for a family wanting to come to Spencer but who couldn't afford one of the larger rental places."

"That does make sense."

"Plus, he's willing to pay my original asking price," David said. "That's an offer too good to refuse."

"Sounds like you've made up your mind."

"Maybe."

"What's stopping you?" she asked. "If Mac's buying it for your original asking price, then you can get a nice place up the mountain; or do you want to live here on the lake? When are you going to start looking at houses? Or do you want to stay in Mac's guest house to save more money for a bigger place?" She fired off her questions like an automatic weapon.

With a toss of his head, he said, "Let's go down to the lake." Tugging on her hand, he led her over to the walkway and the stairs leading down to the boat dock. He kept ahead of her to watch her while easing down the steep steps. Behind her, Molly looked apprehensively down at the dock and the water.

"What's down here?" she asked.

With a wicked grin, David replied, "You know what's down here." He gestured at the boat house next to the dock.

Her pale face turned pink. "You brought me here to seduce me in the boat house? David, we aren't teenagers anymore. If you want me, you could have taken me home for that." She giggled.

David pulled her in close, wrapped his arms around her, and lifted her face up to his. She caressed his firm shoulders.

Gently, he kissed her lips. "I've always liked this place." He brushed his lips against her cheek.

"Liar."

Gazing into her eyes, he said, "Yes, I do have some bad memories of it, but my memories of our time here are good ones—like that afternoon in the boat house, when we first told each other that we loved each other."

She smiled broadly. "And then your father walked in and caught us half naked."

As their laughter subsided, David recalled, "That was when Dad told me about Mac—that I had a brother I never knew about."

"I'm glad you two are friends."

"That isn't why I brought you down here," David said.

She shook her head. "Then why?"

"Do you remember back in December, when those men abducted me?"

He felt her tremble in his arms. "How could I forget?"

"The one person I kept focused on getting back to was you. I knew before they took me that I loved you, but that night, while I was lying there tied up, I vowed to get out of there alive and … when I did … I was going to make things right between us."

"Make things right between us?" she asked. "David, I forgave you for cheating on me. That was eons ago. It's in the past."

"It's one thing to tell you that I love you and to spend every night in your bed," David said. "But you deserve more than that. You deserve a lot more than that."

He knelt down in front of her.

"Chelsea Adams, I have been in love with you since we were kids who thought we knew all the answers to how the world worked. That's why I brought you here, to the beginning, to where I first told you that I loved you."

Her eyes grew wide with wonderment.

David reached into his pants pocket and took a jewel box out. He opened it to display a diamond ring. "Will you marry me, Chelsea Adams?"

Even Molly's dark eyes on her white face were wide at the sight of the ring. She edged forward to sniff at the box. Then, she glanced up at her master as if to declare that it was real.

While David gazed up at her, Chelsea's eyes filled with tears. Her lips quivered. Her mouth seemed to work, but nothing came out of it. Kneeling before her, in a position of complete submission, David felt his heartbeat quickened while the silence grew between them.

"Chelsea, you need to say something," he finally said.

Tears spilled from her eyes.

"Are those tears of happiness or sorrow because you're about to break my heart?"

Sniffing, she thrust her left hand out to him with her fingers spread out.

"What do you want me to do?" David asked.

She shook her hand and pointed with her finger at the ring.

David fought the grin working its way to his lips. "Do you want me to put it on your finger?"

Her head bobbed up and down. When he took her hand, he felt it trembling with excitement. Tears spilled from her eyes to soak her cheeks.

Amusement turned to worry when he remembered her epilepsy. *Suppose this is the start of a seizure.*

Slipping the ring onto her finger, he stole a glance at Molly who appeared curious, but not concerned. She would be barking and pawing at Chelsea to tell her to take her medication if she was. Admiring the perfect fit of the engagement ring on her finger, David stood up. After throwing herself into his arms, she kissed him. Her whole body shook with excitement.

"I guess this is a yes?" he asked into her hair.

Hugging him tightly while holding up her hand to admire the diamond, her reply into his ear consisted of a string of sob-filled words. He didn't understand anything she said.

"Are you accepting my proposal?" David asked with a laugh while stroking her hair. "Just nod your head yes or shake it no."

Letting loose with a fresh batch of tears, she nodded her head.

❧ ❧ ❧

The Next Morning

The delicious scent of a hot breakfast casserole in the oven greeted Mac when he and Gnarly returned from their run.

Every morning, without fail, by the sixth bong of the grandfather clock in the front foyer, Gnarly pounced on Mac to let him outside. While Mac was able to go back to sleep after letting the dog out, an hour later, Gnarly's barking outside his window roused him to demand re-entrance, at which point Gnarly would order breakfast.

By then, Mac would give up on going back to sleep.

Such had been Mac Faraday's life of leisure.

After his last physical revealed that he had gained twenty pounds since his windfall, Mac decided to use the early morning wake-up to add more athletics and get in some cardio before breakfast. A run served two purposes. One, it was exercise for Mac. Two, it served to tire the high energy German shepherd. By the time they arrived back at the manor, Gnarly would be ready to sack out right after gulping down his breakfast.

The absence of David's police cruiser in his space in the garage told Mac that he had spent the night at Chelsea's lakeside condo, which was steadily becoming David's regular routine. Lately, he had been spending more nights with Chelsea than in the guest cottage.

While pacing in front of the garage to cool off from his run, Mac studied the empty space in the garage. After all these months of living here while sleeping there, wouldn't it be more convenient for him to start moving some of his stuff over to her place. With a grin, Mac recalled how Archie had slyly started moving into the master suite one article of clothing at a time until circumstances forced her to make the big move all at once.

"David's coming for breakfast?" Mac asked Archie after accepting her offer of a mug of hot coffee. "You don't usually go to the trouble of making a whole casserole for just the two of us."

"He's bringing Chelsea over before taking her to work." Her smile, broader than usual, indicated that she was definitely keeping a secret—a big one.

His eyebrow arched. "Do they have an announcement to make?"

Bouncing up and down, Archie uttered a squeal and clapped her hands.

"That's what you meant when you told him that we were rooting for him when he was leaving yesterday." Mac tapped the tip of her nose. "Why'd he tell you and not me?"

"Because he asked me to help him pick out a ring," Archie said. "I sent him to your daughter. She's really into that stuff, plus, I know she has a guy who designs custom jewelry." She grasped Mac by both arms. "Oh, it's so beautiful. It's a full carat diamond that Jessica got with a really nice discount and the band is white gold. Chelsea has to love it."

"She said yes?" Mac asked.

With a bark, Gnarly charged for the foyer.

Archie was close behind the dog. "Act surprised!" she ordered Mac.

"Why should I act surprised?" Mac fell in behind them at a more dignified pace. "You're not acting surprised."

Archie threw open the door and flew out onto the front porch. David had pulled his cruiser up to the bottom of the steps. Usually, Chelsea would wait for David to open the door for her, but not this morning. As soon as the two women saw each other, Chelsea threw open the door and jumped out of the cruiser. Waving her left hand, she ran up to Archie who grasped it to admire the new addition to her ring finger. All the time, they were uttering excited squeals and sobs of joy.

"How did he ask you?" Archie asked Chelsea, who responded with a tear-filled, unintelligible response.

Archie replied with a shriek and a hug before escorting her past Mac and inside the house to get all the details.

"I guess you did get lucky last night." Chuckling, Mac strolled down the steps to where David was letting Molly out of the back of the cruiser. The two dogs went racing side by side around the house and out to the rolling garden leading down to the boulder lined shore.

"Congratulations." Mac clasped his hand. "You're a lucky man."

"Don't I know it," David replied. "I've been granted a second chance with Chelsea and this time I'm not going to screw up."

Mac said. "Hopefully, you've come a long way since you two were in high school."

"I'd like to think so," David said. "Is your offer to buy my house still good?"

"Sure. I'll call my lawyer today to get started on the paperwork." Mac clasped David's hand. The handshake turned into a hug. "Have you set a date?"

They strolled up the walk to the steps leading up to the front porch. "Sometime in mid-September, after the end of the season and my next reserve tour. Only it's not going to be like your and Archie's wedding."

"Why wouldn't you want murder and mayhem at your wedding?"

"It sets the wrong tone."

CHAPTER SIX

During breakfast, Archie volunteered to drive Chelsea to Ben Flemings' office, which allowed the two women more time to plan the wedding. This also let Mac and David scope out the scene of Ashton Piedmont's disappearance sooner.

By the time they had finished eating breakfast, it was decided that Molly and Gnarly would play the role of flower dog and ring bearer. While Mac was certain that Molly, whom he called "The Stepford Dog" in reference to the movie *The Stepford Wives*, would do well in her role, he was not so certain about Gnarly. It was not beyond the realm of possibilities that Gnarly would outright rebel at the notion of marching with decorum down the aisle. Somehow, Mac envisioned the roof caving in on the "devil dog."

The cove where Ashton Piedmont had disappeared was less than fifteen minutes from Spencer Point.

"Where does this Carlisle Green, the woman who Ashton was last seen with, fit into all this?" Mac asked while referring to the notes he had made from Ashton Piedmont's case file. "She wasn't at the Diablo Ball. Or rather, she wasn't in the group that got banned."

"The Greens go almost as far back in Spencer history as the Spencers and O'Callaghans," David said. "They're snowbirds from Arizona. I gave Carlisle swimming lessons when I was lifeguarding at the Spencer Inn back when she was a little girl."

Knowing the term, Mac nodded his head. Snowbirds was the term used to describe seasonal residents. Like birds, they wintered down south, where it was warm, and then migrated back north for the summer months.

"Carlisle's grandfather never went to college," David said. "But Ellery was brilliant. Took what little money he had and made a fortune in the stock market. The Greens are billionaires. His son and daughter-in-law enjoyed the good life. Carlisle got tossed out of the best boarding schools in the world."

"Tossed out?" Mac asked.

"Her parents finally decided they had had enough of her and shipped her off to Grandpa Green," David said. "She was sixteen when they were killed in a hotel fire in Europe. Her grandfather was so broken-hearted, he died of heart failure nine months later. Carlisle Green was seventeen years old when she became a billionaire ... and an emancipated minor."

"I can imagine what would have happened to my daughter, Jessica, if she came into that much money at such a young age and had no adult supervision," Mac said. "My son has always had a good head on his shoulders. He'd have been able to handle it ... but Jessica, back when she was that age ..." He cringed at the thought.

David was shaking his head. "I think that's why she and Ashton connected. They both lost their parents and they were close to their grandfathers who they lost. Ellery Green and Ross Piedmont were both brilliant, down to earth men. Practically every morning, they'd be out on the lake fishing during the summer."

"Then it would be natural for Ashton and Carlisle Green to become friends."

"They lived next door to each other during the summer," David said. "Carlisle was about three years younger than Ashton. But, emotionally, she was years older."

"Why wasn't she at the ball the night of the incident?" Mac asked.

"Most likely, she turned down the invitation," David said. "The Diablo Ball was definitely not her bag. It was too tame for her tastes."

The Piedmont estate had remained empty for five years. Even though the family lawyer had the grounds kept up in order to not let the property become overgrown, the mansion was eerily still and quiet.

Slowing down so that Mac could scope out the home of the subject of their cold case, David eased the cruiser past it on the way to the mansion around the bend in the lake shore road. Between the Piedmont and Green estate, there was a grove of trees and a stream that flowed into the lake.

"Carlisle Green makes Lindsey York look like a nun," David told Mac out of the side of his mouth. "Every summer she'd come out here and raise Cain. Her neighbors would call the police almost every night because she'd have the music blasting and she and her friends would be skinny dipping off the dock."

David turned the wheel to ease the cruiser between two stone pillars. They noticed piles of chopped brush, and a wheelbarrow next to the sidewalk that wrapped around to the lake side of the luxurious two-story stone house.

"I've always loved this house." David shot Mac a wide grin.

When the cruiser rounded the curve of the heavily wooded drive, Mac could see why. The Green home was not your average mansion. One would expect a billionaire to have a massive mansion, or at least the biggest house on Deep Creek Lake. Such was not so with Ellery Green's home.

While the lake house was large, it was not massive. From the exterior, Mac estimated it to be the same square footage as Spencer Manor. It was a guess, which was rough, considering that the two-story stone house was round with windows on every wall from floor to ceiling. Like Spencer Manor, it had decking all around from the front to the back. The sloping roof contained close to a dozen sky-lights.

Off to one side of the drive was a four-car garage with what appeared to be an apartment on the second floor.

"Very interesting," Mac said.

"Wait until you see the inside," David said.

"Is this Carlisle Green, witness-slash-suspect, still around?" Mac asked.

"I don't know what happened to her," David answered. "I know she hasn't been to Spencer since Ashton disappeared. Probably hiding out in a country that doesn't have extradition." He brought the cruiser to a stop and turned off the engine.

They heard a chainsaw running when they climbed out of the cruiser. "Must be the yard man keeping the place cleaned up," David said in reference to the sounds of outdoor work.

As soon as Mac opened the rear door, Gnarly leapt out and galloped around to the back of the house.

"Could Carlisle have killed Ashton?" Mac fell in behind David to follow him up onto the walkway leading to the dock and lake where Ashton had last been seen.

"Witnesses said they were having a cat fight."

"Over what?"

The sound of the chain saw grew louder. Determining that the sound was from overhead, they shaded their eyes with their hands to look up into the trees lining the walkway.

"No one knows and Carlisle claimed she couldn't remember," David said.

The chainsaw cut off. "Look out below!" a woman yelled from up in the branches.

Leaves and twigs rained down on them. A thick branch crashed inches from Mac, who grabbed David by the arm and yanked him back toward the house. The heavy branch barely missed them.

"Are you okay, Chief O'Callaghan?" the woman's voice called down to them. Camouflaged by the leaves and branches, they couldn't see her.

"Yes!" David continued to peer up the tree to find the culprit with the chainsaw who almost crushed them. They were finally able to make out a pair of bare legs with the feet encased in heavy work boots making their way downward.

"I'm so sorry." Focusing on the branches she clung to while descending to the ground with the agility of a monkey, she kept her back to them. "Lucky thing your dog came running by. I didn't hear your car. I had no idea anyone was here. Unfortunately, I had pretty well cut through the branch and couldn't stop."

When she broke through the bottom branches to come fully into view, Mac saw that she was a young woman, most likely in her early-to-mid-twenties. She wore her dark hair short in a boy's cut. There was not a hint of makeup on her naturally pretty face. Clad in shorts, with a heavy tool belt, and a tank top, she had a sleek, muscular build that came from hard manual labor—not the gym.

"Please accept my apologies." She offered them her hand.

While David's mouth hung open, Mac shook her hand. "Apology accepted. No harm done. I'm Mac Faraday, by the way. And you are …"

"Carlisle Green." She cocked her head at David. "It's nice to see you again, David. I see you're chief of police now. I'm glad. You deserve it. I'm sure you'll be able to find out what happened to Ashton—better than that other jerk who was running the police department before."

David blinked.

Seeing that he still could not find his voice, Carlisle turned her attention back to Mac. "I assume you're here because you've reopened Ashton's case."

"Yes," Mac said.

The corner of her lip curled up. "I expected you yesterday."

"Why yesterday?" Mac asked.

"That's when I left the note for you at the Spencer Inn."

"That was you?" Mac asked. "Are you behind the phony invitations, too?"

"No," she said. "I believe that's Jasmine and Rock Sinclair's little trick."

David finally blurted out. "What happened to you?"

Carlisle grinned at him. "I died. And then I was reborn." With a wave of her hand, she guided them toward the dock. "Five years ago, I was a pathetic excuse for a human being. I had to be right here when my best friend died and I couldn't help find out what had happened to her because I was too messed up. I admit it. I did have a little bit further to sink before my survival instinct kicked in and I voluntarily spent a year locked up in a rehab center rebuilding myself from the ground up."

They came to the end of the dock. Wistfully, Carlisle gazed out across the water while she recalled, "There, I came to realize that I hated who I was. I hated what my life represented. I was so pathetic that if I'd died, all anyone could say about me was that I took up space and air without giving anything back. So—" She turned to them. "I died. If you don't like who you are, then kill yourself and come back as another person. So that's what I did. I cut off everything and everyone from my old life. I read. I studied and I prayed to God for a clue about what I could offer back to the world. I've spent the last three years growing up into who I am today."

A crooked grin worked its way to her lips when she turned her attention to David. "I'm sorry for the way I treated you before, Chief O'Callaghan."

"Forget it."

"I'd rather not," she said. "It was the height of disrespect—"

"*Forget* it."

Curiosity getting the best of him, Mac asked, "What?"

"Nothing," David said in a firm tone that demanded the subject be dropped. "Can we move on?"

"Where's Gnarly?" Mac suddenly remembered the German shepherd who she had seen running under the tree. They hadn't seen him since he leapt out of the cruiser.

Carlisle pointed. "He took off down the path that leads over to Ashton's house."

"Gnarly!" Mac called in the direction of the mansion next door. There was a bark from in the woods between the two houses. Mac went up the dock to corral his dog.

When he turned back to Carlisle, David spotted the dock to the property on the other side of the Green estate. "Have you seen the Landers since coming back to Deep Creek?"

"No," Carlisle said with a frown. "I guess I'm too ashamed."

"How long have you been back?"

"Only a couple of days," she said. "Today is the first that I haven't been dealing with jet lag."

"Where did you fly in from?"

"South Africa," she replied. "I've been working in partnership with a charitable organization that builds wells for villages so that they can have clean water. I've been living there. This is the first time I've been back in the States for years."

Noting her firm body, with chiseled muscular definition, David guessed the help she offered in building the wells was hands on. He recalled that five years earlier, Carlisle was built like a rail; exceedingly slender to the point of borderline malnourished.

"Have you talked to Parker Lander lately?" Carlisle's voice startled David out of his admiration of her transformation.

"We only just reopened the case," David said. "I will be talking to him again."

"Maybe he'll know what Ashton and I were fighting about," she murmured. "But …"

"But what?" David asked. "Have you remembered something?"

"I remember hearing a woman's voice," Carlisle said. "Ashton and *another* woman fighting. But Parker never mentioned another woman being here." She shrugged. "I guess she could have been me. If Parker had heard Ashton fighting with this other woman and she left before he got here to break it up, he could have *thought* it was me."

"Would you recognize the voice?"

"No," Carlisle said with sadness. "It was a deep voice. Husky. Like a man's, but definitely a woman's."

"Gnarly, where have you been?" Mac yelled when Gnarly came racing out from the woods and across the backyard toward his master. The German shepherd was covered in mud and dirt. "What have you gotten into?"

Carlisle laughed to see the dog playfully bounding toward his master with what appeared to be a tree branch clamped in his jaws. "If he wanted a stick to play with, I have plenty that I've been stacking up."

Gnarly ended his run by jumping up to tag Mac in the chest and leaving muddy paw prints all over the front of his shirt.

"You're going to have to clean him up before he can get back into my cruiser," David warned.

"What do you have there?" Up close, Mac saw that the object was not made of wood. From a distance, its dark color gave it the appearance of a stick. Mac realized that it was, in fact, covered with dirt and discolored after having been buried for years. Wresting it out of Gnarly's mouth, Mac wiped it off.

"David!" Mac turned around to hold up Gnarly's find for the police chief to see.

David trotted up the dock to get a closer look. Carlisle was directly behind him. "What is it?" he asked Mac.

"I think it's a femur." Before Mac could turn to ask Gnarly, the dog was racing back into the woods. "Follow that dog!"

The three of them chased Gnarly down the path, where halfway to Ashton's home, he darted off the path and up an incline. Over the hill, Gnarly zigzagged through a grove of trees until he came to a small clearing where they found that he had begun digging through rotted leaves and twigs, and a tarp that had been recently torn by a determined German shepherd.

David reached the grave first. Gnarly had dug away enough to expose the leg and pelvis. "It's a body all right." He grabbed his radio to put in the call.

His job done, Gnarly trotted several feet away and sat down. His tall ears standing erect, he cocked his head to observe the police chief visually examining the grave.

"Ashton!" Carlisle fell on her knees to dig with her bare hands.

Mac pulled her back. "Don't touch it. It's evidence."

"But it has to be Ashton!" Carlisle looked over her shoulder and pointed. "Her house is only right over there. This is practically her backyard." Her sorrow turned to anger. "She didn't *drown*. She was *murdered* and buried here!"

"There's nothing you can do for her now," Mac said.

"Yeah, but there's something you can do," Carlisle said. "Find her killer … even if it's me. I want to know if I killed my best friend."

CHAPTER SEVEN

"If Ashton didn't drown, how did she die?" Carlisle Green offered a bottled water to Mac, who accepted the refreshment with a thank you.

"Hopefully, there's enough evidence that the medical examiner or forensics people will be able to find out."

Mac had suggested that Carlisle take him inside her home for two reasons. One, he felt it would be easier emotionally for her if she didn't have to watch her friend's body being dug up. Also, being alone, he would have a chance to question her about the last week before Ashton Piedmont had disappeared and, obviously, been killed.

Opening the bottled water, Mac took in the interior of the uniquely designed round house. The interior walls were a mixture of stone and cedar. Floor to ceiling windows provided a gorgeous view from every angle. When they have driven up to the round house, Mac was curious about how the home would be furnished since furniture is usually rectangle. He was surprised to discover that the kitchen's granite counters were indeed curved to fit the wall—as was the rest of the furnishings. The staircase leading up to the second level, where Mac assumed the bedrooms were located, curved along the wall. In the very center of the house the second floor was open to provide an opening to a skylight in the center of the roof.

Unlike his home, Spencer Manor, which rested at the tip of a strip of land that projected out into the lake, the Green estate and neighboring homes were tucked away in a scenic yet secluded section of the lake not frequented by tourists. The cove was wide and deep enough for the residents to enjoy their privacy while taking advantage of the water sports. If Mac squinted, he could just barely make out Spencer Point on the other side of Glendale Bridge.

The Green mansion was the perfect mixture of luxury and rustic charm. Ellery Green had been a die-hard angler who loved nature—judging by several large fish mounted on the walls. A chandelier made up of deer antlers and numerous original oil paintings of nature scenes from around the lake by local artists whose names Mac recognized added to the well-to-do—yet woodsey—feel. Worn leather furniture completed the rustic decor. A layer of dust that covered the hardwood floor and several pieces of furniture was evidence of the home's vacant status.

"Did you receive an invitation to the Diablo Ball this year?" While taking a drink from his bottle, Mac watched for her reaction out of the corner of his eye.

"An invitation I couldn't refuse," Carlisle said over her shoulder from the front foyer. She stood on her toes and cocked her head to watch the crime scene examiners and police collecting their cases and equipment from their vehicles. David was waiting at the edge of the path to lead them on the hike through the woods to where her best friend's decomposed body rested in the dirt and rotten branches and leaves.

Equally curious, Gnarly stood on his hind legs with his front paws resting on the window sill. He pressed his nose against the window to peer out. Occasionally, he would bark at a passing investigator.

"Explain." Mac tried to divert her attention from the happenings outside the window.

"Jasmine Simpson somehow got ahold of my cell phone number," Carlisle said. "Believe it or not, I am able to get a signal in the villages where I work. They can't get clean water, but we mission workers can get 4G on our cell phones. So, she calls and, in this sweet as sugar voice, says she's doing an investigative report on Ashton Piedmont's disappearance for an in-depth journalist program and would I consent to an interview. I told her I had no interest in coming back to the States. That was when she dropped the sweetie pie mask and her claws came out."

"She needed you for the report because you were the last person to see Ashton alive."

Carlisle nodded her head. "She told me that if I didn't come, that they would put the focus on me as the killer and put pressure on the prosecutor to issue an extradition order to have me brought back to the States. Since I was the last one to see her, and I honestly don't know—"

"Have you ever gotten violent when you were drunk?" Mac asked her.

She shrugged her shoulders. "Not that I know of. I was always told that I was a fun, sexy drunk."

"I'll ask Chief O'Callaghan." Mac said, "Their threat seems kind of lame to me. You have the money and means to have fought Sinclair and Jasmine. I'm thinking you gave in rather easily because you do want to know the truth."

"You're a smart man, Mr. Faraday," she said. "That's why I lured you into the case."

"Tell me about our suspects." Mac led her into the living room.

"I didn't really know them," she said. "Sure, I'd socialize with them during the season. Most of them lived here around Millionaire's Cove."

"Millionaire's Cove?"

"You never heard Millionaire's Cove?" Upon seeing the shake of his head, she explained, "That's what the locals here in Deep Creek Lake call this cove because most everyone who lives around here are millionaires. Grandpa was a self-made billionaire."

"And you hung out with Ashton and her friends—"

"I wouldn't call any of them my friends," Carlisle said. "But we weren't enemies either. After Labor Day, I'd go to Arizona or travel elsewhere to hang out. Ashton's friends were all college kids, and I didn't go to college. Plus, they were a few years older than me. They only let me hang around or they hung out here because I always had booze, pot, and other recreational toys for them to enjoy." She uttered a wicked laugh. "No one threw a party better than me. Just ask O'Callaghan. I don't know how many times he had to come out to break up my parties because the neighbors called the police. Probably at least once every weekend."

"A.J. Wagner was Ashton's boyfriend." Mac asked. "How serious were they?"

"Really serious," Carlisle said. "They especially bonded after A.J.'s father died. She had lost her grandfather only a few months before, so they leaned on each other." A solemn expression came to her face. "They always did have a thing for each other."

She giggled. "If you're looking for someone who hated Ashton—"

"That would be good place to start."

"Rachel Breckenridge," she said. "Never did like her. She always acted like she was better than me." She shrugged. "She was right, but she didn't need to be snooty about it."

"Her mother—"

"She was a big wig at the university where A.J.'s father was president," Carlisle said. "I assume she still is. Ashton's grandfather was her mentor. Rachel and Ashton grew up together. I remember they used to hang out together—somewhat—but whatever friendship they had dissolved when A.J. came into the picture."

"Isn't it funny how women's friendships end when a man enters the picture?" Mac noted with a grin.

"Tell me about it," Carlisle said in agreement.

"Then Rachel Breckenridge wanted A.J. Wagner for herself," Mac said.

Carlisle nodded her head. "She and Ashton were pretty chilly towards each other that last summer."

"But Rachel was Corey's date at the Diablo Ball," he said.

Saying nothing, Carlisle shrugged her shoulders while holding up her hands.

Leaning forward, Mac rested his elbows on his knees. "Anyone else in Ashton's life who maybe could have been jealous of her and A.J. getting together?"

"Greaser," Carlisle said quickly.

"Greaser?" Mac repeated.

"I never met him," Carlisle said. "Ashton knew him from school. He met her through Jasmine, who lived in Ashton's dorm. Greaser fell hard for Ashton—"

"That's who I'm looking for," Mac said. "Why was he called Greaser?"

"Because he dyed his hair jet black. Ashton said he always looked greasy. I was the one who came up with the name Greaser. Ashton had too much class to tell me his real name. She didn't want to make fun of him."

"I don't suppose you know what happened to Greaser?" Mac asked. "Even if you hadn't met him …"

"People, places, and things," Carlisle said with a shake of her head and a wave of her hand. "I left that whole world behind a long time ago. That's one of the main reasons I didn't want to leave the jungles of Africa. Less temptation there."

Seeing the concern for her sobriety in her eyes, Mac felt a tug of sympathy for her. "If you ever need someone to talk to—"

His sensitive ears picking up the footsteps on the back deck, Gnarly whirled around from the window to race to the door to greet David when he came in. "Doc's here," he said in reference to the medical examiner. "My deputy chief, Bogie, and the crime scene people have marked off the whole clearing and are searching for what they can."

"Considering that it's been five years …" Mac said.

Not holding out much hope for clues to Ashton's killer being found in the area around her grave, they exchanged glances.

David broke the silence. "Doc needs to get the body back to the morgue for a thorough exam, but we did find several fractures on her skull. Upper right side of the skull. It's very possible she died from blunt force trauma to the head."

"In other words," Carlisle said, "someone bashed her head in. Like in a drunken fit of rage?"

David's eyes locked with hers. "Very possibly."

"And then she dragged Ashton's body all the way down the path and over the hill to that clearing to bury her in a shallow grave," Mac said.

"You just saw how Carlisle hoisted that chainsaw and climbed up and down that tree like a monkey," David said.

"Could she have done that five years ago?" Mac asked.

"No," David said with a sigh before turning his attention back to Carlisle. "Were you missing a blue tarp back then?"

In silence, she stared at them. Mac could practically see the wheels turning behind her eyes before she answered in a slow steady tone, "I think … now that you mention it … there was a blue tarp that I used to cover the firewood to keep it dry from the rain. I remember noticing it was missing shortly before I left here." She shook her head. "I had so many blackouts back then, I don't remember when I noticed it was gone. It could have been before Ashton disappeared."

"You said you recall two women arguing," David reminded her. "A woman screaming—"

"But it wasn't Ashton screaming," Carlisle said. "This woman had a lower voice—gravely."

"You remember hearing, but not seeing them?" Mac asked her.

"A lot of that evening is in a fog," she said.

Mac gestured for her to sit down in the living area. "Okay, how about if we do this? Let's go back to the beginning."

After inviting David to sit down, Mac went behind the counter in the kitchen. "Forget we're the police and we're just sitting around having a nice chat about the last time you were here." He yanked open the refrigerator door. "I assume you don't have beer."

"I have green iced tea," she said. "Unsweetened."

"You really have changed," David noted.

"I'm totally vegan now," she said. "No processed food, meat, dairy or sugar. I don't even take aspirin. Only homeopathic medicine."

Having found the ice, Mac poured a glass of iced tea and brought it into the living room, where he handed the glass to her. He took a seat across from her.

"Now just relax," he said while she sipped the tea. "The last time you were here in Deep Creek Lake. You got into town and you caught up with your good friend Ashton. Imagine that we're a couple of good friends, we're just sitting around having drinks." He held up his bottled water in a toast, tapped it against her glass, and took a sip. "Tell us about your good friend Ashton. You said you and the gang from here on the lake didn't see each other off season, so, tell us about when you saw her for the first time that last season. How was she? Did she have any big news about anything?"

Carlisle took a deep sigh. She fell back against the seat. Staring at the wall behind them, she brought her fingers to her mouth and bit down on her thumbnail. "She was mad about something," she mumbled around the thumb clinched between her teeth.

David pounced. "What?"

Meeting David's eyes, she pulled her thumb out of her mouth. "I don't know. Back then, I only cared about my next binge." She brought her fingers back to her mouth. Cursing, she placed her hand under her thigh. "Nervous habit," she mumbled.

Mac noticed that, unlike any of the other pampered rich women in Spencer, Carlisle's fingernails were dirty, chipped, and some were bitten down to the quick.

She continued, "Ashton could have told me exactly what she was mad about and I wouldn't have paid any—"

"Forget about that," Mac interjected. "Tell us what you do remember."

"She was going through her grandfather's things in the lake house," Carlisle recalled with a shrug. "Maybe she found out a dirty family secret about her father." She sighed. "I really wasn't part of that crowd with all of their drama and all that."

"What type of drama?" Mac asked in a casual tone.

"Who was hooking up with whom?" Carlisle replied. "Ashton and A.J. were especially tight that summer. I expected them to announce they were getting married or were married." She cocked her head. "Now I remember. Those two were really secretive—getting together at Ashton's place. I assumed it was sex or they were planning to elope. They were definitely up to something."

Mac said, "Depending on what that secret was, maybe that's what got her killed."

❧ ❧ ❧

"Carlisle doesn't strike me as the hell-raiser you described," Mac commented with a grin when he and David, with Gnarly trotting ahead, went around the outside of the round house to return to David's cruiser.

The driveway was filled with law enforcement vehicles, including the medical examiner and crime scene investigators.

"That's not the same woman I used to arrest for drunk and disorderly back five years ago," David said.

"I believe that."

"I don't," David said.

"Don't you believe that people can change?"

"One-hundred and eighty degrees? She's a vegan!"

Mac's wordless response was a shrug of his shoulders. "Nothing wrong with that. If it works for her …"

"You never met the old Carlisle," David said.

"No, I didn't," Mac said. "But I have investigated numerous murder cases in which the killer, in the past, was the sweetest most stable guy or woman you would ever meet. And then, something happened. Usually it was drugs or booze. Addiction has a way of transforming someone—changing them."

David was nodding his head in agreement. "I've met more than one guy like that. The wrong type of woman can change a good man pretty fast."

"And the wrong man can do the same to a good woman," Mac said. "So … if something or someone can do a one hundred and eighty degree transformation for the bad to a good person, why is it so unbelievable that a person can't do a complete turnaround to the good?"

"Chief O'Callaghan?"

The call of David's name drew their attention to the end of the driveway where an older man with thin gray hair and flabby jowls gestured for their attention.

"Who's that?" Mac asked David while holding the rear door open for Gnarly to jump into the back of the cruiser.

"Parker Lander. Carlisle's neighbor." David approached the man watching them a questioning expression on his face.

"What's going on?" the older man asked. "Did Carlisle have an overdose?"

David shook his head. "The decomposed body of a woman was found in the woods between the Green and Piedmont properties."

Parker Lander's small eyes grew wide. His mouth hung open. "Ashton?"

"The body hasn't been identified." Feeling someone approaching behind him, David turned to see Mac joining them.

Parker blurted out, "I told you about Carlisle and Ashton fighting when she disappeared how many years ago."

"Why would Carlisle kill her?" Mac asked.

Instead of answering, Parker looked Mac up and down.

"This is Mac Faraday." David introduced the two men. "He works on contract with our police department on homicide investigations."

"Well," Parker said, "the night Ashton disappeared, she and Carlisle were drinking and probably doing some other stuff, too. They started fighting like a couple of hellions."

"What were they fighting about?" Mac asked.

"I have no idea," Parker said. "It was late, like eleven or so, and suddenly all hell broke loose. My wife was threatening to call the police and I didn't want to make things worse." He asked David, "You remember how Gloria could be."

Being diplomatic, David cleared his throat. "She could be difficult."

Parker snorted. "You always were too kind, O'Callaghan."

"If she's so difficult, why did you marry her?" Mac blurted out.

"She got knocked up, that's why. Now I am a free man," Parker said with a grin.

"Divorced?" David asked.

"She's dead."

Each one trying to decide how best to respond, Mac and David exchanged glances.

"A little over a year ago." Parker Lander broke the awkward silence. "Gloria took a header down the stairs and broke her neck."

"I'd say I was sorry for your loss, but I can see you're not in mourning," Mac said in a deadpan tone.

"It is what it is," Parker said, "Gloria was—"

"Difficult," David interjected.

"Can you get back to the night Ashton disappeared?" Mac urged him back on topic.

Parker extracted a handkerchief from his pants pocket. While mopping his sweaty face and flabby jowls with his left hand, he tugged up on his pants to cover his tubby belly. "I came over to break up that fight between those two so that Gloria wouldn't call the police and start another battle with Carlisle—only she turned on me."

"Gloria turned on you?" Mac asked.

"Carlisle." Parker turned to David. "You saw the scratches. I really hate bringing this up again." He told Mac, "My wife insisted that I tell the police about Carlisle attacking me back when Ashton disappeared. She scratched me up on my arms and neck and even my face."

"Why did you leave if Carlisle was so out of control?" Mac asked.

"I was scared for my own safety."

"In which case," Mac said, "you would have been concerned for Ashton's safety. So why didn't you call the police?"

"They were both drunk and out of control," Parker said. "They did it to themselves and were on their own property.

As long as they weren't out on the road, I figured let them be. Things were bad enough between Carlisle and Gloria as it was. Why make things worse?" He pointed at the round house. "She was living right next door. This is our summer place—our vacation home. The last thing you want on your vacation is two women screaming at each other from the docks."

"In other words," Mac said, "you just didn't want to get involved."

Parker shook his yellowed handkerchief at Mac. "Hey! I came over here. I was coming over here all the time trying to keep the peace. I couldn't win no matter what I did. If I did nothing, then I got it from the old biddie at home. So I'd come over here, trying to help those poor girls out by keeping Gloria off their backs—trying to do them a favor—and what did I get for it?" He stuck out his chin. "She had the nerve to call me a pervert!"

"Who called you a pervert?" Mac asked.

For a long moment, Parker glared at the detective. He turned to the police chief to see that he, too, wanted an answer. "They were out here swimming around with no clothes on and I happened to see them. If they didn't want that type of attention, then they shouldn't have taken off all their clothes." With an exasperated sigh, Parker shoved the handkerchief into his pants pocket.

"Thank you, Mr. Lander," Mac replied.

"It doesn't take a rocket scientist to crack this case," Parker said to Mac's back when he went back to the car. "Carlisle Green killed Ashton Piedmont. Mark my words! Carlisle did it and I'll testify to it in court!"

CHAPTER EIGHT

Death and decomposition can render a once lovely young woman unrecognizable—which is why dental and DNA records were needed to confirm that the body found wrapped in a blue tarp in a shallow grave was indeed Ashton Piedmont.

The day after Gnarly had found the missing young woman's skeletal remains, Mac met David at the morgue. Mentally, he prepared himself for the medical examiner's report by pushing the thought from his mind of how Ashton, at the time of her disappearance, had been the same age that his own daughter now was.

"Both dental records and DNA confirm it," Dr. Dora Washington told Mac and David when they stepped through the door into her lab. "It's Ashton Piedmont. Such a pity." Swinging around in her chair at her desk, the graceful, statuesque woman rose to cross to the drawers where Ashton's remains were being stored and refrigerated. "I knew her grandfather. Brilliant man. I wrote a letter of recommendation for her to medical school—not that she needed it. Her grandfather was head of the medical school in Maryland until he died. Then she disappeared the summer before she was to start." With a shake of her head she yanked open the drawer and pulled back the sheet to reveal the human skeleton.

"Any chance on determining cause of death?" Mac asked.

Doc picked up the skull to show them several breaks along the side of what would have been her head. "These weren't done after she had been buried," she said. "Someone bashed her head in." She held up the skull to illustrate the blows. "Above the ear, toward the front. If the killer was in front of her, that would make him or her left handed."

"That narrows it down a little," David said. "Can you tell what was used to do that much damage?"

Narrowing her eyes, Doc peered at the cracks across the side of the skull. "The pattern is rough and we found dirt embedded in the breaks." She pressed her finger tips along the bone. "The tarp actually protected the body from the dirt and roots where it was buried. In my professional opinion, the murder weapon was a rock."

"That would mean a lot of force was used." Mac took the skull from her to study the breaks in the bone.

"No less than three blows," Doc said.

"A lot of rage," Mac said.

"Did you find anything else?" David asked her.

"Am I correct that the body was too badly decomposed to determine any sexual activity?" Mac asked.

"You're correct there," she replied to Mac. "But we are not exactly dead in the water." She lifted the skeletal arm to show them what had once been Ashton Piedmont's hand. "We have fingernails. Do you know how long it takes fingernails to decompose?"

David guessed. "A long time?"

Doc Washington flashed a smile from one of them to the other. "Thousands of years. Like I said, that tarp actually worked to preserve evidence. While her body did decompose, which degraded evidence—like semen if she had been sexually assaulted, if she managed to scratch her attacker, we may have his or her skin and DNA under her fingernails."

"How long will it take to get a DNA profile back if there is any?" David asked her.

"At least a week," she replied. "That's if it hasn't been degraded over the last five years."

"If," Mac repeated.

"If," David said with a sigh.

❀ ❀ ❀

Spencer Inn

"Flowers?" In spite of her obviously intoxicated state, Lindsey York was coordinated enough to toss her reddish blonde hair over her bare shoulder while throwing the bouquet of flowers Mac had brought for her over onto the table. "They're pretty while they last, but they always end up dead in the end." She sashayed across the suite she had rented at the Inn and plopped down in the chaise out on the patio.

Mac followed her. "I just thought I'd bring you a welcome gift from the Spencer Inn. What do you like?"

"Something that isn't going to die. A nice bottle of wine is always nice."

"That just ends up getting peed out in a couple hours," Mac quipped.

She removed the cigarette she was in the process of lighting out of her mouth to let out a laugh. "Touché!" She eyed him. "I like you, Mr. Forsythe. You're not a tight ass like your old lady."

"It's Faraday," Mac replied.

"Whatever," she scoffed with a shrug.

With a slight shake of his head, Mac chose to ignore the insult. He had encountered more than his share of women like Lindsey York back in his day when he had been a detective. They believed their wealth and beauty gave them a license to get away with anything—from rudeness to murder. The rules applied to everyone except them. Sometimes, they went so far as to believe they were permitted to make up the rules to suit themselves as they went along.

One rule they never seemed to learn was that you pay for a life of total indulgence. They never seemed to notice that they paid with the very thing that they thought had given them the license of privilege—their beauty. In some cases—if life was kind—it would fade with the passage of time. It would creep up with lines on their face or a thickening in the waistline.

In other cases, which it seemed to be with Lindsey, it looked as if it had appeared overnight—in the form of bags and dark circles under her eyes, which she fought to keep focused during their conversation. There was none of that youthful glow on her face. In contrast, her face was as color-less as an old hag.

Lindsey had greeted Mac in a black swim suit with gold trim that did little to conceal her body from him. Mac was sure that, in her mind, she visualized her figure as sensuously slender. In reality, he could see that the drugs she indulged in had eaten away at her body to leave her with nothing more than skin and bones on her frame.

Reminding himself that David had commented on Carlisle Green making Lindsay look like a nun, Mac marveled at the transformation that the change in the young woman's lifestyle had done. He imagined what such a change would do to Lindsay, who was not unattractive.

"Call me curious," Mac drawled while sitting in the chair across from her chaise. "If you didn't like my mother, why are you coming to the Diablo Ball?"

"Money," she snorted before covering her red and puffy eyes with a pair of big sunglasses. She laid her head back to catch a ray of sun. "I never turn down the chance to make money."

"How?" Considering that guests were expected to make large donations to the Humane Society for attending the ball, Mac found it impossible to connect the dots for her to make money by flying to Spencer to attend the formal affair.

"Rock Sinclair, the producer, persuaded me to accept the invitation." She grinned with pride. "He's paying me a lot of money to let them interview me for Jasmine's in-depth investigative report."

"You are aware that they're looking for a killer?"

Lindsay lifted her sunglasses from her bloodshot eyes. "It's all publicity. Everyone knows Ashton drowned. No one will watch the show if they say that. So they're selling it as an unsolved murder."

Mac slowly shook his head. "We found Ashton's body. She didn't drown. Someone killed her."

"How was she killed then?"

"I can't say," he replied with a shake of his head. "Her body was found far away from the water. Someone killed her and buried her to make everyone think she was at the bottom of the lake. Now, who do you think would want to do that to Ashton Piedmont?"

Lindsay replied by laughing loudly. A note of insanity crept into her cackle. "It wasn't me."

"If not you—"

"I barely knew the bitch," she interjected. "Stick up her butt thinking she was too good for me because her family was doctors and her parents died putting band-aids on skinny runts from third-world countries—" She sprang upright. "I bet she died a virgin. Can they find that out in an autopsy?"

Mac ignored the question. "If you knew her well enough to know you didn't like her, then maybe you knew her well enough to want to kill her. When was the last time you saw her alive?"

A sly grin crossed her face. She looked like the big bad cat who just ate her master's favorite canary. "When she walked in on me hooking up with her boyfriend."

"A.J. Wagner?"

Lindsey smiled broadly.

"What was Ashton's reaction to that?"

Slipping her fingers underneath the top of her suit, she eased it down to expose her breast. "What would your old lady do if she walked in on you doing the horizontal boogie woogy with me?"

Staying on topic, Mac adverted his eyes and asked, "When did this alleged connection happen?"

"The afternoon before Ashton disappeared," she said. "We got together at his folks' summer place. It used to be next to my daddy's place. He sold it after Ashton disappeared. Corey Haim was there, too." She giggled. "We had a threesome. It was a blast … until Ashton showed up and threw a hissy fit." With a shake of her head, she added, "I wouldn't bother asking them to confirm it. They'll deny it ever happened."

With a smug grin, Mac asked, "Why aren't you staying at your daddy's summer place now?" He already knew the truth to the answer, but was curious about her response.

Her eyes clouded over. She dropped the sun glasses down to cover her eyes. "He's a bigger tight-ass than your mother ever was."

Seeing her lounging on the chaise, smoking her cigarette, with her puffy eyes hidden behind a pair of dark sunglasses, he could see her life was quite a tragedy. She had looks and money and all the resources necessary for a good education. But somehow, she had ended up being a pathetic figure. Maybe because she had too much of all that.

He reminded himself about the Diablo Ball and the mysterious invitations that seemed to have gone out. "About your invitation to the Diablo Ball—"

"What about it?"

"When did you get it?"

She shrugged. "I don't remember. I was going to toss it out, but Rock called and asked if I had gotten one. Then he said he and Jasmine was going and if I was going, too, then it would be great to revolve the investigation of Ashton's disappearance around the ball."

"Do you have the invitation with you?"

"I don't know." She made no move to look for it.

"Are you friends with Jasmine Simpson now?"

"Why wouldn't I be?"

"You threw a table at her at the Diablo Ball," Mac reminded her. "That's why you got banned."

"Obviously not since I got an invitation."

"So you are friends now."

She lifted her glasses. "I have no friends."

"That's pretty sad," Mac said.

"Who needs friends?"

"Everyone."

"I have money to buy my toys." She dropped the glasses back onto her face. "Live fast. Die young and leave a good-looking corpse. I don't need friends for any of that."

"Did you know the other guests at the table you turned over before the ball?"

"We all knew each other from summers here at the lake." Annoyed by his questions, Lindsey sat up and whipped off her sunglasses. "Anything else?"

"Yes."

"What?"

Mac looked at her. "What started the fight? What was it about?"

"That I do remember," she replied in an even tone.

"Tell me."

"Someone threatened me and no one threatens me."

"How?"

"They left a note on my plate. It was all fancy in an envelope. I opened it. It said that they knew my secret and I wasn't going to get away with it because they had proof that I was a fraud." She glared at him. "No one calls me a fraud."

"Have you ever found out who sent it?"

"No. No one had the guts to own up to it." She scoffed. "Wouldn't if they know what's good for them. Me? Secrets? I don't have any secrets. I learned a long time ago, don't keep secrets. When you have secrets, people try to use them against you. That's why my life is an open book. Ask anyone. What you see is what you get."

Mac sighed. "I can see that."

CHAPTER NINE

With the sun beaming on Deep Creek Lake, Mac was speeding around the lakeshore with the top down on his Dodge Viper when he heard the mechanical British voice in his Bluetooth announce that David was calling him.

"Accept call," Mac instructed the device in his ear. "Hey, David, what's up?" he asked when the police chief came on the line.

"Did you get your fill of Lindsey York?"

"She's a piece of work."

"Told you," David said. "Hey, I thought you might like to know, we got a call from the security company protecting the Piedmont place. Their system reported a break-in. Specifically, someone entered the place using an old security access code. I've sent Fletcher and Brewster over to check it out. Considering that Ashton's body was just found—"

"I'm on my way." After ensuring no one was behind him, Mac made an illegal U-turn to head to the other end of the lake.

Two Spencer cruisers were already in the long driveway outside the Piedmont mansion when Mac pulled in to park on the grass behind them. Seated in his cruiser, Officer Brewster was reporting into the station on his radio. When he had finished, he told Mac from over his shoulder. "Whoever it is took off out of the rear basement door as soon as we pulled in. He went down the path into the woods."

"Did you get a look at him?" Mac asked.

"Moving too fast," Brewster said with a shake of his head that shook the tight salt and pepper curls on his head. "Couldn't even say if it was a man or woman." He nodded toward Office Fletcher who came around from the corner of the house to confirm his report. "Whoever it was, they had to have a key."

"No sign that they forced their way in." Officer Fletcher flashed a wicked grin. "Maybe it was the ghost of Ashton Piedmont. Gnarly raised her spirit by finding her body and she decided to go home to make a sandwich."

They turned around to note David pulling into the driveway in his cruiser.

"She would be hungry after five years," Brewster said in agreement.

David heard their chuckling when he stepped up to them. "What have we got?"

"The ghost of Ashton Piedmont using an old pass code to go inside to make sandwich," Mac summarized before adding, "Guy or girl got away out the back while they went in the front."

"Was anything taken from inside?" David asked.

Fletcher reported, "Nothing looks like it was disturbed—probably just some curious kids."

"Curious kids would not have access to an old security pass code." After instructing his officers to search the grounds for the culprit, David gestured with a wave of his hand and a toss of his head for Mac to check the inside of the vacant home with him.

When he saw the dimly lit and dusty interior of the empty home, its furniture covered with once white, now gray sheets, Mac said, "It feels to me like they were looking for something."

"Something that is or not connected to Ashton Piedmont's murder," David asked.

"Carlisle Green said Ashton and A.J. were pretty secretive shortly before Ashton disappeared," Mac said while randomly lifting up sheets to peer at the furniture underneath. "The note Lindsey intercepted at the Diablo Ball claimed to know a secret."

"Are you thinking Ashton Piedmont's murder is about a secret?" David asked while opening a closet door to find no sign that anything inside had been disturbed.

"Considering that someone broke in here," Mac said, "I think it's a good possibility that after all these years, someone is still looking for whatever it was that got Ashton killed."

"But we don't know if Ashton was keeping a secret or had uncovered someone else's," David said.

Mac laughed, "Must everything be handed to you?"

After searching the main floor of the mansion and finding no sign of a disturbance, Mac took the stairs down to the lower level while David went upstairs to the bedrooms.

The ground floor contained a spacious game room with all the toys that a wealthy man and his family could want. A pool table took center stage. A bar ran along one side of the room. Everything was covered with a layer of undisturbed dust. Mac checked the patio through the sliding glass doors. The doors were locked from the inside. A huge hot tub rested in the corner of the patio. The cover was caked with a layer of encrusted dirt. Through the window, Mac could see that the spa was unplugged. The cord was slung across one corner of the tub with the plug hanging limp.

Nope, no skinny dippers here.

Mac made his way down a dark and musty hallway to what he guessed to be Dr. Piedmont's home office, which resembled a laboratory more than a wealthy man's study. One wall of the room had built in bookcases filled with thick books and notebooks. One side of the room consisted of a long counter with a built-in sink, portable burners, and microscopes of various types and sizes, including a computerized model. The door leading to the side yard and the path around to the other side of the cove was on the opposite end of the room.

Many of the doors to the bottom cabinets of the counter were open to reveal boxes of computer floppy discs scattered on the floor. Mac knelt down to read the labels on the disks. The shaky handwriting was in pen.

"Upstairs hasn't been touched," David called out in the hallway before entering to discover Mac examining the old boxes of disks. "What did you find?"

Mac held up one of the boxes. "Would bored kids be interested in files about liver cancer in pigs?" He restacked the disks and placed them back in the cupboard. "Whoever broke in had an access code, even if it was old. Ashton was dating A.J. Archie told me that he just got into town last night and is staying with the Breckenridges—right here on Millionaire's Cove. My vote is to stop in to see him next."

"Are you thinking he used that old code to drop in for old time's sake?"

"Even if he didn't, he knew both Ashton and her grandfather," Mac said. "He'd probably know what our housebreaker was looking for. They didn't touch the spa, but it looks like he or she went through these disks. Most computers nowadays don't even have drives that can read these types of disks."

"Didn't Carlisle tell us yesterday that Rachel Breckenridge's mother was Dr. Piedmont's protégé?" David asked while lifting the lid off a large plastic box that resembled an odd looking aquarium. Instead of water or dirt for a terrarium, it contained tiny plastic beads.

"Which means she could have had the old pass code and or possibly know what someone was looking for in here." Mac rose to his feet.

"What's this?" David peered down inside the aquarium.

"I have no idea." Mac noticed an electrical cord hanging out of the back of it. "Whatever it is, it looks expensive. So don't touch it."

"If it's expensive, then why is it here?"

"Because your police department is good at what you do." Mac urged him toward the door. "Let's go play bad cop good cop with A.J. Wagner."

"Dibs on being the bad cop."

"Are you kidding?" Mac said, "I'm the natural bad cop. Look at you."

David looked down at his gold badge. "This badge can be pretty intimidating."

"A.J. Wagner is only a few years younger than you," Mac said. "You'll be like his big brother." He grinned, "Whereas I can come across like the big bad old man."

"Seriously?" David said, "Lately, you've been as intimidating as a fat and comfortable house cat."

❧ ❧ ❧

Neither Mac nor David missed noticing that the Breckenridge estate was a short run along the lakeshore path from the Piedmont mansion—very conveniently located for a burglary suspect.

They found Dr. Elizabeth Breckenridge and her daughter, Rachel, sunning on the dock behind the sprawling French country style home.

Even with the money from her position as chairperson of a prestigious medical school, Dr. Breckenridge looked every day of her plus-fifty years. Her face was bloated to make her eyes look like tiny brown circles with heavy bags hanging underneath. Her gray hair hung limply down to her shoulders. She covered her doughy figure with a robe, allowing only her plump legs to get the sun.

In contrast, Rachel Breckenridge wore a demure royal blue two-piece swimsuit. Her long dark hair was pulled back into a tight ponytail. She kept her head back and her body spread out to allow the sun access to every inch of flesh.

While David explained the reason for their visit to ask if they had noticed anything suspicious at the Piedmont estate, which was in plain view across the cove, Mac saw the small stone cottage tucked away in a grove of trees off in the corner of the estate. He also took note of a face peering out at them from between the curtains. Seeming to notice Mac peering in his direction, the figure in the window stepped back and the curtain fell limp.

"I'm sure no one who lives here on the cove would go breaking into houses, especially Ashton's house," Rachel was saying.

"Except Carlisle," Elizabeth interjected in a low voice that would have been considered sexy in her younger years. Now she almost sounded like a man.

Recalling Carlisle's description of the woman she heard Ashton arguing with as having a low voice, Mac's head jerked around from where he had been watching the guest cottage.

"She's back, you know," Elizabeth Breckenridge said. "I saw her out on the dock this morning doing what looked like yoga. At least this time she was dressed. I don't care how much money her parents and grandfather left her, you know how quickly you can blow a billion dollars up your nose when you have a habit like hers? It's her fault Ashton is dead. She was so drunk that she couldn't get up off her knees to help her." With an arched eyebrow, she jerked her head in the direction of the round house across the cove. "That's where you should be looking for your burglar—not here."

"Do you mind if we look around," Mac said before David could respond. "Hate to leave you ladies to your sun bathing only to find some desperate junkie hiding out here to attack you as soon as we leave."

"Your desperate junkie is over there," Elizabeth said.

Rachel had already settled back onto her chaise. "Feel free. We have nothing to hide."

When Mac stepped back up the dock in the direction of the guest cottage, Rachel sprang up on the chaise. "Don't go in the guest cottage. We've got guests. Their plane came in late last night and they're asleep."

The corner of Mac's lips curled when he glanced back at David, who replied, "We'll be as quiet as mice."

Mac waited until they were out of earshot before whispering to him, "Wagner is wide awake."

"Good," David replied. "Then we won't have to wake him up."

Instead of A.J. Wagner answering their knock on the door, a young man with long dark hair and piercing dark eyes opened the door a crack. He took a long moment to take note of David's police chief's badge before asking, "Can I help you?"

"We'd like to speak to A.J. Wagner, please," David replied.

"He's—"

"Let them in, Corey," they heard called out from further in the cottage. "I've been expecting them."

As ordered, Corey stepped back and opened the door to allow them entry.

Wearing a polo shirt, khaki slacks, and loafers on his feet, A.J. Wagner stood to meet them in the cozy living room. With his neat blond hair and square jaw and straight nose, he looked like half of the young men Mac saw hanging out at the Spencer Inn's sports club.

The difference between A.J. and those young men was a smoldering look in his eyes. Mac had seen it before in many a young man's eyes. Fury was brewing beneath the surface.

When David made the introductions, A.J. was quick to place Mac while shaking his hand. "You own the Spencer Inn. You're hosting the Diablo Ball."

"And you've already RSVPed," Mac said.

"Like he had a choice," Corey muttered.

"As in you didn't?" David replied.

"Jasmine Simpson and Lindsey York made sure of that." With a wave of his arm, A.J. gestured for Mac and David to take a seat in the two chairs in the living room, while he eased down onto the sofa.

"They needed you for their show about Ashton's murder," Mac said. "It wouldn't be much of a show without the victim's boyfriend."

The smoldering fury in his eyes sparked. "I never wanted to come back to this place. Everywhere I look I see Ashton. As a matter of fact, I sold the family summer place. My plan was to get through medical school and move on with my life. But then Rachel and her mother got their claws into me, and then that invitation came—"

"If he refused, they'd kill A.J.'s medical career before it even started with one phone call," Corey said.

"I was still going to say no," A.J. said.

"What do they have on you?" David asked. "Did you kill Ashton?"

"No!" Corey answered in an angry tone. "A.J. loved Ashton. He'd do nothing to hurt her."

"I'd like to hear him say that," Mac said. "You two do know that we found her body. She didn't drown. She was murdered."

"I thought she'd drowned," A.J. said. "Carlisle told everyone Ashton had drowned while they were skinny dipping."

"And you weren't there," Mac said. "Why not?"

"He was partying with me," Corey said too quickly.

Mac turned his attention to A.J.'s devoted best friend. "What were you doing?"

"Drinking."

"Why?"

"Why not?"

"Could you have been drowning your sorrows because you had a fight with Ashton?" Mac asked A.J.

"Why would we have been fighting?" A.J. asked.

"You tell me."

"Does A.J. need a lawyer?" Corey stepped between them.

"Maybe I should ask Rachel and her mother what they got that was good enough to put their claws in you and drag you back here," Mac replied. "Or should I talk to Lindsey, who also seems to have something on you?"

"What have you two done?" David said. "If it wasn't murder—"

Corey was ready to do battle when A.J. replied, "Ashton and I weren't fighting; she disappeared—or was murdered—before Lindsey could tell her."

"Tell her what?" David wanted to know.

"That summer," A.J. said slowly, "that day, that afternoon as a matter of fact, Lindsey came over to my place—the lake house my family had left me. She said she was looking for Ashton for some reason and, since she wasn't at her house, she assumed she'd find her with me. Well, Ashton wasn't there. Lindsey had a bottle of something and offered me a drink. I had one drink—"

"A.J. is not a drunk," Corey interjected.

"No, I'm not," A.J. said. "Lindsey drugged me. I have no doubt about that. By the next day, Ashton had disappeared—murdered, I guess—and Lindsey had a sex tape of her and me together in bed."

"How did she make a tape if she was at your place?" Mac asked.

"She had a special camera on her phone that she had positioned in a pocket of her purse so that she got everything."

"What did she want from you?" David asked.

"Money at first," A.J. said. "Then …"

When A.J.'s voice trailed off, Corey jumped in. "You might as well tell them everything, A.J. Lindsey was keeping you busy in bed while Dr. Breckenridge was killing Ashton." His southern roots and accent came out in his excitement.

"Why would Dr. Breckenridge want to kill Ashton Piedmont?" Mac replied.

In a steady tone, A.J. said, "She killed my father and then she killed Ashton."

"And now they're trying to force A.J. into a shotgun wedding," Corey said.

David asked them, "Did she murder Ashton to make you available for Rachel?"

"And your father?" Mac noted. "Why would she kill him?"

"This all has to do with Dr. Ross Piedmont, Ashton's grandfather" A.J. said. "Dr. Breckenridge was his protégé. Dr. Piedmont was a brilliant doctor. Ashton would have been, too. She graduated top of her class from pre-med. Her grandfather was very proud of her." He stopped to swallow. "I loved her. We were going to start a clinic together in the northern Alaska—in the wilderness region."

"But Ashton wasn't an arrogant bitch about being the brightest," Corey said. "I was barely scraping by in pre-med. I was about to drop out when both Ashton and A.J. took me on. They spent so much time working with me that I could graduate. I never would have gotten into med school if it wasn't for them."

Taking note of the passion in Corey's tone, and his long dark hair, Mac wondered if Corey was the Greaser that Carlisle

Green had told them about. "Ashton sounds like a great young lady."

"She was," A.J. said.

"Which makes me wonder what she was doing skinny dipping with Carlisle Green, a known drug addict, at the time of her disappearance," Mac said. "What's the connection between a brilliant scientist and a party girl?"

"Don't you ever need to blow off steam, Mr. Faraday?" Corey asked.

Before Mac could answer, A.J. said, "Carlisle Green was a lot deeper than people gave her credit for. Sure, on the surface, she'd come across like a Lindsey York, but she wasn't like that at all—and Ashton saw that. Ashton used to babysit Carlisle during the summers here on the lake—being next door and all. Ashton's folks died when she was just a little girl. When Carlisle's parents gave up on her, and then died—followed by her grandfather, Ashton knew her well enough to see beneath the drugs and booze to know that Carlisle was really hurting, but too proud to ask for help."

"That's why Ashton took time to hang out with Carlisle," Corey said. "A.J. and I tried to suggest that she cut things off with her—that Carlisle would ruin her reputation with her drugs and partying, but Ashton refused because she was loyal to her friends."

"Plus, Ashton did confess that Carlisle knew how to have a good time," A.J. said.

"I remember that last summer," Corey said with a sad tone, "Ashton told us that one day, Carlisle would surprise everyone. That when she grew up, if she learned how to use her inner strength, that she was destined to be a great lady, and do great things in this world."

"Sounds like Ashton was quite a perceptive lady," Mac said.

"That still doesn't explain why Dr. Breckenridge and her daughter would want her dead," David said.

"Because Dr. Breckenridge stole Dr. Piedmont's book," A.J. said. "The book and research that made her who she is today—the world's number one expert on using three-dimensional technology to replace body parts in medical research. Dr. Breckenridge wasn't the expert. Dr. Piedmont—and Ashton—were. All Dr. Breckenridge did was assist *him* in his research and keep track of his notes. He was writing his book while doing his research—here at the lake house."

"Dr. Piedmont died while Ashton was in Europe doing an internship at Oxford," Corey said. "By the time Ashton got back, Breckenridge had submitted all of Piedmont's material to a publisher in New York, who accepted it as hers."

"Dr. Piedmont had died before he could copyright anything," A.J. said. "Breckenridge had stolen everything. But my father knew the truth because he and Dr. Piedmont were friends. He was going to expose Breckenridge." With a wave of his hand, he announced, "Suddenly, my father was dead of a heart attack … when he had a medical only six weeks before in which they declared his heart completely healthy."

"Don't you think that sounds like a very strong motive for killing Ashton?" Corey asked them.

"The note that Lindsey found at the table at the Diablo Ball," Mac said, "was that meant for Dr. Breckenridge, who was originally assigned at your table?"

A.J. nodded his head. "Ashton had left it for her. She was determined to expose Dr. Breckenridge for the phony she is."

"Sounds like quite a conspiracy they have going," Mac said with a hint of doubt in his tone. A.J.'s and Corey's youth made him wonder if they had possibly let an active imagination get the best of them. "Lindsey happens by your place to seduce you—"

"She drugged me," A.J. said. "Why would I want to be with *her* when I had Ashton?"

"Then, while you were being otherwise occupied with Lindsey and out of the way," Mac said, "Ashton, who is out to expose Dr. Breckenridge for plagiarism and theft and possibly murder, ends up being murdered. And now, you're being blackmailed—have been for years—by the very two women behind all of this."

"I'd let them post the sex tape on the Internet," David said. "Everyone in Spencer has had a sex tape posted on the Internet."

"Not me," Mac interjected.

"That's because you're boring," David told him out of the side of his mouth.

"Is there a sex tape of you—"

"There's something you're not telling us," David interrupted Mac's question by returning to the topic of their discussion.

"Positions at the best medical centers are very competitive," A.J. said. "They do a search of the Internet to determine character of the applicants. If that sex tape ends up on the Internet with my name attached to it, I won't be able to get a job anywhere."

"When A.J. said he didn't want to be in the investigative report," Corey said, "Lindsey gave a copy of that tape to Jasmine to use for leverage. It's dated and time stamped—proof of his infidelity and motive for killing Ashton during a lovers' fight."

"Lindsey is claiming that Ashton walked in on us and that the last she saw Ashton, we were fighting about my sleeping with her," A.J. said. "Never happened. She's giving that recording to whoever she has to in order to get what she wants." He shrugged his shoulders. "I might as well let her post it on the Internet."

"They actually expect A.J. to marry Rachel," Corey said.

"I can't see how they can do that," David said. "What would they have to gain by that?"

"I don't have to be faithful," A.J. said. "I just have to give her my name, which will give them my unofficial endorsement. My father, Dr. Howard Wagner, was the university president. He had a lot of contacts and influence in the academic community. Dr. Breckenridge has faked her way through the medical community and squeezed everything she can out of Piedmont's research. Now she wants to be university president before conning her way into politics."

"You wouldn't believe how much money she rakes in for speaking engagements," Corey said. "She makes more demands than a rock star, and these medical associations and conferences are paying it because they believe she's a pioneer in medical research."

"But she's smart enough to see that the ride is coming to an end," A.J. said. "Other researchers have been making headway, based on the research she published, while she hasn't set foot in a lab since. She announced a few months ago that she's going to retire from medical research and go into academia. The university president who took my father's place is retiring. Now Breckenridge wants it. If I marry her daughter, and whisper the right words to the right people, she could get the job."

"Can you help A.J.?" Corey asked.

"Where were you while your friend was being raped?" Mac asked Corey.

"I was down in central West Virginia," he replied.

"You mean you didn't take part in Lindsey's party?" Mac asked while recalling Lindsey claiming that her encounter with A.J. was a threesome that included Corey.

"I wouldn't touch Lindsey York with a ten foot pole." Corey laughed. "I was visiting my fiancée back home. She's a school teacher. I can give you her phone number if you want. Everyone in town saw me there."

"What do you think, Mac?" David asked.

Mac looked from Corey to A.J. Both young men seemed to be holding their breaths. "Did either of you just break into the Piedmont home a little while ago?"

"We both did," A.J. confessed without hesitation. "Right before Ashton disappeared, she had found proof positive that Dr. Breckenridge had stolen her grandfather's research."

"That's what she meant in the note that Lindsey intercepted at the Diablo Ball," Mac said. "The note said she had proof."

"Exactly," A.J. said. "Ashton had found an earlier draft of the book. It was dated the year before her grandfather died and had his name on it. I saw it. It was like six inches thick. After Ashton disappeared, it was gone."

"Dr. Breckenridge must have gotten her hands on it," Corey said with a growl deep in his throat.

"But it occurred to us that there had to be a digital version of the book," A.J. said. "Dr. Piedmont and Ashton had been researching 3D printing for over a decade. During that time, they had upgraded their computers and had to transfer their research from one system to another. So what if we could find a backup copy of that book and research on an external hard drive? We figured since we were here that we would take a look around to see if we could find something else to prove that Ashton's grandfather and Ashton were the real pioneers. I was looking while Corey was acting as my look out."

All eyes were on Mac for his decision. Without a word, he rose to his feet and went to the window. Parting them with his fingers, Mac peered out at the two women sunning themselves on the deck.

Several conversations replayed in his mind.

Carlisle Green recalled two women fighting. One had a deep voice. Elizabeth Breckenridge had a deep voice—she almost sounded like a man.

Such perfect timing. Lindsey chose that day, and time, to drug A.J. and bed him in order to get him under the Breckinridge's thumbs, while Ashton Piedmont, a determined young woman, disappears—along with the threat of ruining their scheme to steal her grandfather's research.

Then, there was Jasmine Simpson, who was using Ashton Piedmont's murder as a springboard into a journalism career—using whatever means necessary to do so—threatening and blackmailing Carlisle Green and A.J. Wagner.

People using others' tragedies for their own gain. His thoughts wandered to an observation he had made long ago while investigating murder cases on the streets of Washington, D.C., among street people who worked the system in order to collect disability, welfare, and food stamps so that they wouldn't have to get a job and work for a living.

The creative ingenuity some of those people displayed.

Now, here on Deep Creek Lake, among the upper crust, at the other end of the social ladder, the same thought came to Mac's mind.

Theft. Rape. Extortion. Murder. If these women exerted their creative energy in positive directions, think of what they could accomplish.

"I think I'm going to be sick the night of the Diablo Ball," Mac finally said.

CHAPTER TEN

"Let the festivities begin." Archie paused in touching up her lipstick to tell Mac. "Are you ready for this?"

"Nope. I have a really bad feeling about tonight." Mac pulled his black SUV up to the end of the line of cars waiting for the valet at the Spencer Inn.

A bank of news and network cameras wanting to record the event of the social season got an interesting shot of the SUV with a large German shepherd sticking his head out the rear window. Being the host of the event, Mac Faraday had the privilege of including Gnarly on the guest list. After all, it was the *Diablo* Ball, named after the sidekick of the Mickey Forsythe Mysteries—that being a German shepherd.

Even Gnarly, freshly bathed and blown-dry, was stylish in his own doggie jewels. Archie had located a dog collar with real diamonds. It was only one-hundred-and-fifty thousand dollars, which caused Mac to choke on his breakfast when she told him. While Archie thought Gnarly was worthy of real diamonds, Mac did make a good point when predicting that the unruly shepherd would eat the valuable jewels, which would result in a very expensive emergency room visit and surgery to extract them. With Mac winning the argument, Gnarly's jewels were downgraded to a twenty-five dollar rhine-stone collar and leash.

The ballroom was one of the most elegant rooms at the Inn. It had an entrance out onto the patio and gardens. Two grand staircases from the main floor descended to the floor below to provide guests the opportunity to make an entrance. In the alcove between the staircases, a pianist had been hired to provide elegant background music on the Inn's white grand piano, which had once belonged to George Gershwin.

"We have both the police and Hector's security force swarming all over the resort." Archie waved her long, elegant hand bejeweled with gold and gemstones in the direction of the mass of people leaning towards their vehicle to identify its occupants. "What could go wrong?"

Mac pulled the SUV up to the end of the red carpet. The valet opened the car door and held it for Mac to step out. On the passenger side, an attendant opened the door and helped Archie out. Gnarly seemed to have heard her instructions before leaving Spencer Manor to pretend to have manners. After climbing over the front seat from his seat in the back, he jumped out onto the carpet and paused to allow Archie to grasp his jewel studded leash.

The party waited for Mac to take his place on the dog's other side. After pausing for pictures from those lining up the red carpet, Archie led Mac and Gnarly up to the main entrance.

Below the camera line, Archie kept a tight hold on Gnarly's leash. Instead of red or black, the usual star colors that she expected the other women to wear for the event; Archie had chosen a shimmering gold gown that hung off her shoulders. The shimmer of the gold in her dress matched that of the diamonds she wore around her neck and from her earlobes.

Archie Monday was not a clothes horse. Nor did she go in for a lot of jewelry. But on those rare occasions when she chose to, she never failed to surprise Mac by how she stood out in the crowd.

While to those along the carpet Mac was smiling and saying hello, they did not know that he was studying each of them as closely as they may have been eying him. He noted hands that he could not see. Was anyone holding a weapon? With his arm around Archie's waist, he ushered her up the carpet, across the Inn's front steps, and through the doors into the lobby.

The white spots from the camera flashes were still clearing from Mac's eyes when he heard loud voices coming from the coat room nearby.

"Listen to me, you little twerp! I told Rock how I wanted this show shot and he agreed that we would do it my way! So cut the crap! You got that?"

Mac could hear Jasmine Simpson hissing her threats. Gesturing for Archie to keep quiet, he eased the door open a crack and stepped back out of their line of sight.

Jasmine Simpson was chewing out a young man dressed in black slacks and a black button down shirt. "Have you forgotten that I'm the producer?" She jabbed him in the chest. "You're the director. *You* work for *me*."

In contrast to the producer's fury, the director appeared unimpressed, as evidenced by his smirk—which Mac recognized.

Samuel Nash. Jasmine Simpson's date at the last Diablo Ball. He was now directing the film project being produced by his former date and her current lover.

"Oh, yes, baby," Samuel responded in a cool tone, "this is your show all right. All you did was spread your legs for Sinclair. I'm the one who did the real work coming up with the premise and pitch."

"With your body, Samuel, your pitch wouldn't have gotten us out of the bus station," she said.

"Okay, so we're a team," Samuel said. "I have the brains and the talent and you have the body."

"You think I'm just a body," she replied with a laugh. "Wait until you see my twist on this whole Piedmont murder."

"What twist?" Samuel asked. "It's an investigative report. We interview everyone involved and present the most likely killer."

"You haven't been paying attention, darling." She was on the verge of giggling. "We don't have to prove our case in court. We prove it to the public. And the public loves nothing more than a juicy story, especially with a compelling twist that leaves them breathless and the police looking like fools for not discovering it before us."

"Have you forgotten the laws against slander, Jasmine?" The amusement slipped from Samuel's tone. "We can't just go making things up."

"We don't have to make it up, just spin the facts around to make it believable without actually pointing the finger."

"I didn't sign up to be on the wrong end of a lawsuit," Samuel said.

"You signed a contract." Jasmine's voice was hard. "Rock agrees with me. If any network is going to pick up our show, there has to be intrigue, drama, and—"

"Murder?" Mac interjected.

Jasmine regarded Mac with annoyance for interrupting her meeting.

"I thought the whole point of this investigative report was to get to the truth about what happened to Ashton Piedmont," Mac said. "Now that Ashton's body was found and it has proven to be murder, suddenly you're more interested in making up the most entertaining story for your audience. Why is that? Are you afraid of what would be found out if you actually did conduct an investigation?"

"Afraid? If I was afraid of anything, I wouldn't have brought Rock and gotten you and Chief O'Callaghan off the stick to find Ashton's body." With a smug grin, Jasmine said, *"This whole investigation* is my baby. I got all of the suspects together, including Carlisle, which was a major coup."

Mac asked, "Wasn't Ashton a friend of yours in college?"

"Yes," she answered, "her death hurt all of us."

Mac glanced at the director. "Did you know Ashton?"

Jasmine said, "Mac Faraday, this is Samuel Nash, our director."

"I knew Ashton in college while I was dating Jasmine," Samuel said with a bored tone while taking his cell phone out of his left pants pocket to check a text. Upon hearing Jasmine scoff, he continued, "Funny how some people deny their baser needs once they get within reach of their goals."

With a curse, Jasmine whirled on her heels and hurried out of the closet. She was in such a hurry that she almost knocked Archie and Gnarly over.

Chuckling, Samuel Nash brought his cell phone to his ear and sauntered after her.

"What was that about?" Archie whispered to Mac when he joined them outside the closet.

"Looks like our party is off to a rip-roaring start."

❧ ❧ ❧

Sophisticated in a floor length, off-the-shoulder, red gown, Catherine Fleming was perched at the entrance at the top of the stairs leading down into the ballroom. With her silky blonde hair falling in a single wave to brush her shoulders, she reminded Mac of Lauren Bacall.

Upon entering, the guests would give their name to Catherine so that she could announce them. The guests would think it was so they could make their entrance down the grand staircase into the banquet room filled with deep pocketed guests dressed in formal fare.

In reality, it was so Chelsea Adams could compare their name to the guest list at the registration table behind the senator. Those not on the list, they would know did not receive their invitation from Archie, but rather Jasmine Simpson and Rock Sinclair for their investigative report.

So quiet that only those looking would notice her, Molly laid at her master's feet under the table. Upon entering, Gnarly practically knocked over the table charging underneath to greet Molly with a lick on the snout. Startled out of her sleep, the white German shepherd rose up. With shrieks, Chelsea and Catherine dove on top of the table to keep the paperwork in order. A catastrophe was adverted only due to Mac quickly grabbing the table while Archie pulled Gnarly out.

"Why couldn't my mother have chosen a less difficult charity?" Mac hissed to Archie. "Like disaster relief?"

Chelsea Adams's wavy platinum blonde hair was swept up into a French twist. She showed off her model thin figure in an ivory cocktail dress with a lacey overlay. In front, the dress looked demure with a high neckline not unlike a turtle neck. But when she turned around to re-take her seat, Mac discovered that the dress was back-less, revealing her sensuous back down to the waist. She contrasted her pale features and dress with sapphire drop earrings and matching stiletto shoes.

Before Mac, Archie, and Gnarly made their way down the stairway, Catherine gave a status report on the attendees. "So far only those guests who we have already identified as not being officially invited have appeared on our crashers' list."

Archie sighed with relief.

Catherine was equally pleased. They had visions of dozens of crashers. "Do we have actual proof that the invitations were sent out by Rock Sinclair and Jasmine Simpson?"

"Not yet," Mac said. "But they have the most to gain by this reunion and they've been strong-arming anyone saying no to the invite. That tells me they sent them out."

"Rock Sinclair and Jasmine Simpson have arrived." Catherine said. "When they came, they gave her name, Jasmine Simpson. Rock Sinclair is her guest."

"So the quote-invitation-unquote was sent to her," Archie said. "I hope you're not solo tonight, Chelsea."

The arch of Chelsea's eyebrow answered their question. "David is here, but don't be looking for him in a tux. He's upstairs in the security office with Bogie, some officers, and the security staff."

Seeing the disappointment in her eyes, Mac said, "I'm sorry about this, Chelsea. It's our fault."

"No, it's not," Chelsea said. "You didn't dig up Ashton Piedmont."

"No, Gnarly did," Archie said.

Chelsea shook her head. "This is just one of the things that comes with falling in love with a law officer."

"That's right," Mac said.

"And David is going to have to get used to the junk that comes with falling in love with a future county prosecutor." Catherine pointed a long fingernail dipped in bright red in Chelsea's direction. "This is going to be a working event for you, young lady. All of the movers and shakers with the power to get you elected prosecutor are here tonight and Ben intends to introduce you around."

"I didn't know Ben was planning to retire," Chelsea said.

"Not tomorrow, but one day he will and it's never too early for you to start networking."

Mac patted Chelsea's hand. "You don't have to schmooze us. You already have our vote and support."

"Don't you think I should graduate from law school and pass the bar first?" Chelsea reminded them.

In the ballroom, Mac snagged two flutes of champagne, with the Spencer Inn logo carved into the crystal, from one of the many servers offering guests refreshments. Dressed in black with knee-length stark white bib aprons marked with the Spencer Inn logo, the servers flitted throughout the ballroom with serving trays filled with drinks and other goodies.

Tucking her clutch bag under one arm, Archie grasped Gnarly's leash with one hand while taking the offered glass with the other.

Above them, the doors flew open and Lindsey York stepped through with what could only be described as an *entourage*. Her reddish hair fell down her bare back. She showcased her body in bright red with a plunging neckline that threatened to show more than her shapely breasts. The front of her gown was cut so low that any mismanagement of her body threatened to reveal all of at least one naked bosom, something she seemed to be well aware of by the naughty smile on her face.

Her escort sent chills down their spines.

He was a head taller than Lindsey. Falling to his shoulders, his jet black mane came from a bottle. His menacing expression seemed to come from hell, from his dark eyes that lacked any emotion or compassion to his stride to the bulge that Mac noticed under his tuxedo. His bow-tie was untied and the top buttons of his shirt was opened to reveal tattoos coiling around his thick neck.

Noting their names on the uninvited list, Catherine announced the party. "Ms. Lindsey York and her guest Raul Zernbog."

In a suite of offices in the Inn's business wing, Police Chief David O'Callaghan whirled around from a security monitor to ask Hector Langford, the Inn's director of security, "Who's Raul Zernbog?"

"Who's Raul Zernbog?" Hector was asking one of his officers who was manning a computer that was already patched into the police database.

A lean, gray-haired Australian, Hector Langford had been with the Inn for over twenty-five years and had been a trusted employee of the late Robin Spencer. Mac had heard unconfirmed rumors that the smooth-talking foreigner had been a spy during the Cold War. Sometimes, the Australian's expertise in collecting information and slick manner made Mac wonder if the rumors he had heard were simply that.

"Whoever he is, I have a very bad feeling about him," Mac muttered, knowing that his earpiece, connected to the radio, was picking up everything he said.

"That's called vibes," Archie whispered while tightening her grip on Gnarly's leash. She noticed the dog's hackles rising on his back. "I get bad vibes from him. It might just be his tats."

In the security office, David took notice of Raul's tattoos as well. He instructed Officer Brewster to zoom in on Lindsey's date from another angle using a different security camera. "Several summers ago, the drug traffic around here practically doubled. DEA came in. The drug connection ended up being Lindsey's flavor of the season, a drug dealer she had met in Rio during Spring break."

"Great," Mac muttered with heavy sarcasm.

"Mr. Faraday." Mac was startled out of his conversation with David by a barricade made up of two bodies that suddenly appeared between him and the bar.

"I'd like you to meet someone." Jeff Ingles, the Inn's manager, continued, "Mac Faraday,—"

"We've already met." Dr. Elizabeth Breckenridge stuck out her hand in a businesslike fashion.

Mac took her hand, which she shook in a firm grasp. "Dr. Breckenridge, pleasure to meet you again."

Before he could react, the doctor turned to flash a smile for two photographers who swooped in to snap a picture of them.

Across the room, her daughter Rachel was engrossed in a conversation with A.J. and Corey. Her hair fell to her shoulders in brunette waves. She was dressed in a becoming black backless cocktail dress. Mac noted that Rachel did not appear to be totally engaged in the conversation between the two men. Rather, her eyes were narrowed in a piercing glare at something or someone across the room. Mac followed Rachel's line of sight across the room to where Rock Sinclair and Jasmine Simpson were engaged in a friendly conversation with Lindsey and her date.

I guess A.J. and Corey and Carlisle aren't the only ones being dragged into this thing.

Elizabeth was telling Mac, "Rachel has just finished medical school. I had promised myself that I would retire from medical research once she was able to take the reins of our family profession. She's taking off this summer to consider which of the dozen offers she wants to accept. Or, she may open a clinic with A.J. after they get married."

"In Alaska?" Mac asked.

"Excuse me?" the doctor's nose wrinkled at the suggestion. "Alaska?"

"That's where A.J. was planning to open a clinic with Ashton Piedmont," Mac said.

"Ashton is dead," she replied without emotion.

Jeff whispered to Mac, "Rachel and A.J. Wagner have booked this banquet room for Fourth of July weekend for a private party. Keep it under your hat, but they're planning to announce their engagement." Seeing a matter that demanded his attention, Jeff hurriedly excused himself and trotted across the room in a flurry leaving Dr. Breckenridge alone with Mac.

Watching Jeff scurrying away, Mac noticed that Rachel Breckenridge was no longer with A.J. and Corey. With a quick glance around the crowded ballroom, he saw her nowhere.

Elizabeth recaptured Mac's attention with a question. "Speaking of Ashton Piedmont, when are you going to arrest Carlisle Green for her murder?"

"When I determine that she did it and uncover evidence to prove it." Mac replied. "So far, neither has happened."

Dr. Breckenridge laughed. "Carlisle Green is a crazed drug addict and was the last one to be seen with Ashton. The fact that Ashton didn't drown proves what I've always believed. Somehow Ashton set Carlisle off and Carlisle killed her." She lowered her voice. "I can't tell you how many times I tried to warn Ashton to cut off her friendship with Carlisle, but Ashton was a dear sweet girl who believed that there was something good in everyone."

"Carlisle Green," Catherine Fleming announced from the ballroom entrance above.

Hearing the name of the topic of their conversation, Mac and Dr. Breckenridge turned their attention to the top of the stairs.

To look at her, no one would guess that she was the richest woman in the room. She was dressed in a demure blue sleeveless dress that reached down to her knees. Instead of high heels, she wore flat blue shoes. Her hair was neatly combed. She wore plain gold posts in her earlobes and a simple gold necklace. At the bottom of the staircase, she met with Ben Fleming, who introduced her to Chelsea. After a polite greeting, she knelt to pet Molly, who offered her paw.

"Yeah, I can't see where there is any good in that woman," Mac said with sarcasm.

"You didn't see her five years ago," Dr. Breckenridge said.

"No, I didn't," Mac agreed.

"Money doesn't buy class ... or the hunger to succeed." She gestured across the room to where Corey Haim and A.J. were talking to Samuel Nash, who had an ear mike attached to his head.

Elizabeth was on a roll. "Corey Haim should have been kicked out of pre-med years ago, but Ashton and A.J. believed that he had the heart to be a doctor. He's a sweet compassionate man, who wants to open a free clinic to treat the poor in the Appalachia where his family has been working in the coal mines that the EPA has been shutting down." She paused to roll her eyes. "That's a nice dream, but Corey simply doesn't have the drive to do what he has to do."

"Because he's not cut throat?"

She said, "There's nothing wrong with being ambitious—doing whatever is necessary to make it to the top."

"By whatever is necessary, do you mean steal, threaten, and even kill to get there?"

She glared at Mac as if he had thrown down the gauntlet.

Mac flashed her a wide grin. "I'm a retired homicide detective. You'd be surprised how many murderers I've arrested who killed all in the name of ambition."

"We are doctors," she said. "We've taken oaths to save lives, not take them."

"But you can't deny that medicine is still a cut-throat game when it comes to getting the most prestigious, high paying jobs," Mac pointed out. "How much does a university president make nowadays? I heard it was more than the governor. Is that true?"

"Yes, it is." She cleared her throat. "To get back to what we were talking about, if it wasn't for A.J. pushing for Corey Haim, probably out of his devotion to Ashton's wishes, I would have kicked Corey out his first year of medical school. As it is, he only graduated in the middle of his class and he's been adequate during his residency—not a failure, but no shining star either."

"Somebody has to be in the middle of their class," Mac noted, "and at the bottom. But that doesn't make them a bad doctor. As long as they know their weaknesses and are humble enough to ask for help when going up against them, then they can still succeed. Sometimes, what's in the heart can make up for what you lack in book knowledge."

Leveling his gaze on her, he added, "Everyone has weaknesses. It is the great man and woman who are honest enough to not try to take credit for other people's work and success, who rise to the top."

With a snort, Dr. Breckenridge dismissed him. "Excuse me, Mr. Faraday. I need to talk to Dr. Wilkins about an important matter concerning DNA going to civil court this week." Having no further need to talk to him, she and her two photographers hurried across the room in the direction of a robust man with a gray beard.

CHAPTER ELEVEN

"There you are." Archie slipped up behind Mac to loop her arm through his. "You're supposed to be mingling with the guests."

"I am."

"No, you're not," she chastised him with a grin. "You're interrogating suspects."

"You call it interrogating, I call it mingling."

"Mac," she said in a sultry tone while brushing imaginary dog hair from the lapel of his tuxedo, "this is our first big social event since we got married. Now I love solving murder cases almost as much as you do. And I know that you love a good juicy case as much as your mother, but the Diablo Ball really meant a lot to her. She did it every year for the animals. Please, for Gnarly's sake and his fellow furry friends, don't ruin this by inviting murder and mayhem tonight."

As if to add his plea for good measure, Gnarly pressed his cold nose against Mac's palm.

Archie slipped Gnarly's leash into Mac's hand. "Be a good host and really go mingle so we can score some big donations."

"Donations?" Mac replied. "These people already paid two thousand dollars a plate to come to this thing. Are you saying they have to pay more money if they want food on that plate?"

With a wink of her eye, she brushed her hand across his cheek. "You are so adorable." Caught up in a crowd of chattering women, she drifted away.

"Hey, Mac," David's voice abruptly called into his earbud, "have you got eyes on Lindsey's date?"

Mac turned around on a complete circle while scouring the faces of more than a hundred guests at the benefit event. "No. Why?"

"He's a member of a very dangerous South American drug cartel that's been making a big splash on the west coast."

"What's he doing here in Deep Creek Lake?" Mac hissed while trying to appear hospitable as the event's host.

Gazing up at his master, Gnarly was sitting in front of him. With a questioning expression, he cocked his head at Mac.

"Lindsey York," David growled. "Need I say more? Bogie and Hector are on their way down to collect him. The feds say he's suspected in four drug related assassinations."

"Then what's he doing at a party hosted by a retired homicide detective?" Mac asked before coming up with his own answer, "Lindsey's probably his partner in crime."

Grabbing Gnarly's leash, Mac began elbowing his way through the crowd of guests as best he could. Abruptly, seeming to catch onto the scent, Gnarly picked up speed and determination. Intent on reaching his goal, the German shepherd dragged Mac through the guests. It was all Mac could do to keep from spilling drinks on the party-goers or himself.

Suddenly, a hand struck out of the crowd to grab Gnarly by the collar. "Whoa, handsome. Women find you more attractive when you play hard to get." Carlisle knelt down between Gnarly and Molly to accept licks on both cheeks.

Laughing, Chelsea patted Molly on the head. "You certainly have a way with animals, Carlisle."

"I have a pet leopard back home," Carlisle tilted her head back to give Gnarly access to her chin.

"Leopard?" Mac parroted. "Really? An honest—"

"In Africa," she explained. "I took her in as a baby. Her mother had been killed by poachers. She was young enough that I was able to domesticate her." She peered into Gnarly's eyes while petting the top of his head with such enthusiasm that it bordered on a head massage. "You remind me of her. Big. Strong. Smart and noble."

Holding a serving tray with a single champagne flute, a server stopped next to Carlisle. "Ms. Green, a gentleman over at the bar asked that I bring you this drink. It is a red velvet champagne. He told me to tell you that it would bring back fond memories of the last time you were at Deep Creek Lake."

Rising to her feet, Carlisle looked at the glass and then over toward the bar. "I don't get it. Who?"

The server searched the faces of the people crowded around the open bar. "I don't see him now." He held out the drink. "Even so—"

"I don't drink," Carlisle said in a firm tone. "Take it back."

Passing by, Lindsey York snatched the drink from the tray. "No sense in letting a perfectly good cocktail go to waste."

"But—" the server objected while hurrying after her.

After Lindsey disappeared into the crowd, the server gave up. Shaking his head, he returned to the bar.

"What's wrong?" Mac asked Carlisle. "What significance is there to a red velvet champagne cocktail?"

"I have no idea," she said. "But then, back when I was here last, I did a lot of stuff, most of which I don't remember. Maybe I spent an evening downing red velvet cocktails with whoever it was that sent it over."

Chelsea said, "Since he didn't stick around to see you accept his drink, maybe he realized he had mistaken you for someone else. If you were such a mess back then, I'm sure your appearance has changed a lot."

"That's true," Carlisle said.

In Mac's ear, David's voice broke through to drown out Chelsea's question about what Carlisle fed her pet leopard. "Is that Carlisle Green and Chelsea?"

Keeping his voice as low as possible, Mac whispered, "Yes."

"What are they talking about?"

"Right now they're talking about what leopards like to eat for dinner."

"What did you say?" David asked with disbelief in his tone. "Did you say *leopards?*"

Preoccupied by David's conversation in his ear, Mac almost missed Carlisle admiring Chelsea's engagement ring.

"Who's the lucky man?" Carlisle was asking.

"David O'Callaghan," Chelsea said. "He's the chief of police. I believe you've met him."

"Congratulations." Her grin stretching across her face, Carlisle rose to her feet. "I'm sure you already know how blessed you are to be engaged to a man with such integrity."

"Now, they're talking about you," Mac whispered.

"What?" Mac didn't miss the note of panic in David's tone.

Mac almost jumped out of his skin when he felt a hand clasp him on the shoulder. "Mr. Faraday, I'm sorry to disturb you." Turning around, Mac saw a young man clad in a tuxedo, which from how it hung on his slightly built frame, was not tailored, but taken off the rack. The jacket hung off his bony shoulders and the pants were baggy down his legs to where they pooled on top of his scuffed loafers. Seeing the question on Mac's face, he reminded him, "Rudy Crowe, from the Inn's public relations department."

"I'm just surprised to see you here, Rudy," Mac lied about the source of his expression.

"I'm covering the gala for the Inn's blog," Rudy said. "The only way I could cover it was to be here myself. Anyway, there's someone here who wants to meet you."

Without giving Mac a chance to refuse his offer in order to return to his search for Raul, Rudy led Mac, who dragged Gnarly, who really wanted to get back to a wonderfully relaxing head massage, across the ballroom to where Vincent Van Dyke was watching his daughter holding court by the bar.

"Mr. Van Dyke," Rudy stepped into his line of sight, "I'd like to introduce you to Mac Faraday, the owner of the Spencer Inn."

Vincent Van Dyke tore his attention from where Kassandra was entertaining a group of middle-aged men overtly admiring her overflowing cleavage. He stood up to take Mac's hand.

Seeing pride on Vincent's face while he watched the group of men practically pawing his daughter, Mac lost every ounce of admiration for his former screen detective idol. Mentally placing his own daughter Jessica, who was approximately the same age as Kassandra, in her place, he knew that pride would be the last sense he would feel. Rather, he would be out of the chair, grabbing his daughter by the arm, and dragging her outside to put some clothes on her—after punching every one of the horny old men in the nose.

At least, he would have a very strong urge to do it. Archie would put a stop to it before things got that far.

Mac had met many celebrities since his windfall and had found it to be disappointing. He discovered that often there was a great divide between someone's public image and reality. Meeting Vincent Van Dyke was no different. His once blond locks had all but disappeared along with his six-pack abs. Mac doubted if he still ran the five miles a day he once bragged about to the media to explain how he stayed in shape and did his own stunts.

Gnarly's whine seeped into Mac's assessment of the aged actor. Behind Vincent Van Dyke, Mac saw Chelsea and Carlisle, with Molly in between them, going through the exit. They looked like lifelong friends.

David's going to have a cow. Amused at the thought, Mac fought the grin working its way to his lips.

"Excuse me, gentlemen," Rudy's voice broke through Mac's thoughts, "I need to go check with Mr. Ingles about a matter that needs taken care of." Without waiting to be excused, he hurried away into the crowd.

"Mickey Forsythe," the actor said while studying his face. "I met your mother, Robin Spencer, once."

"Mac," he corrected him. "Mac Faraday."

"Sorry," Vincent Van Dyke said. "You look like him. Your mother interviewed me for Mickey's part in *Dead Men Don't Lie.*" The star went on to remind Mac that a famous producer had bought the film rights to three of Robin Spencer's biggest books in the eighties, which featured her most famous detective, and wanted Vincent Van Dyke to play the starring role in all three films. "As part of her agreement to sell the movie rights to Lee, Robin Spencer insisted on being involved in the casting. So I had to interview with her." He grinned. "She liked me. So did Lee. We all but signed the contract."

Recalling that Vincent Van Dyke did not appear in the three movies that went on to become blockbusters and won the lead actor, who had been an unknown, an academy award, which shot him to stardom, Mac asked, "What happened?"

"*Hawaii Night Watch's* producers refused to let me out of my contract." The actor's tone and sour expression betrayed a long time lingering resentment over the turn of events.

Abruptly, the actor excused himself and rushed across the room to grab Rock Sinclair by the arm. Mac noticed that a look of displeasure crossed Rock's face when he turned to see the former television star.

"Is this the infamous Gnarly?" A.J. Wagner was kneeling next to the German shepherd to give him a good scratching behind the ears. "I always wanted a German shepherd. My father was allergic to dogs. Now I'm too busy to care for a gold fish. Maybe when I open that clinic in Alaska. I'll get a malamute."

Gnarly greeted the doctor with a lick on the nose.

"Where's your date?" Mac asked him.

"Good question." A.J. was more interested in petting Gnarly, who enjoyed the attention at his level. "Of course, you can see how hard I'm looking for her."

Taking the opportunity to question A.J. alone, Mac said, "Speaking of dating, did Ashton ever mention someone who was obsessed with her? She may have referred to him as Greaser."

His eyebrows furrowed, A.J. paused while stroking Gnarly's fur all the way down his back. The German shepherd had a dreamy expression on his face. He was in heaven.

Mac wondered if A.J. would admit to knowing who he was asking about if Greaser was his devoted friend Corey Haim.

"I seem to recall Ashton and Carlisle talking about a Greaser," A.J. said. "It was like a code name between them. Girl talk. Carlisle would say Greaser and they would giggle like a couple of hyenas." He stopped petting the dog and shot a look up at Mac. "You don't think he killed Ashton, do you?" He let out a low gasp. "I guess it is possible. I never thought— No, it has to be Breckenridge. She's the one who's made out since Ashton disappeared." He stood up.

"There are other ways to gain by someone's death other than money," Mac pointed out.

"Have you talked to Carlisle?" A.J. asked. "What does she know about this Greaser? Who is he? Did he ever threaten Ashton?"

The questions were coming at a mile a minute.

"Carlisle told me to talk to you," Mac said. "She'd never met Greaser. He was someone Ashton knew from school."

A.J. was shaking his head. "That's not possible. I knew all of Ashton's friends."

"He was infatuated with Ashton," Mac said.

"You mean like a stalker?"

"Possibly. Who would fit that description?" Mac asked him.

"If it was someone from school who Carlisle had never met," A.J. said, "then why would he come all the way out here to Deep Creek Lake to kill Ashton?"

Mac shrugged. "One rejection too many. He snapped."

"Let me think about it," A.J. said. "I'll ask Corey. He might be able to come up with a name."

Feeling the need to be blunt, Mac asked, "Could it have been Corey? He does seem—"

"Corey and Ashton were friends—that's all," A.J. said. "Corey brought the two of us together. He noticed Ashton following me around like a puppy dog and slapped me alongside the head to point out how she was right for me. Now would he do that if he wanted her for himself?" He chuckled. "Besides, he has a girl back home in West Virginia that he's head over heels in love with. They've been together for over ten years. She teaches grade school and doesn't even make enough money to buy a house—but she's loyal to her friends and family—just like Corey." He shook his head. "Corey kill Ashton? Not on your life."

While Mac could see that A.J. believed in Corey's innocence with all his heart, he had seen too many instances where a cunning killer had fooled everyone, including his closest friends.

With a quick "excuse me," Samuel Nash inserted himself between the two men, stepping on Gnarly's toes, which prompted a loud yelp. Oblivious to the crowd of party guests turning to see who had hurt the canine guest of honor, Samuel asked A.J., "Where's Rachel? We want to have a sit down interview with all of you."

"I'm not her keeper, Samuel," A.J. replied.

Archie appeared at his elbow. "Mac, it's time for them to start serving dinner and everyone is going to be expecting you to speak." Noticing A.J. being led away by Samuel, she asked, "Have you been soliciting donations or interrogating suspects?"

"Both," Mac lied. "Am I allowed to go freshen up before begging for dollars?"

"Be quick," she replied while tapping his chest, "and no more interrogating our guests."

Approaching from Archie's other side, Chelsea tapped her on the shoulder. "We have a problem."

"What kind of problem?" Archie asked.

As if to answer her question, a high-pitched scream came from the corridor outside the banquet room. The scream was followed by a crash, and another crash, and scream, and more crashes and more screams.

"What was that?" Archie blurted out.

"It's called a fight," Chelsea answered. "I believe a woman is trying to kill one of our guests. That's the problem I wanted to tell you about."

Ben fell in behind Mac to wade through the panicked guests to get out onto the corridor where Jasmine was screaming hysterically. Rock was shielding himself as best he could while one piece of Spencer Inn china after another was being hurled at him from a service table that Riva Sinclair had managed to hijack from a bus person.

"And this is for that trip to Nice that you never took me on!" Riva threw a tea cup that smashed against the wall above Rock's head to shatter into china dust which rained down onto his head.

Riva picked up a dinner plate. "And this is for abandoning Pugsy."

"No one cares about that rat dog of yours!" Jasmine yelled.

"Pugsy has gone into a depression because of his daddy abandoning him," Riva said. "The doctor has had to put him on anti-depressants." She punctuated her announcement by throwing a saucer at her runaway husband.

"Why aren't you in jail?" Rock ducked to avoid being hit in the head by a saucer. "I thought they arrested you!"

"Oh yeah!" Riva hurled a plate like a Frisbee at him. "And that is for the thousands of dollars bail money I had to pay out after being busted by a flea bitten mutt for carrying the gun I was going to blow you and your slut away with!"

"Gnarly is not flea bitten!" Archie yelled out.

"She's trying to kill him!" Jasmine said. "Where's that police chief? Why isn't this psychopath locked up?"

Samuel Nash was laughing loudly. "You know what they say about a woman scorned, Jasmine."

"Mac," David's voice asked in his ear, "what's going on?"

"We have a distraught abandoned wife trying to kill her estranged husband and lover."

"I'm sending Fletcher down to break it up," David reported.

"What's happening here?" Jeff Ingles shrieked and grabbed his head with both hands upon seeing the growing pile of broken hotel china in the hallway.

"You didn't even leave me enough money to live on!" Riva yelled. "Phony skirt chasing con man!"

"Do we have to go through this here?" Rock hissed. "Can't you see that I'm working?"

"Is that what they call it now?" She roared, "You shut off my credit cards!"

"They're my credit cards!"

"How am I supposed to live?" Riva shouted.

"Can you say 'Get a job'?" Jasmine spat out.

"That's an idea," Riva said. "Maybe I'll take up the same career as you. Hooking!"

Jasmine lunged for her.

Mac and Ben forced their way in between the two women.

"You husband-stealing bitch!" Riva raised up her hand in which she clutched a dinner plate. "I'm going to get you for this! I'm going to get you like no one has ever done before. When I'm done with you—"

"That's enough, Ms. Sinclair." Mac thrust Gnarly's leash into Ben's hand and grabbed Riva's arm, poised to hurl a dinner plate at her cowering husband.

"Oh, I'm only getting warmed up," she argued while Mac pinned her arms behind her back. "I'm not some chewing gum that you can just spit out after wringing the best out of me." Seeing Jasmine helping Rock to his feet, she shouted at the couple. "I'm not finished, Rock."

Mac had her pressed against the wall when Officer Fletcher jogged around the corner. Struggling against Mac, she continued to hurl threats at the couple. "By the time I'm through with you, every husband will think of how you ended up before stepping out on his wife ever again."

"You all heard that," Jasmine shouted to everyone within ear shot while clinging to Rock. "Riva Sinclair is threatening to kill us. If anything happens to either of us, you all heard her." She pointed at Riva who Mac handed off to Officer Fletcher.

"It's not a threat," she said while eying her estranged husband and mistress. "It's a promise."

"Mrs. Sinclair," Ben warned, "you're not doing your case any good throwing out threats like that in public. As it is, because of this attack, your bail will have to be revoked. We have no choice but to lock you up again."

"That china is special order," Jeff said.

"Don't worry," Mac said while glaring at Rock and Jasmine. "They're paying for the damage."

"She attacked me," Rock said.

"She wants to kill us," Jasmine added.

In contrast to his bosses' dismay, Samuel Nash was doubled over in laughter.

"Do you find this funny?" Mac asked him while taking Gnarly back from Ben, who accompanied Officer Fletcher and Riva Sinclair out of the hotel to attend to his duty as the prosecuting attorney.

Seemingly unembarrassed, Samuel grinned like the Cheshire Cat in *Alice in Wonderland*. Turning his back to Mac, he sauntered down the hallway.

It must be something in the water in California. These Hollywood types are just plain nuts.

Beyond Samuel's departing figure, Mac spotted David's deputy chief, Art Bogart, called Bogie, gesturing for his attention. In sharp contrast to his age, which was sixty-five years old, the silver-haired deputy chief, who sported a thick, bushy mustache, possessed the solid build of a wrestler, which commanded respect from every officer in the area—far and wide.

Keeping hold of Gnarly's leash, Mac jogged to the other end of the corridor, which opened up into the reception and lounge area where a painting of Robin Spencer hung above the mantel of a stone fireplace.

Beyond Bogie, Mac saw Raul step out of the servant entrance. His hand flew up to point at their suspect. "Zernbog! Stop! Police!"

It was only when Gnarly barked and charged, yanking Mac's arm out of its socket, that Mac remembered he still had the hundred pound German shepherd on his leash.

How Gnarly knew they were pursuing the tall dark haired man with the tattoos, Mac didn't know. He was too busy trying to get back up onto his feet or release Gnarly from his leash in order to stop being dragged down the carpeted hallway.

Finally, Mac was able to untangle the leash from around his wrist, which was already burning like hellfire. Bogie and Gnarly, barking up a storm, disappeared around the corner at the end of the hallway.

Mac tried to climb up onto his knees, but a sharp pain in his shoulder stopped him. He knew the instant it happened what it meant; his shoulder was dislocated. "Gnarly," he muttered to the absent German shepherd, "I'm going to kill you."

The pain heightened Mac's distaste for the formal affair. Grabbing the gun out of his ankle holster, he ran down the hallway in time to see Raul dart back across the hallway and down a servant stairway.

Doubling back. Very clever. Mac heard Gnarly barking. Following Raul's scent, the German shepherd was closing in. *Not clever enough.*

Mac reached the door and held it open in time for Gnarly to charge through.

The door was to a small employee stairwell that descended to the event kitchen. This kitchen was used exclusively for affairs like weddings and benefits. The separate kitchen kept the catering staff from interfering with the daily operations in the main kitchen for the inn's five-star restaurant, which was located on the opposite end of the hotel.

There was only one place for Raul Zernbog to go—down to the kitchen, which was filled with busy hotel employees. Gnarly was hot on his heels. There were three ways out of the kitchen—the back door to the loading dock where food supplies arrived, backup the stairwell, which Mac was blocking, and through the banquet room door into the ballroom filled with over two hundred guests.

A woman's scream came to Mac's ears when he stepped out of the stairwell with his gun drawn.

Coming down the stairs behind him, Bogie said, "That doesn't sound good."

Familiar with the kitchen's layout, Mac instructed Bogie, "Keep him busy," before ducking down a galley way filled with hot burners and stoves. A delicious blend of culinary scents met Mac's nostrils to remind him that he hadn't eaten since lunch. From his left came the smell of prime rib, while chicken cordon bleu drifted behind him. The lobster was wafting up ahead not far from the freshly baked bread, rolls, and desserts.

In the middle of it all, Bogie held up his hand in a fist to signal for Hector, who was directly behind him, to hold his fire.

Keeping his gun aimed at the floor, Mac made his way past a collection of cooks and servers frozen in fear and gazing pleadingly for him to help them. On the other side of the counter where they prepared the plates of hot food, Gnarly was barking and snarling while a man yelled above the barking and a woman sobbing—"Call off the dog! Now! Or I'm going to kill her—I swear—I'll blow a hole right through her head!"

Finally, Mac was able to spy Raul. Gnarly had him backed into a corner. The tall drug dealer was using one of the Inn's young servers as a human shield. With his arm grasping her across her shoulders, he held his gun pressed against her temple.

Mac knew her. Her name was Savannah Cosgrove, the registration manager's daughter. She had dark hair and big dark eyes. A tiny little thing, she didn't look old enough to be legal. But she was—barely.

"Gnarly! Stand down!" Bogie ordered.

Instantly, Gnarly stopped barking and backed up. He didn't sit. Instead, he stood ready to pounce when Bogie or someone gave him the word.

Mac saw that Bogie held his hands up. "Now, Zernbog, we can talk about this. There's no need for anyone to get hurt."

"No talk," Raul said. "You let me out of here and she lives. You don't back off and let me go—she dies."

"Let her go," a male voice announced from among the huddle of employees.

While Bogie tried to hush him, Brian Gallagher elbowed his way through the crowd of frightened kitchen staff. He held up both hands. "I'm a better hostage than her. You can take me. They'll all step back. You can take me out of here and I'll take you wherever you want to go. I can give you all the money you need to get anywhere you want."

"How's that?"

"My father is a billionaire," Brian said. "He'll pay whatever you ask for to get me back." He gestured. "I'll go with you willingly, without any trouble, if you let Savannah go."

Raul's grin, filled with bright white teeth, crossed his face. For a moment, everyone held their breath, anticipating the drug dealer accepting Brian Gallagher's offer. Then, he started to laugh. "Ah, a hero, eh?"

"I don't want to see Savannah hurt," Brian said.

Savannah whimpered. "Brian, don't."

Pushing through the sharp pain in both his shoulder and his wrist, Mac hunkered down behind the counter. He was aware of more than a dozen pair of eyes watching him while he took aim on Raul. When he pressed his finger against the trigger, a sharp pain shot in all directions from his wrist. His hand shook. With a grimace, he shifted his position and moved the gun to his left hand. He was going to have to shoot with his weaker hand.

Peering over the counter at the man holding the server close to him, Mac had a target of Raul's side, but it was slim. While he was an excellent shot, Mac preferred it if Raul offered a clearer target.

No one was breathing.

"You like the lady, huh?" Raul asked. "You try to be a hero to save her and maybe impress her to get into her pants, huh?"

Brian's eyes narrowed. "Don't talk about her that way."

"I'm the one with the gun!" Raul said, "I'll show you what we do to heroes where I come from." Abruptly, the gun that had been pressed against Savannah's temple rose up and across her shoulder to take aim on Brian's chest.

"Zernbog!" Mac bellowed as sharply as he could.

As Mac expected, Raul instinctively turned in the direction of where he had heard his name called, exposing half of his body.

Mac fired off three shots.

Every hotel employee in the kitchen moved to get out of the way. Savannah dove into Brian's arms. He plunged her to the floor and landed on top of her to shelter her from any bullets coming their way.

In the same instant, Gnarly charged. From four feet away, he became airborne. His jaws clamped down on the hand grasping the gun. The force of Gnarly's attack spun both of them around three hundred and sixty degrees. Grasping at the bullet wounds that Mac had put into his side and chest, Raul was unprepared for the hundred pounds of fur and teeth that knocked him off his feet. He was grappling for whatever senses he had left from the bullets that punctured his lungs and heart when the two of them sailed through the swinging kitchen doors to land on the carpeting inside the ballroom.

Mac and Bogie were giving chase.

After ensuring that Brian and Savannah were okay except for being horribly frightened, Hector followed them out into the banquet hall where stunned guests gazed silently at the bleeding guest gasping his last breath with Gnarly standing over him. Behind Gnarly, Mac, Bogie, and Hector stood over him with their guns drawn.

Archie Monday broke the silence. "Mac, what are you doing?"

Her voice made Mac aware of how the scene must have appeared to the hundreds of guests who had been invited to make donations to the humane society. He looked up at a sea of expressions filled with confusion.

Holding his gun up for everyone to see, Mac looked around the banquet room and asked, "Anyone else want to leave without making a donation?"

CHAPTER TWELVE

"Yes, you definitely have a dislocated shoulder." Doc Washington proceeded to wrap the bandage around Mac's shoulder and around his chest. "This is only temporary until you go to the hospital to get that shoulder and wrist x-rayed."

Mac lifted the ice pack from his wrist that the medical examiner had applied upon discovering his injuries when she has arrived to examine the dead drug dealer. Jeff Ingles had offered his office for her to give Mac a quick examination.

"Gnarly did that?" she asked with a frown.

"He's passionate when it comes to catching bad guys."

She tossed his tuxedo coat at him. "I have a dead man waiting for me."

Noting her skinny jeans and polo shirt, Mac said, "You didn't come tonight. You and Bogie were on the invite list."

"Bogie had to work," the stunning woman grinned when mentioning the name of the deputy chief who was twenty-five years older than she. "It wouldn't have been any fun without my favorite handsome man escorting me." Her smile was demure.

Mac felt a tug of guilt. "I'm sorry, Doc. I feel like this is all my fault. Chelsea came without a date and you ended up sitting home alone."

"Both Chelsea and I signed on for this when we fell for the men we love." The corners of her lips curled. "We may miss out on fancy dress balls, but our men more than make up for it in other ways."

Recalling arguments from the distant past about missing out on affairs that were only a fraction as fancy as the Diablo Ball, Mac said in a low voice, "My first wife was not quite so understanding. Maybe she was at first, but as the years wore on ..."

"Your first wife had issues," Doc said, "and none of them were your fault." Her dark eyes met his. "You have nothing to worry about with Archie."

"Do I look worried?"

Snapping her medical bag shut, she ordered, "Go get that wrist x-rayed and tell Gnarly to take it easy next time."

❧ ❧ ❧

"Do you have any idea how stupid that was, Gallagher?" Hector was chastising Brian Gallagher in a low voice when Mac went back into the kitchen to check the status of the crime scene investigation. As the shooter, he was certain the state police would have questions for him.

"Even if he believed you," the security chief was telling the intern, "you would have been dead the second he found out the truth."

Savannah's mother, Betty Cosgrove, had been called down from where she was managing the registration desk. Twenty-one years old, Savannah had only been working for the Inn for six months. Her divorced mother Betty had been with the Spencer Inn for more than twenty-five years—working her way up from housekeeping to managing the registration desk after getting her bachelor in business management. She did it all while raising her daughter alone.

A single mother, Savannah had a two year old little girl. Mac had been told that the child's father had abandoned Savannah in the same manner as her father.

Blinking away tears of relief along with the other employees, Jeff ordered the two women to go home. Police Chief David O'Callaghan consented to getting any statements they needed in the morning.

Before leaving, Savannah wrapped her arms around Brian's shoulders and kissed him tenderly on the cheek. "That was the sweetest thing anyone has ever done for me, Brian," she said in a whisper that Mac heard.

"I didn't do anything," Brian said.

"You offered to take my place," she said. "You lied to make him take you. Mr. Langford is right. He would have killed you when he found out that you'd lied about being rich."

"But you would have been safe," Brian said. "That's what was important. You being safe."

The puzzlement in Savannah's eyes struck Mac. It was plain to him that never had she heard those words from a man before. Maybe she had, but if so, they had been lying, and she had been made a fool afterwards when the man abandoned her the same way her father had deserted her mother. But here was Brian Gallagher who had put his life where his mouth was by offering up his life in exchange for hers.

Savannah was still staring with awe at Brian when her mother ushered her, with one of the Spencer police officers, out through the loading dock doors to go home.

Hector Langford waited until they were gone before having another go at Brian. "She's right, you know."

"Let him go, Hector," Mac said in a firm tone. "Everything is fine. We have our man."

"But the banquet is a disaster," Jeff said.

"No," Mac said, "Archie and Catherine are predicting that this is a record breaking year for Robin's Pets. The guests are throwing money at them faster than they can keep count."

"Can't imagine why," Hector quipped, miming a gun with his hand and holding it straight up in the air.

"Right now, I care more about getting my hands on Lindsey York," David said. "I want to know what she knew about this monster and why she brought him here. I know she did it for a reason and I want to know what that is." He turned to Hector. "Have any of your people located her yet?"

"I have all of my people looking for her," Hector said. "She hasn't been in her room and Jasmine Simpson and Rock Sinclair claim that they never saw Raul before tonight."

Bogie came in from the ballroom. His stern expression and posture was enough to make everyone pause in what they were doing. "We have another problem."

"*Another* problem?" David asked. "As if we don't have enough."

"Rachel Breckenridge appears to be missing," Bogie said. "Her mother says she hasn't seen her for hours."

"A.J. Wagner is her date," David said. "What does he say?"

"He says he was talking to her a couple of hours ago, she excused herself to go to the ladies room and he hasn't seen her since."

"Hector," Mac said with a sigh.

"I've got my people on it." While pressing the button on his radio, Hector whirled around on his heels and hurried out of the kitchen.

David's eyes met Mac's. There was a long moment of silence between the two men while officers and security personnel rushed about to make sense of the chaos. Finally, David stated, "I hate your party."

"Not as much as I do."

Stepping in close, David whispered, "What was Carlisle telling Chelsea about me?"

Mac gazed long and hard into David's eyes. "Huh?" he asked.

"You said Carlisle and Chelsea were talking about me earlier."

"Carlisle noticed Chelsea's engagement ring and was admiring it," Mac said. "Chelsea told her that you two were engaged and Carlisle congratulated her. That's all." The thought struck his brain like lightning. "Did you sleep with Carlisle Green?" The question came out as a hissed accusation.

"No," David answered in a harsh whisper. "Why would you even accuse me of that?"

"Because you have a very bad habit."

"I do not."

Narrowing his eyes, Mac peered at him. "Do you want to rethink your response to that accusation?"

"Okay, it's a long list but ..." David grit his teeth. "I did not sleep with Carlisle Green." Brushing past Mac, he said, "I need to go check in with Brewster and Zigler about our witness statements."

Seeing David heading for the door leading into the ballroom, Mac said, "Chelsea's out there."

Spinning on his heels, David turned to the stairs leading to the main floor.

"Carlisle's upstairs in the lobby."

"Don't make me shoot you, Mac," David said before pushing through the doors leading out to the loading dock.

Chuckling at David's dilemma, Mac went back out into the banquet room to collect his wife and go home to have a long soak in his hot tub.

He found Archie, Catherine, and Chelsea huddled together at a table. Cash, credit card receipts, and checks were organized into several neat piles in front of Catherine. Archie had a calculator in front of her and a ledger sheet to keep track of the accounting for their records while Chelsea was keeping a list of names and contact information for sending out thank you notes and receipts for tax purposes.

Lying together next to the table, Gnarly was licking Molly's ears for all they were worth while the white German shepherd appeared to be making a grand effort to ignore him.

Ben Fleming was sitting back in his chair with his arms folded across his chest. A bottle of very expensive cognac rested on the table in front of him. Seeing Mac, Ben sat up and poured the cognac into an empty snifter he had waiting for their host. While holding up the glass in an offer of a drink, he gestured at the ice pack wrapped around Mac's wrist. "Some old-fashion medication to ease the pain."

After taking the drink, Mac gestured at Gnarly. "He doesn't even look guilty."

With a sigh, Gnarly rested his head across Molly's back. When the white German shepherd rolled over to press against him, Gnarly resumed licking her ears.

"He did help capture Raul Zernbog," Ben said, "and, while I hate it when a suspect forces the police into a shootout that ends up with someone dead, I can't deny that I do love it when you guys make it easy for me by eliminating the bad guy before he can get his day in court."

"Still creates a ton of paperwork," Chelsea said.

"And anymore it doesn't make for good public relations," Catherine pointed out.

"Raul left us no choice." Mac took a sip of the cognac and uttered a sigh of both exhaustion over the night and pleasure over the smooth taste of the liquor. "He was going to shoot Brian Gallagher in front of more than a dozen people, including a uniformed deputy police chief."

"Because Brian offered himself as a hostage," Archie said. "Talk about gallant."

"He almost got himself killed," Mac said.

"To save Savannah." Archie told Catherine in a low voice. "I think he has a crush on her. Have you seen the way he looks at her?"

"Sounds like suicide by cop," Chelsea said without looking up from where she was writing out an address. "I feel sorry for the officers who get put in that position. David always has trouble sleeping when someone forces him to shoot him. I don't imagine you ever get used to it, do you, Mac?"

"No," Mac replied before taking another sip of his drink.

"Usually those hard core types would rather go out in a blaze of glory than be snuffed out in prison by a rival gang or one of their own for being a suspected snitch," Ben said.

"Why would someone like that come here?" Mac asked. "He had to know that with all the A-listers coming to this thing that the police would be out in force to protect them. Everyone knows I'm a retired cop." He gestured at Catherine. "A United States Senator was one of the hosts. Wouldn't he assume the Secret Service would be here? What was he thinking?"

"I don't have a Secret Service detail," Catherine told them what they already knew. "I turned it down. The last thing I want is a dozen men following me into the ladies room."

"But the average drug dealer doesn't know that," Ben said. "Mac has a point. What was Zernbog doing here?"

"Besides a dead drug dealer," Mac said, "we also have two missing women. Rachel Breckenridge—"

"We know about that," Archie said.

"We're also looking for Lindsey York, who brought the now dead drug dealer," Mac said.

"You'll find her in her room," Ben said, "sleeping it off."

"Hector checked already," Mac said. "She's not there."

"Then check all of the other beds here at the inn," Chelsea said. "It's common knowledge that she doesn't like to sleep alone."

Mac brought the cognac to his lips. He was about to take another sip when a scream echoed in his ears. He looked up and saw Archie covering her mouth with one hand while pointing across the room and up.

From the top of the grand staircase, Lindsey York tumbled over the railing and plummeted down through the air— like a duck shot out of the sky—to crash into George Gershwin's white grand piano below.

While everyone stared at the body of the young debutante sprawled out across the musical instrument below, Mac followed her flight path backwards to where Brian Gallagher was peering at her lifeless body from over the railing.

CHAPTER THIRTEEN

With wide eyes, Brian Gallagher stared down over the banister at Lindsey York's body sprawled among the ruins of the once impressive white grand piano.

Mac and Ben Fleming were the first ones to come out of their shock and react to the catastrophe. While Ben rushed to help his wife and Chelsea shovel the donation funds into a money bag, Mac stepped into the remains of the piano to check for any signs of life in Lindsey York. Grabbing Gnarly's leash, Archie urged both German shepherds to their feet and ushered them out of the banquet room so that they could not be accused of contaminating a potential crime scene. As soon as the bag was sealed shut, Chelsea followed her service dog, Molly.

"Oh, man! Did that really just happen?" Mac heard from up above him. One of the camera operators he had seen flitting about the Inn while filming Kassandra and Lindsey had his mouth hanging open. "Is she—"

Wordlessly, Mac shook his head in response to everyone's question about if Lindsey was still alive.

David pushed the growing crowd pouring in from the kitchen out of the way to join him. "What happened?"

Mac noted foam around Lindsey's lips. "Could be a heroin overdose."

While David took control of the scene, Mac galloped up the stairs to where Brian Gallagher was staring down at the fallen body. He clutched the banister in a white knuckled grip. "Brian, what happened?"

Mac saw that the young man was breathing hard.

"She came out of the bathroom and went bonkers," the camera operator said. "Foaming at the mouth. It was like she had rabies or something."

"Brian …" Mac touched his arm. "Did you see what happened?"

Slowly, Brian nodded his head. "I didn't want …" he whispered.

"You didn't want what, Brian?"

"She didn't deserve …"

Mac's brow furrowed. "Did you know Lindsey York, Brian?"

The young man started. He turned to Mac and seemed to finally notice that he was there. "I need to go make a phone call."

"You need to talk to the police." With a toss of his head, Mac gestured at David trotting up the stairs toward them.

Brian Gallagher was taking his cell phone out of his pocket. "Sure, but I need to call someone first."

❧ ❧ ❧

Inn manager Jeff Ingles didn't need to be told to have his staff seal off the entrances and exits to keep any possible suspects from slipping out. While Police Chief David O'Callaghan was taking charge of the scene, Mac zeroed in on the camera operator who had been tailing Lindsey the whole evening.

Mac managed to scurry him away before his boss, Vincent Van Dyke, got word of the possible goodies he had on his camera and could confiscate the possible evidence—or destroy it if it was in his interest.

Clutching the arms of his chair in the lounge, the camera operator, who went by Gopher, looked like he was going to faint while recalling the events leading up to Lindsey's dive over the banister. Overcome with shock, he let the camera drop to his feet and covered his face with his hands. "I thought it was all part of the show," he muttered.

The name Gopher was fitting for the young man who was short, tubby, and had bucked teeth. Mac could see that he was not much older than his own son, who was a third year undergraduate studying natural science at George Washington University. He had chosen not to follow in his father's footsteps, which was fine with Mac.

"Part of the show?" Mac pretended to be skeptical, though he had his suspicions. "I thought none of this was planned."

Under Mac's gaze, the kid shook his head like the weak link in a childish conspiracy to pull a prank on the teacher. "That's what they want the viewers to think. Everything is planned. I mean, it's not scripted like they have lines to memorize and stuff is rehearsed, but we do have an idea of what will happen. Both girls had a cameraman assigned to her. I was assigned to Lindsey and was to follow her everywhere, except when she went to the bathroom. I think she got sick in the bathroom before this happened." He gestured at the body across the hotel lobby and out of sight, now being examined by the medical examiner.

"You just said you didn't go into the bathroom with her," Mac said.

Gopher shook his head so hard that his plump cheeks jiggled like gelatin. "No, but she was staggering all over the place and suddenly she took off running." He explained, "Lindsey was the party girl. That's why I asked for her. She was the one who would stir things up. You know, getting drunk and making passes at other women's men. Kassandra Van Dyke is gorgeous, but … really, she's as dumb as a stick. Always wants

to be nice to everyone and doesn't like to make waves. That's what makes them a good pair. Kassandra is the dumb blonde and Lindsey is a bitch."

"Just because someone is nice doesn't make them dumb," Mac said.

"Maybe not in Deep Creek Lake," Gopher said.

Mac asked, "How did Kassandra feel about working with Lindsey?"

"I don't think she's smart enough to care," Gopher said. "But Vincent Van Dyke is another story. He had hired us to make this pilot for the show to revolve around Kassandra and him—a father-daughter show. Lindsey was only going to be in the first or second episode because Kassandra was coming to the ball and Rock Sinclair was shooting his investigative report. But then, the director showed the footage that we had shot so far to Sinclair and he said he would buy the show but only if Lindsey was in it—shared billing with Kassandra."

"Was Van Dyke's name being scratched off the billing?" Casually, Mac picked up the camera the operator had used to record his part of the show. It recorded onto a memory card. "I'll bet he wasn't happy about that at all."

"Not in the least. But it's the only offer on the table." Gopher nodded his head. "I grew up in Hollywood. It's a buyers' market. Everyone has a project that they're promoting. If Van Dyke turned down Sinclair's offer, he may not get another."

"But if he took it," Mac said, "It's a given that Lindsey would have squeezed him out and his chance of a comeback as a reality star would be gone." He gestured at the camera operator's earpiece he wore in his right ear. "Who gives you your direction?"

He fingered the earpiece. "The director."

"What's his name?"

"Samuel Nash." Gopher paused to swallow.

"Isn't he the same director working on Rock Sinclair's investigative report?"

"Yep."

"Where is he?"

"In the control room." Gopher gestured up the staircase and down the hallway. "They booked one of the suites. That's where the crew works."

Mac noticed that he was still fingering the earpiece. "Were you following Lindsey all evening?"

"All day."

"Which means you recorded everything—"

"Her getting ready for this evening." His naughty grin reminded Mac of his son. "Even her bubble bath. She met with Kassandra and Vincent for drinks her in the lounge before going to the banquet." Gopher nervously wiped his face. "Was she murdered?"

Mac searched the camera for the compartment that housed the disk. "We won't know that until the autopsy."

"Is that where they cut them open?" Gopher's face turned green.

"Y-incision from both shoulders, through her ribcage, then a straight line down to her crotch."

As Mac had expected, Gopher's face turned greener.

"Did Lindsey take any drugs? Cocaine? Heroin? Pills?" Mac opened the compartment and found the memory disk. "You don't have to answer. We'll find that out ourselves when the ME cuts open her stomach and dumps it. After they sort through the bile they'll find out what she ingested. Do you know what bile straight out of the stomach looks like?" He screwed up his nose. "Nastiest thing you ever want to smell—especially when a body has been sitting out in the open for a couple of days."

Gopher covered his mouth and turned away to hold back his dinner, during which time Mac slipped the disk into his jacket pocket and slapped the camera door shut.

After handing the camera back to Gopher, who seemed to not have the strength to hold it up, Mac went in search of Brian Gallagher, whom he assumed had finished talking to David and Bogie.

"Gopher, there you are!" Vincent Van Dyke rushed into the lounge to nab the camera operator. "Tell me you got Lindsey's somersault over the railing."

"Yes, sir! I got it all." He held up the camera which Van Dyke snatched out of his hands.

Clutching the disk in his pocket, Mac dove into the guests, out of the lounge, across the lobby, under the crime scene tape stretched across the entrance to the ballroom, and down the stairs to where Doc Washington was showing the foam on Lindsey's lips to David and Bogie.

"Drugs," David said. "Knowing Lindsey, it was an accidental drug overdose or poison."

Mac grabbed David's arm and whispered into his ear. "I have something for you, but you need to take it now."

Annoyed by the interruption, David glanced at Mac over his shoulder. Mac directed him to look at the object he slipped out of his pocket only enough for him to see. "It's the recording of what the camera operator following Lindsey shot this evening. I stole it from his camera."

"That's theft."

"What do you intend to do about it?" Mac asked. "Arrest me and take this into evidence?"

"I should." A grin came to David's lips.

"Chief O'Callaghan!" Vincent Van Dyke bellowed from the barricade David's officers had set up. "I need to talk to you! Now! I think you have something that belongs to me!"

Slowly, David turned around to face the former star shouting at him from the top of the stairs. "What did you just say, Mr. Van Dyke?"

"You heard me!"

In the other direction, Mac slipped under the barricade into the kitchen and up the back stairs until he came out into the lobby where he found Archie and Gnarly with Ben, Catherine, and Chelsea.

Mac grasped Archie by the arm. "I need your help." He glanced over her shoulder to see the county prosecutor shadowing them.

Vincent Van Dyke's voice rose above the crowd when the police chief led him away from the crime scene into the lobby. "Someone stole one of our disks for the show from my camera and if I don't get it back right now, I'm suing your police department, Chief O'Callaghan!"

"I don't want to know about this." Ben Fleming slipped his arm around his wife's waist. "Catherine, we're leaving. Now! Chelsea, we'll give you a ride home." They trotted out the door. Without waiting for a valet, they hurried in the direction of the parking garage.

Mac slipped the memory card into Archie's palm. "I need you to copy this disk ASAP."

Archie whirled around on her heels. "Give me five minutes."

"My lawyer is on his way!" Vincent Van Dyke announced.

"You have two!" Mac hissed while she and Gnarly hurried across the lobby in the direction of Hector's security office to find a computer with a drive from which to copy the disk. "Now!"

❧ ❧ ❧

"I'm going to need all copies of what you shot tonight—un-edited." David O'Callaghan wasted no time in telling Rock Sinclair after tracking him and Jasmine down in their suite.

Rock Sinclair threw back his head and laughed. "Not without a warrant." His expression and tone was not unlike that of a bully who had stolen the neighborhood geek's money and was now daring him to go tattle to his mommy. "Do you think I'm going to let you and your neighborhood rent-a-cops take my award winning film to leak all over the media before I get my shot at airing it? Not a chance. No one is seeing it until my network premiere."

"You are aware that two people are dead, one being one of your stars—"

"We don't have stars," Jasmine corrected David. "This is an in-depth investigative report. If anything, Lindsey was a suspect. Maybe she was a witness who knew too much and Ashton's killer had to silence her." With a low laugh, she cocked her head. "Just think," she said with a broad smile. "There's a murderer right here at the Spencer Inn, right under your noses, and you don't even know it."

"Maybe even right here in this room." David stepped up to her. The accusation in his eyes made her back up a step. "Maybe you weren't content to investigate a cold case, but you wanted a hot one as well."

"Anything we've recorded involving Lindsey stopped a good hour before she collapsed," Samuel Nash volunteered from a desk off to the side. Texting away on his phone, he slouched in the chair and one very long leg crossed over the other. He was clad in black slacks and a button down black shirt. David was surprised to discover he had been paying attention. He had seemed more focused on the phone.

David bypassed Rock and Jasmine to stand over Samuel. Ripping the phone from his hand, he said, "As director, you must have been in a keen position to notice Lindsey's relation-ship with the other interviewees in this report."

"In other words you want to know who Lindsey had problems with."

"Exactly."

"That's an easy question to answer." Samuel snatched the cell phone back and shoved it into his left pants pocket. He looked up to meet David's eyes. "Everyone. She caused prob-lems with everyone from her hair designer to Jasmine to the server who brought her breakfast to the Inn's public relations guy."

"As a matter of fact," Jasmine said, "I saw her arguing with him when we left the ball after Mac Faraday killed her date."

"Do you mean the tall man with red hair and freckles?" David asked. "Brian Gallagher?"

While Jasmine said yes, Samuel Nash shook his head and replied a notch louder. "No, this guy was shorter than the Gallagher dude and his tux looked like his tailor was drunk when he fitted it. He tried to take her champagne before she was finished with it and she went ape on him."

"Like *he's* going to *kill* her for that." Jasmine scoffed. "The police chief is looking for suspects."

"I'm just saying …" Samuel replied. "The chief is asking me who Lindsey had trouble with so I'm telling him. For all we know this guy in the bad suit is a whack job who decides to go on a killing spree because Lindsey reminded him of his demented mother who hugged him too much when he was a baby."

Rock turned around to say to Samuel, "Tell me you didn't miss that altercation with the whack job."

Samuel bit his lip, causing his goatee to twitch. "Our communications went down temporarily and I had to go check on the system."

"But the cameras would record everything to their smart cards, wouldn't they?" David asked.

Jasmine and Rock waited for Samuel's response. "If the camera operators weren't on break at the time. They had been working all evening. When our server went down—it wasn't able to sync everything they were recording, so I told them to take thirty minutes while I fixed it. Now Van Dyke is writing the pay checks for his people, so they most likely kept on recording."

"Is the server working now?" The annoyance in Rock's tone was evident.

"What happened to the server?" Jasmine asked before Samuel could answer.

"Our wi-fi went down," Samuel said in a snarky tone. "I rebooted and it's working now." He turned his attention back to the police chief. "Lindsey York has been nothing but trouble during this whole production."

"Now that she's dead," David said, "things should run more smoothly for you."

The three of them exchanged telling glances while David smirked at them.

Samuel extracted his cell phone from his pocket. "Like I said, Chief, Lindsey York had problems with everyone."

❦ ❦ ❦

Mac found Brian Gallagher directing the bartender to continue providing drinks on the house to the guests in the lockdown until the police released them. With two people dead in separate incidents, the Inn's guests were becoming more anxious as time passed.

"Mr. Ingles told me that we would have an open bar until the police released them," he told Mac to assure him that he had not made the decision to offer thousands of dollars of free booze on his own.

With other thoughts on his mind, Mac brushed past the excuse. "Where is the control room for Vincent Van Dyke's show?"

"They booked the Lake Room Suite." Brian explained. "Vincent Van Dyke threw a fit when he found out that it was only the second largest suite on the top floor and Rock Sinclair had already booked the biggest one with the view of the lake. Van Dyke got the view of the valley."

"Walk with me," Mac ordered.

Brian fell into step with him to leave the lounge. "Is it always so adventurous here?"

"Do you mean do high society girls take high dives off of stair landings onto grand pianos just after international drug lords get shot down in the main ballroom? No."

The intern paused to hold open the cut glass door for Mac to step through into the Inn's lobby. Mac spied the bright lights of the media's cameras jostling outside to catch a glimpse of the action inside.

Brian led him across the lobby to the penthouse elevators.

"I assume you've had time to make your phone call," Mac said while allowing Brian to press the button for the floor. "Was it to your lawyer?"

"No," Brian said, "it was … a friend." He went on to explained, "He knew Lindsey. I didn't want him to find out on the news."

"Was he a close friend?" Mac asked. "A suspect?"

Brian shot Mac a sidelong glance. "No … to both questions. He was close, but not terribly close and he had no reason to want Lindsey hurt. He's not even in town."

"But you are," Mac said. "And you're his friend. Maybe you decided to do him a favor—"

"I would never hurt Lindsey."

The elevator doors opened, but neither man stepped off.

"I noticed that you were directly behind her when she went over the railing," Mac said casually.

"The camera man was there," Brian said. "He'll tell you. I never touched her."

Mac glanced Brian up and down before stepping off the elevator into the corridor. When the intern did not immediately follow, Mac paused to wait for him. The doors were about to close when Brian hurried off and fell into step beside Mac.

"Did you notice anything about Lindsey's behavior before she went over the banister?"

Brian quickly shook his head. "Only that she was higher than a kite. A guest came to get me at the front desk because the cameraman was in the ladies room. I went in—"

Holding up his hand, Mac stopped. "Wait a minute. The camera*man* was in the *ladies* restroom?" He recalled Gopher specifically saying that he did not follow Lindsey into the bathroom, which was how he did not know if she was taking recreational drugs.

"Yes," Brian nodded his head. "I went in to shoo him out."

"Did you see him in the restroom?"

"Yes, I did," Brian said. "Both he and Lindsey were in the bathroom stall."

Mac stopped and turned to face him. "The cameraman was recording her *in* the bathroom stall?"

"No, the camera was on the counter," Brian said.

"If he wasn't recording—" With a firm shake of his head, Mac asked, "Did either of them throw something into the garbage can after they came out?"

"If you're asking if they were shooting up, yes, I think that's what they were doing."

"Did you touch the garbage can?" Mac took out his cell phone to send a text to David.

"No, I wanted no part of that," Brian replied. "I just wanted them out of the restroom so that the rest of our guests wouldn't see that going on here at the Spencer Inn. It's not good for our five-star image, you know."

"I know." Mac imagined Jeff Ingles' reaction to learning that guests were shooting up in their bathrooms.

"They weren't wearing gloves," Brian said, "so you should be able to get fingerprints or DNA or whatever off it. The camera man was the one who got rid of the syringe and stuff. Lindsey came out of the stall looking like hell. She shoved me out of the way and almost fell through the glass doors on her way out. I followed her to make sure she was all right, but before I could stop her, she went flying over the railing." When Mac turned to continue down the hall, Brian stopped him. "Was it a heroin overdose?"

"Why do you mention heroin? Why not LSD or crack cocaine?"

"Lindsey was in rehab a few years ago for heroin addiction."

"How do you know that?" Mac asked. "I notice that you call her Lindsey, not Ms. York. Brian, did you know Lindsey York before you came to Spencer?"

"My friend told me about the rehab, which is not exactly a state secret considering her public life." Brian threw open the double doors to a conference room.

The suite looked like another world—the world of motion pictures.

A short man in jeans and a short sleeved shirt, with tattoos all over his arms, rose to block their entrance. "You're not allowed in here!"

"Oh, yes, I am." Mac rose his voice for them all to hear. "Who's in charge here?"

A tall, rail thin man with bright, white hair under a baseball cap, and small round glasses, was yelling into a wireless mike. "What do you mean you don't know where she went? It's your job to follow her." He scanned the bank of monitors. "We're getting award winning stuff happening right on camera—one of our stars died on camera during the debut episode—and you've lost one of our main attractions!"

"Excuse me!" Mac interjected while coming up behind him. "Are you in charge?"

The yelling man whirled around. "Who are you?"

"Mac Faraday, the Inn's owner. Are you the ring leader of this circus?" He saw what he had first taken to be a smudge of dirt on his chin was, in fact, a small, black goatee.

"That would be me." He glanced back at the monitors. "Henry Dolan."

"You're the director?" Mac asked.

"Assistant director and writer."

Mac played dumb. "Writer? I thought this was a reality show."

"Even reality needs a little help sometimes to keep the audience interested," Henry said.

Mac brushed past him to study the panel of monitors. He was correct. They were recording David and the police in action.

One of the monitors caught his attention when he saw Kassandra Van Dyke's face. Tears filled her eyes while she gestured angrily at the camera. He peered to see that the background was not the banquet room, but rather what appeared to be a hotel suite.

"Where is this being recorded?" He laid his fingertip on the monitor's screen.

"The room next door," Henry answered with an impatient sigh. "That is where the girls go to tell the audience their impressions about the show."

"Is this happening live?"

"Yep," the director said. "We wanted to get as much on the scene response to Lindsey's dive as possible while it was still fresh and raw."

"Certainly looks raw to me," Mac commented on Kassandra's tears. "Turn up the volume."

Henry pushed a lever up on the control panel.

"What kind of animals are you?" Kassandra yelled in the direction of the camera. "A woman has died. She's dead and you want to know what I think? You want to know how I feel? I'll show you how I feel!"

The camera shot dodged when she took a swing at the operator.

"Don't you even care? She's a human being, damn it." Kassandra broke down into sobs. "And all you care about is getting some great action on camera!"

While Mac's heart ached for the sobbing woman in the room next door, he heard Brian's voice behind him mutter, "She's right."

Henry was chuckling with glee. "Oh, this is great stuff. There won't be a dry eye in the room when we air this."

"I've seen enough." Mac spoke into the mike. "This is Mac Faraday, owner of the Spencer Inn. I want all camera operators to cease and desist recording now! Anyone who does not turn off their camera will be evicted from my premises immediately. Have I made myself clear?"

Instantly, the bank of monitors turned royal blue with the shutdown of the cameras.

Henry objected, "You can't do that!"

"I just did. Two of my guests are dead and I want to know why. Considering how you, Van Dyke, and your director have jumped onto the sensationalism bandwagon, you're beginning to look like suspects to me. Now, if you can't change my opinion, you may find your butts in Spencer's jail."

Henry threw up his hands. "Wait a minute! This is reality television! Stuff you don't expect to happen happens all the time. If you stop recording as soon as it gets unpleasant—"

"A woman bringing a known drug dealer, armed and dangerous, to a public event and then getting killed herself is more than unpleasant! Lindsey York put innocent people, many of whom I love, in danger. I personally know that server who York's date took hostage—her and her family! Now," Mac poked Henry in the chest, "if I find out that you put her up to bringing him here to my Inn in order to make your reality show a little more interesting for the audience, I will hold you personally responsible."

Henry's face turned white. "She messed herself up and fell over the banister," he said. "Too bad for us, too. Lindsey was supposed to be the live wire that kept all the action flowing on this show."

"I thought Van Dyke and his daughter were supposed to be the live wire."

"Not since Van Dyke sold the show to Sinclair," Henry said. "He gave us orders to make Lindsey York the star."

"What happens now that your live wire is dead?"

Henry gazed at Mac with no answer.

"I guess Lindsey's death opens the door to several possibilities," Mac said. "Who supplied the drugs she was taking tonight?"

Henry said, "Lindsey did all that on her own. She's got big and powerful friends, as you saw for yourself in the date she brought tonight."

Brian said, "The cameraman was shooting her up with something in the restroom minutes before she went over the banister."

"Most likely it was her shooting Gopher up," Henry said. "Since her father cut her off, Lindsey has been forced to go into business on her own. She's not just a consumer, but a supplier." He rubbed his finger over his goatee. "But then, Lindsey isn't very good with needles. She was pretty unstable the last hour or so of the shoot. She may have asked Gopher to help her out."

"In which case Gopher would be criminally liable for homicide," Mac said.

Henry's hands went up in a signal of surrender. "I'm only guessing based on what you guys told me. I *saw* nothing. I *know* nothing."

"The police are going to want copies of everything you recorded, including after Lindsey's death."

Henry shook his head. "Van Dyke already put out the word, no one gets anything. He's aiming for the big time with this."

"And what are you aiming for?" Mac asked. "Jail time for obstruction of justice?"

Without waiting for his answer, Mac left the suite and rushed downstairs in time to see Archie making her way across the lobby toward him. Along the way, she crossed to where Vincent Van Dyke's camera crew was talking together while waiting for Police Chief David O'Callaghan to release them.

After catching Mac's eye, Archie spied Gopher among the group.

Snatching a glass of wine from a waiter, she elbowed her way through the group. "Hey, Jeff—" Tripping, she fell into Gopher in what appeared to be a full body slam. "Oh, excuse me!" she shrieked while attempting to wipe away the spilt wine from his jacket. "I hope I didn't hurt you."

Saying that he was okay, Gopher brushed away the drink.

"I am so clumsy. I hope they let us go soon," she said. "I mean if I have any more free drinks I won't be able to go home. I hope I didn't break anything."

With a slight nod of her head in David's direction, she made her way through the crowd. While she exited the group on one side, David and Bogie made their way to Gopher from the other.

"Justin Smith, you're under arrest for suspicion of homicide." David slapped the cuffs on Gopher's wrists before he had time to react.

"What the—"

While the camera operator sputtered, David stuck his hand into his jacket pocket and extracted the memory card that Archie had dropped inside. "What's this?"

Bogie held out an evidence bag. "Looks like evidence to me."

"Where did that come from?" Gopher asked. "My boss has been looking for that. Hey, Vince!"

"He can see it at your trial," David said while leading the camera operator through the crowd and out the door.

"That was slick," Mac whispered into Archie's ear.

"I learned from the best."

"I take it you were able to copy it?"

"Copy plus a backup."

"Good," Mac said. "While Ben gets to work on the warrants to make the original footage admissible as evidence, we can get to work solving the case using our bootleg copy."

CHAPTER FOURTEEN

"You do realize that it's okay to wake up after six o'clock in the morning, right?" Mac asked Gnarly around the two maximum strength aspirin between his lips. He washed them down with a swig of orange juice.

Focused on the empty dog food bowl on the kitchen counter, the German shepherd was oblivious to the bags under Mac's eyes. After leaving the Spencer Inn, they had gone to the emergency room where Mac had his shoulder and wrist x-rayed. As Doc Washington had diagnosed, he had a dislocated shoulder. Thankfully, his wrist was only badly sprained. They put his hand and wrist in a brace and his arm in a sling that was secured to his chest.

With only two hours of sleep, Mac planned to return to bed right after filling the bowl with dog food and plopping it onto the floor next to Gnarly's water dish.

"I knew you'd be up." Carrying her laptop tucked under her arm, Archie trotted into the kitchen. She was still clad in one of his pajamas tops, which she wore for bed clothes. On her petite frame, they hung down to her upper thigh, not unlike a short nightie. As always, her feet were bare. Archie only wore shoes, usually sandals that let her feet breathe, when she needed to get into public establishments.

"To tell you the truth, I was planning to go back to bed. I wanted to sleep in, but the morning dog had other plans."

Gnarly stomped his front paws and let out a yelp. When Archie arrived to snatch a kiss, his master had become distracted in his duty. The dog dish was still resting on the counter.

"Sorry," Mac apologized before placing his dish on the floor.

Gnarly dove in.

"He's allowed to be a morning dog." Archie patted the German shepherd on the back. "He gets to nap all day long. On the other hand—" She sat down at the kitchen table. "I would have thought you wouldn't have slept at all after last night." She opened the lid to her laptop.

"I tend to sort things out in my sleep." Seeing that she intended to stay, Mac hit the button on the coffeemaker to start the coffee brewing. "What did you find out while mingling with the witnesses last night?"

"Not much," she said. "To tell you the truth, I ended up with more questions than answers. I'm still trying to figure out who sent out the bogus invitations and why."

"You don't think Rock Sinclair did it to bring together all his suspects for his show?" Mac asked.

Archie shook her head. "Neither he nor Jasmine had access to the invitation list. The phony invitations only went out to the suspects in Ashton's murder who had been banned from the Diablo Ball." She tapped his hand with her fingertips. "Not only that, but the counterfeits that Catherine and Chelsea had confiscated are identical to the real invitations."

"That means whoever sent out the phony invitations had to have access not only to your guest list but the custom invitations," Mac said.

"Mac, the only ones who had access to both were me, Catherine, Chelsea, and the event coordinator at the Spencer Inn."

"I'll check with her to see if she has any ideas of who else may have accessed it," Mac said. "Did you discover anything from the recordings on the memory card?"

"It only has shots of Lindsey acting like the bimbo that she was," Archie said.

"Now don't go speaking ill of the dead," Mac said. "Kassandra Van Dyke was devastated by her death."

"I have to admit, she did surprise me." Archie slid the laptop over to rest in front of Mac's seat. "Exhibit A." She had brought up the video player on her laptop. "From the video we stole—"

"Confiscated," he corrected her.

She explained, "According to the time stamp, this was recorded at twelve minutes after seven—before you spotted Raul and chased him down into the kitchen, which was around seven-thirty."

Reminding himself of the sequence of events, Mac asked, "Riva Sinclair attacked Jasmine and Rock outside the ballroom around twenty after seven."

"This was a little more than five minutes before that." She pressed the play button.

The scene opened with a shot of Lindsey's back while she was making her way across the crowded hotel lobby. She turned to the camera. "Well, this is some banquet," she said in a tone laced with heavy sarcasm. "I mean, like, I show up with Raul and everyone disappears."

With a glance over her shoulder, Lindsey seemed to spot her friends. "There they are." Her grin was brimming with evil. "Time for some fun."

Judging by the swing of her hips, Lindsey was in full trouble making mode when she swaggered across the lobby in the direction of the massive stone fireplace that served as a central focal point for the Spencer Inn lobby. A life-size portrait of Robin Spencer, in her later years, sitting in a chair with a German shepherd resting at her feet hung above the mantle.

In a natural reaction to get out of the way of the woman and her camera operator, the sea of guests parted to allow her a clear path to the lounging area in front of the fireplace. Along the way, Lindsey reached out her hand to take a champagne flute with the Spencer Inn logo etched on it from a server.

"Hey," he objected off-camera. "That was for—"

"Whatever!" Without the courtesy of looking in the server's direction, Lindsey waved her hand at him in a sign of dismissal.

Their heads close together, Carlisle was showing pictures on her phone to Kassandra. "I call her Sunshine because, when I see her smile, it's like a ray of sunshine on my whole day."

The warmth on Kassandra's face was genuine. "She does have a lovely smile."

"You should have seen it before her operation."

"What operation?" Kassandra passed the phone to Corey.

"She had a cleft lip," Carlisle said. "I had to take her to Johannesburg to have it fixed."

Lindsey took the phone from Corey to study the picture of a little African girl with a wide toothy grin. "Hey, Corey, where's Rachel?"

"Don't know," Corey replied in a cold tone. "Haven't seen her."

"That's one of Carlisle's kids," Kassandra interjected to tell Lindsey. "She has thirteen children."

With a quick glance at the picture, Lindsey noted with a naughty tone, "You've obviously been busy since the last we saw you."

"They're adopted," Corey looked at Carlisle with admiration. "They're orphans in a village where Carlisle was helping build a well for clean water. The village was hit with Ebola and these children lost their parents."

Her eyes narrowing, Lindsey peered across at Carlisle with distaste.

"What about schooling?" Corey was asking off-camera.

Watching the film, Mac noted the fire brewing beneath the surface while Corey and Kassandra ignored Lindsey to discuss Carlisle's mission work. "She really can't stand not being the center of attention."

Archie said, "Keep watching Kassandra."

While Carlisle went on to explain about the regular ordeal of transporting the children on an old bus to a village over an hour away, Kassandra's face softened as she was visibly filled with compassion. The sexy playmate being groomed for reality stardom was transformed on camera into that of a woman filled with empathy for the hardships of the children she had never met.

Carlisle concluded her tale by announcing that she was looking for volunteers to help build a school in the African village. "There are two other villages nearby who have children they could send to our school," she said. "I have the money, of course, but I need people to travel there to help me build it. Educators, doctors—"

"I'll go," Kassandra blurted out with childlike enthusiasm.

Carlisle and Corey stared at Kassandra in disbelief.

Almost choking on the champagne, Lindsey laughed loudly. "You have got to be kidding."

Kassandra's face turned bright pink. Her eyes moist, she gazed down at the picture of Sunshine on the phone. Carlisle reached over. It appeared as if she were reaching for her phone. Instead, she grasped Kassandra's hand. Kassandra raised her eyes to meet Carlisle's.

"They laughed at me, too, Kassie, when I first went to Africa," Carlisle said in a soft voice. "I thought the only help I had to offer was to write out checks. But the Lord knew that I was willing, and in no time, He showed me that I had many other talents to offer. And the joy that I have experienced using those gifts ..." Squeezing Kassandra's hand, Carlisle's voice dropped to a whisper, "There's no recreational drug on earth that can match that high."

"I'm not smart enough—"

"All you need is an open heart and a willingness to serve. God will place you where you're needed."

Lindsey blurted out so loud that heads turned from across the lounge area. "Bull—"

"God gives everyone spiritual gifts," Carlisle said. "If Kassie looks for hers, she'll find them—"

"We're talking about *Kassandra*," Lindsey said in a disinterested tone.

"I like the name Kassie," Kassandra said.

"Whatever."

Mac could see that Lindsey's attention was drawn to something or someone off camera. Her eyes narrowed to focus.

Off camera, the recording picked up Gnarly barking and Mac's voice yelling, "Zernbog! Stop! Police!"

Abruptly, the recording shut off.

"Then we have the shootout in the kitchen off the ballroom," Archie said while fast forwarding.

"Sorry about that," Mac said while getting up to fill their coffee mugs.

"That's okay, darling." Archie shot him a crooked grin. "I love you anyway." She reached up to kiss him on the lips.

The door to the deck abruptly opened. "Don't you two ever stop?" Dressed in his police chief's uniform and looking as fresh as if he had a full night's sleep instead of only a couple of hours, David stepped into the kitchen and slammed the door behind him. "I thought I smelled coffee." He took a mug out of the cupboard and filled it.

"I'm surprised you didn't stay at Chelsea's." Archie held out her mug in a silent order for David to refill it.

"Are you in a hurry to get rid of me?" David poured the coffee into her mug. "I got in so late that I didn't want to disturb her."

"Any leads on Rachel?" Mac asked.

"None," David said. "I checked first thing when I got up. Nada." He paused to take a cautious sip of the hot coffee. "But Doc did get the results for the tox screen on Lindsey York. Turns out she didn't die of a drug overdose. She was poisoned with belladonna."

"Belladonna?" Mac repeated the name.

"Comes from a plant that has dark blue, almost black, berries," Archie said. "Ten berries is enough to kill you. Actually, it's an old poison. Was used in Ancient Rome. Very sophisticated … and deadly." In response to questioning looks from Mac and David, she added, "I researched it for one of Robin's books."

"Lindsey had ingested it at some point during the evening," David said. "Doc told me that it was less than two hours before she died. Maybe as short as an hour. Turns out the heroin that Gopher shot her up with was the final nail in her coffin."

"What was Gopher's story?" Mac asked.

"Lindsey supplied the drugs," David said. "We found a bunch in her suite at the hotel to confirm that. Gopher claims Raul brought them and shot Lindsey up before she left the suite to go down to the gala. Raul was already dead when they went into the restroom. Between the booze that she had been drinking all evening and the heroin that she had before coming downstairs—"

"And the poison that she had in her system," Mac interjected.

David agreed with a nod of his head. "She asked Gopher to shoot her up. He agreed if he could have some. So he shot her up and was shooting himself up when Brian came in and chased them out. He confirms Brian's statement that he never touched Lindsey." He added, "We found no evidence of drugs in Gopher's room, so Ben told us to let him go for now until we can get evidence that he poisoned her. My people are keeping an eye on him."

"Well," Mac scratched his ear, "nobody had a chance to eat before the chaos started. Lindsey was drinking like a fish. So I suggest we start looking for the poison in the drinks."

"According to what we just saw on the recording we confiscated from last night, Lindsey was looking for Rachel who is now missing," Archie said. "Maybe while going around stirring up trouble for the show, Lindsey saw something that she shouldn't have seen … or knows too much about Rachel's disappearance."

David's brows furrowed. "Why was Lindsey looking for Rachel? I wonder if it has anything to do with Lindsey's role in seducing A.J. so that the Breckenridge's could blackmail him."

"Now that Ashton's body has turned up, Dr. Breckenridge has more at stake than just her reputation," Mac said.

"You might want to take a closer look at how Dr. Piedmont and A.J.'s father died," Archie said.

"This case is about strange bedfellows," Mac said.

She asked, "What about strange bedfellows?"

"According to you and Catherine, Lindsay York and Kassandra Van Dyke did not travel in the same circles as the Breckenridges, Greens, and Piedmonts," Mac said. "However, according to A.J. Wagner, after Lindsey drugged and seduced him, the Breckenridges got what they needed in order to blackmail him into silence. That circumstance alone makes me suspect that they hired Lindsey to do it. But, everyone here on Deep Creek Lake knows Lindsey and her reputation. If I was a blackmailer, she'd be the *last* one I would enlist into a conspiracy. She has—had zero belief system. She'd be willing to turn the tables in a heartbeat."

"Now that you mention it …" David mused, "if it was a matter of drugging A.J. to seduce him, why didn't Rachel do it? He knew Rachel. She belonged to his social group. She was at the Diablo Ball. At the medical school, they had plenty of access to the drugs to do the job."

"Why did Dr. Breckenridge and Rachel take the risk of enlisting Lindsey's help?" Archie asked.

"Maybe Lindsey's dead now because she *did* turn the tables," Mac said.

"Speaking of blackmail …" The corner of Archie's lips curled. "How is Lindsey paying the bills without her daddy supporting her?" She took a cautious sip of the hot coffee. "Daddy cut her loose after her fourth stint in rehab a couple of years ago. So, how was she able to afford that twelve thousand dollar dress that she was wearing?"

"Don't designers sometimes lend their insanely expensive clothes to celebrities for public appearances?" David asked.

"According to information I uncovered last night, she went into the pharmaceutical business," Mac said. "Van Dyke's assistant director and writer told me that Lindsey was very tight with major drug dealers from South America. Why else would she have brought Raul Zernbog last night?"

Mac went back to the table to see where Archie had fast forwarded the recording. When he sat down, he inadvertently bumped his right wrist on the tabletop, jostling his dislocated shoulder, which caused him to yell out.

Startled, Gnarly yelped from where he had laid down under the table.

"You *should* yelp," Mac grumbled.

"It's not Gnarly's fault." She turned his attention back to the laptop. "You're going to want to see this."

According to the time stamp, the recording was captured at fourteen minutes after eight, fifty minutes after Raul had been shot in the kitchen.

Leaving the elevator in the lobby, Lindsey struggled to stay steady on her feet. Abruptly, she stopped. "You! What are you doing here?"

"Now what?" Mac peered at the screen.

"Something interesting." Archie set the mugs on the table.

"I work here."

"Here? What are you doing in Deep Creek? Son of a bitch!" Lindsey's voice rose.

The picture blurred while the camera operator fought to turn and focus on who she had seen to upset her.

"I have every right to work wherever I can get a job."

The picture focused to show Brian Gallagher, embarrassed to be captured on camera while Lindsey targeted him to star in a scandalous scene.

"And out of every place throughout this whole country you decided to come here to Deep Creek Lake, the Spencer Inn, to get a job."

"In case you were unaware, which I'm sure you are, this country is in a recession right now. Jobs are hard to come by. I was very lucky to get offered this internship, so I grabbed it."

"And you had no idea that I was going to be here?" Lindsey said, "Everyone knows that I spend every summer at our place on Deep Creek Lake."

"You haven't been here in years," Brian shot back.

"You bastard!" Lindsey yelled. "Bastard! You're fired! You just wait! When I'm done with you, no one is ever going to give you another job anywhere anyway anyhow!"

Turning away, Brian attempted to head to the corridor leading back to the offices.

"Don't you turn your back on me, you bastard!" She lunged for him. "I'm talking to you!"

While Brian tried to grab her claws to fend off the attack, Lindsey continued to slap at him.

"What's going on here?" They heard Jeff Ingles' voice off camera. "Is there a problem?" The camera focused in on down the hallway where the hotel manager trotted into view. "This is not one of your party clubs, Ms. York."

Pointing a finger at the object of her fury, Lindsey screamed. "I want him fired! He's a stalker! He's been following me for years! The only reason he came here is to follow me!"

"That's not true!" Brian told Jeff who held out his arms to hold him back from Lindsey.

"Fire him!" Lindsey shouted hysterically. "I want him out of here! Now! Tonight!"

Jeff replied in a calm voice. "Brian, I suggest you go home."

Brian objected, "But—"

"We will talk about this in the morning. Right now, I suggest you take the rest of the evening off and go home."

While Lindsey laughed gleefully at her success, Brian glared, "You little bitch! One of these days you're going to run into someone who's going to give you everything that you have coming—in spades."

"Bring it on!"

Turning on his heels, Brian stormed in the direction of the lobby.

Jeff glared at her. "Any more trouble from you, Ms. York, and I'll have security remove you from the premises with orders to not allow you on our property again."

Her reply was a curse that made Jeff's pale face flush a deep red.

"Did you really fire him just because she was upset to see him?" Gopher the camera operator asked the hotel manager from off camera.

Jeff directed his attention to the camera operator. "Aren't you supposed to be following Ms. York around?" The manager turned his back to the camera and hurried down the hallway.

A wicked grin crossed Lindsey's lips. "My work here is done," she told the camera. Grabbing the wall to steady herself, she made her way into the ladies room.

Pausing the recording, Mac sipped his coffee. "Very interesting. Contrary to what Brian told me last night, it looks like he and Lindsey York have a past of some sort."

Giggling, Archie turned from David to Mac and then back again. "Have we ever investigated a murder where *someone* wasn't lying about *something*?" Seeing the time on her laptop, she uttered a gasp and slammed down the lid. "I have to go. I'm going to be late."

"For what?" Mac called after the woman running from the kitchen.

"Chelsea and I are going shopping for wedding gowns today." They heard her running up the stairs and then the door to the master suite slam shut.

Shaking his head, David turned his attention to the coffee in his mug. As hard as he could, he tried to shake off the feeling of Mac's attention focused on him—studying him in silence.

Finally, in a quiet tone, Mac asked, "Are you going to tell me about it?"

"About what?" His confusion was genuine.

"Why you freaked out when Chelsea became BFFs with Carlisle Green?"

David chuckled. "Be serious. One, Carlisle would not strike up a friendship with someone as tame as Chelsea. Two, even if they did become friends, I wouldn't freak out about it. I'd have no reason to."

Mac peered at him with one eyebrow arched. He took a long sip of his coffee. "Okay," he said, "it was all my imagination." Aware of David's attention focused on him, he slid Archie's laptop around and opened the lid.

David waited until Mac started the recording again before he dropped down into the chair that Archie had vacated. "They didn't really talk to each other that much, did they? I mean, they were just being polite ... mingling ... right? Like, you don't think they're going to be seeing and *talking* to each other now that the ball is over, do you?"

Forcibly, Mac turned to look David in the face. "Did you sleep with Carlisle Green?"

"No!"

Mac sighed with relief.

"I *almost* slept with Carlisle Green." When Mac turned back to him, David rushed on. "It was the summer before Ashton disa—"

"How old was Carlisle?" Mac's voice went up a full octave.

"She was legal," David said. "She was an emancipated minor—I swear."

Unable to think of what he wanted to chastise David for first, Mac sputtered. Finally, he forced out, "David! What is wrong with you?" He pointed at him. "You have a very bad habit!"

"She was legal."

"That's rationalization and you know it," Mac said. "You know damn well that you were in the wrong. If you weren't, you wouldn't be worried about Chelsea finding out about it. Innocent people don't run around covering their butts."

"She seduced me," David said.

"You were the adult," Mac said. "I don't care how many judges emancipated her, she was still a minor—a teenager. You were the adult."

In silence, David stared at Mac. Guilt washing over him, he turned away. "Do you want to hear what happened?"

"I might as well."

David let out a deep breath. "One night, I got lonely—"

Mac sighed. "As long as I've known you, you have never been *lonely*, David."

"Okay, I was bored," David shot back. "Do you want to hear about it or not? Shut up and listen to me."

Mac had to grit his teeth to refrain from chewing him out.

"I went to that dive bar out by the main road, where none of the tourists go," David said. "Carlisle came in and they wouldn't serve her, of course. I could see that she was on something. She wasn't high out of her mind—she clearly had a buzz on. I knew that she would get pulled over or get into some trouble. So, I drove her home. She was chatty and managed to make me laugh. I wasn't in my uniform and maybe that made a difference between us. I wasn't a cop and ..." He shrugged. "So, she invited me inside and offered me a beer. I accepted. She went into the kitchen. I was looking out the windows at the view of the lake. When I turned around, she was coming out of the kitchen with the beer and wearing nothing but a red thong. Next thing I knew, I had her pressed up against the wall. I tore off the thong, which went flying across the room." He avoided Mac's piercing glare. "We came this close." He held up his thumb and forefinger to show him. "Then, she pushed me away and said, 'Let's go to bed.' She went upstairs to the bedroom and I ran out of there like a scared rabbit." He drained the coffee in his mug. "End of story."

"You were a *police officer*," Mac reminded him. "She was a teenaged *girl*. You were and are an authority figure. Even now, today, as chief of police, if your enemies on the town council got wind of what happened—with your reputation with the ladies—Even if nothing had happened that night, I'll bet money the media would make it look like something did and the town council would fire you." With a shake of his head, he sighed, "Thank, God, you came to your senses and got out of there."

David nodded his head. "I'd actually forgotten all about it until I heard Chelsea's voice over your com talking to Carlisle. The memory came back and I felt like someone had dumped cold water over my head."

"The fact is, you didn't do anything, David," Mac said. "If you're telling the truth, all you did was kiss her. Plus, if she was high, she probably doesn't remember anything about it, either." He patted him on the shoulder. "Consider yourself lucky and learn your lesson. Next time, call a female officer to drive the girl home."

"What if Carlisle didn't forget about it?"

"That day we ran into her at the Green place, she told us then, the old Carlisle died," Mac said. "What happened is in the past. It's done—gone. She's forgotten about it." He took his and David's coffee mugs to the sink.

"What if she hasn't?"

Mac turned around. Leaning against the counter, he folded his arms across his chest. "Then she'll tell Chelsea who will kill you—after breaking off your engagement."

"Do you really think she will … break off our engagement, I mean?"

"She's your fiancée," Mac reminded him. "I think you're worried for a reason."

David looked down into the coffee in his mug. "She was devastated when I cheated on her back in school," he said. "I've worked so hard to get her to trust me again."

"Chelsea wasn't in the picture six years ago," Mac said. "She knows you haven't been celibate all this time." Narrowing his eyes, he studied the concern etched on David's face. "Trust is a huge thing in a marriage. If Chelsea doesn't trust you, you two are going to have a lot of problems. If you don't believe me, think about your parents' marriage."

"I did not have sex with Carlisle," David said. "Things are so good with Chelsea right now. It's best if she just doesn't know."

"Oh, yeah, that's the way to go," Mac laughed in a heavily sarcastic tone. "Keep it from her. First, it will be this secret, and then another, and then a bigger one. Then, you'll have to start lying to cover up the first secret. Then, you'll need to re-member the lies you told to keep the other secrets. Next thing you know, you'll be moving back into my guest house." Still chuckling, he gave David a head slap on his way to the kitchen door. "I always love a good plan."

Rubbing the well-deserved head slap, David sighed. *Mac's right. Lack of trust ruined Mom and Dad's marriage and contributed to Mom's dementia.* For the first time, he admitted to himself that his past behavior was destined to ruin his life with the woman he loved if they both weren't able to put it behind them before they got married.

Feeling like he was being watched, David looked up to see Gnarly staring at him from across the table. The German shepherd's tall ears standing at attention. "What are you looking at?"

Gnarly cocked his head at him.

"I didn't have sex with her," David said in a firm tone. "Come hell or high water, I'm not going to break Chelsea's heart again."

He swore he saw Gnarly shake his head before standing up and pressing through the swinging kitchen door to go upstairs.

The Dogs of Clark and the Dead Indian Standing
up and was fighting by her side, instead as to go
the

CHAPTER FIFTEEN

A cloud of shock at the events of the previous night hung over the Inn. Even with forensics officers searching every crevice, utensil, and instrument in the banquet room and kitchen for clues, guests and employees gazed at each other in disbelief that two people had died the night before, and in such dramatic ways.

Upon his arrival with Gnarly on a leash, Mac heard guests whispering to each other, "Can you believe it?"

Across the lobby, Mac's attention was drawn to Corey Haim and Carlisle Green, who appeared to be in an animated conversation. Abruptly, Carlisle let out a squeal of delight and hugged Corey, who returned her embrace. After they parted, she whipped out her cell phone and hurried off in the direction of the outdoor cafe.

"Looks like you made someone's day," Mac said when Corey turned around to leave.

Corey opened his mouth to respond, but before the words could come out, the enthusiasm on his face clouded over when his eyes made contact with someone behind Mac.

Mac turned around to see Dr. Elizabeth Breckenridge sail through the front doors with her assistant by her side.

Dressed in crisp tennis whites, she carried an athletic bag and tennis racket. Seeing Mac, she paused. After ordering her assistant to check in with her tennis instructor, Elizabeth addressed Mac without wasting any time on a greeting. "Have you and your security staff located my daughter yet?"

"I was just on my way to the security office for a status report," Mac replied.

Noting Gnarly glaring at her, she asked, "Is that a search and rescue canine?"

Mac glanced down at Gnarly. "More like a breaking and entering canine."

Failing to see the humor, the doctor said, "I thought the security staff here at the Spencer Inn was supposed to be the best. If it turns out—"

"With all due respect, Dr. Breckenridge," Mac interjected, "if you're so worried about your daughter, why aren't you waiting at home for her in case she returns. You must not be very concerned about her welfare if you're traipsing out here for tennis lessons."

Elizabeth dropped her athletic bag to the floor and stepped towards him. "Who are you to judge my relationship with my daughter?"

The menace in her gaze would have made any of her underlings back down. Not Mac. Instead, he stepped forward to hold her glare. "I'm trying to find her and in doing so, I need to examine *every* possibility and you're not behaving like a distraught mother. You're acting more like a suspect." He narrowed his eyes into blue slits. "Are you aware that Lindsey York died here last night?"

"She fell over the railing in the ballroom and smashed the grand piano," Corey told her.

Elizabeth scoffed. "While I'm always sorry for the loss of a life, I can't help but think that it was bound to happen sooner or later."

"She was only twenty-three years old," Corey said. "She had her whole life in front of her. If she had put as much energy into helping others instead—"

"Your Good Samaritan crap is wearing thin on me, Haim," she replied.

"I suppose you think this is wearing thin, too," Mac said. "Homicide has not been ruled out in Lindsey York's death."

"Pul-eze," she replied with a roll of her eyes. "She was a known drug addict. Ask her father how many times she went through rehab." After picking up her bag, she tried to step around Mac, who stopped her with his hand on her arm.

"How well did Lindsey and Rachel know each other?" he asked.

Elizabeth shook off his arm. "They were acquaintances, nothing more. They were the same age and would see other on the lake during the season, but they weren't friends by any means." She sighed. "If you're thinking that Lindsey's drug overdose has anything to do with Rachel, you're completely wrong."

"You did point out that Lindsey was a drug addict," Mac said, "and Rachel was a doctor, which means she could write prescriptions or supply—"

"Don't even go there, Mr. Faraday." Bringing her face to his, she lowered her voice to a hiss. "If you even so much as breath an insinuation like that to the media, then I'll bring my lawyers down on you like a ton of bricks. Have I made myself clear, Mr. Faraday?"

"Crystal."

Tucking her bag close to her, Dr. Elizabeth Breckenridge stalked across the lobby.

"I wouldn't be surprised if Rachel faked her disappearance to get away from her mother," Corey Haim said with a chuckle from behind Mac.

"Are you saying they weren't that close?" Mac turned around to him.

"Let me put it this way," Corey said with a cock of his head, "I heard Rachel say more than once that her mother was a psychopath, incapable of feeling love, regret, or remorse." He jerked his chin in the direction of where Elizabeth Breckenridge had hurried toward the sports club. "This is par for the course with Breckenridge. You or any other parent would be pacing the floor waiting for a call. That would only be possible if she was able to think of anyone but herself and that's an impossibility for a narcissist." He added with a hint of amusement in his tone, "Do you always let your dog carry your cell phone?"

"What?"

Corey pointed to where Gnarly was lying down. Clutched between his front paws was a smart phone which he was gnawing on with a sense of accomplishment.

"Hey!" When Mac reached for the phone, Gnarly jumped to his feet to make a break for it. Luckily, Mac had a tight hold of his leash in his left hand, since his right arm was in a sling and his wrist in a brace. When Gnarly reached the end of his leash, he was jerked back. Still, Gnarly kept the cell phone clutched in his teeth.

"Who did you steal that from?" Mac reeled Gnarly in by wrapping the leash around his hand and wrist until he got him close enough to grab the dog by the collar. But the large German shepherd wasn't giving up his prize without a fight. When Mac grabbed hold of him with his injured right hand, Gnarly turned his head and pulled away. Unable to keep a tight grip, Mac threw his leg over Gnarly's back and pinned him between his knees while prying the phone out of the dog's jaws. "Drop it. I said drop it." He had just managed to extract the phone when he heard Jeff Ingles' voice behind him.

"Mac, don't you think it would be … more fitting for you to play with Gnarly outside instead of here in the lobby?"

Mac was too busy checking the phone to identify its owner to answer. The home screen had a picture of Dr. Elizabeth Breckenridge. "Great," Mac murmured with sarcasm. "You must have taken it out of her bag."

The phone vibrated with the arrival of a text. The message read:

```
Booked on U.S Airways Flight 5349 to George
Town. Leaving @ 11:42 am. Will text when
arrive.
```

"Now I wonder who that is. Considering how calm, cool, and collected Dr. Breckenridge is, I think it's maybe her daughter." Easing Jeff out of the way, Mac hurried across the lobby to the security offices.

"Mac," Jeff yelled after him.

Mac whirled around. "What is it, Jeff?"

The manager pointed at Gnarly, who was sniffing Jeff's pockets. "Can you take your klepto dog with you? Please?"

❦ ❦ ❦

"I thought I'd find you here," Mac greeted David who was engaged in a conversation with Hector. Before David could respond, Mac thrust the cell phone, still coated in dog droll into the police chief's face. "I think I found Rachel Breckenridge. She's alive and well and on her way to the Cayman Islands."

"Where did you get this?" David took the cell phone from him.

Shooting a sideways glance at where Gnarly was sitting by his side, Mac's tone oozed with innocence. "We found it."

Wiping the dog drool from his hand on the thigh of his slacks, David said, "We need to find out where that flight is leaving from and pick up Rachel before she gets on that plane." He took his radio out of its case.

"Whose cell phone is that?" Hector asked Mac when David stepped away to issue a BOLO on Rachel Breckenridge to be picked up before she left the country.

"Dr. Elizabeth Breckenridge," Mac said.

"Are you kidding me?" Hector's voice went up two octaves. "Isn't she the one who reported her missing? We've been tearing this resort apart looking for Rachel. My staff has been scouring the security videos and here her mother knew all along—"

"We don't know that," Mac interjected.

"Yes, we do," David turned around to tell them. He was thumbing through the text messages on the phone. "Last night, Dr. Breckenridge texted her daughter, 'Where are you?' Some time later, Rachel replied, 'Got to leave. In trouble. Will call later to explain.' Dr. Breckenridge then replies telling her that Lindsey is dead. Rachel replied that that was why she had to get away. Then, a second text message thread starts this morning from a different number asking Dr. Breckenridge for advice about what country to escape to."

"A burner phone," Mac said.

"Point is," David said, "Dr. Breckenridge knew her daughter was safe and didn't tell us to call in the hounds. That's filing a false police report—"

"Unless she didn't know where Rachel was at the time she told us she was missing," Mac said. "Rachel was reported missing before Lindsey died. So this exchange appears to be after Dr. Breckenridge told us that she had disappeared and continued after Lindsey's murder and on through to this morning."

"Rachel's a doctor," David said. "It would have been a cinch for her to poison Lindsey and then get out of Dodge before it took effect."

Mac asked, "Do you want my suggestion?"

"No, but I'm going to get it anyway," David replied.

"True," Mac said. "Let's slip the cell phone back into Dr. Breckenridge's bag and say nothing to her. Have the police pick up Rachel and then build our case against the doc from there. If Rachel's mother even suspects we know where Rachel is, she'll give her a heads up and be out of the country so fast that we'll be lucky if we can ever lay our hands on her again. "

"Mac's got a point," Hector said.

"He always does." David handed the phone to the security chief. "Take this phone to the front desk. Let them notify Dr. Breckenridge that someone had found it."

"How do we explain the teeth marks?" Hector showed Gnarly's bite marks in the corner of the phone to the police chief.

"We don't," David said. "We never saw it."

"Works for me." In response to a call on his security radio, Hector tapped the button on his ear piece. "Langford here." Dismay crossed his face. "Seriously?"

Not liking Hector's expression, Mac and David exchanged glances.

"I'm with O'Callaghan and Faraday now," Hector said. "Don't touch anything. We're coming right up." He tapped the radio button to disconnect the call.

"What is it?" Mac asked.

"Jasmine Simpson," Hector reported. "She's dead."

CHAPTER SIXTEEN

Smart phones have made it possible to communicate while on the run. By the time Mac, David, and Hector boarded the elevator to go up to Rock Sinclair's suite, the police chief had his desk sergeant on the line.

Exasperated, David was asking, "When did she leave?" He turned to Mac. "Eleven o'clock *last night*?"

"Last night?" Mac told David, "Riva Sinclair had been arrested for assault and vandalism."

Hector interrupted to add, "Plus, her bail would have been revoked for the charge of carrying a concealed weapon without a permit."

"It's Sunday," Mac said, "Bail would not have been set until Monday morning when she was arraigned—" He stopped speaking in response to David holding up his hand while turning away so that he could listen to his desk sergeant.

"And no one thought to check with me?" David's voice went up a full octave in his attempt to not yell.

Gritting his teeth, Mac turned to Hector, who grumbled, "We are so screwed."

The elevator doors opened. David disconnected the call and thrust out his hand to hold the door open for Mac and Hector to step off. "Tonya says the night shift desk sergeant got a call from the Spencer Inn saying that Jeff told him to call and tell them that they didn't want to press charges against Riva Sinclair—at the request of Rock Sinclair, who said that his lawyer had advised him to drop the whole thing and to pay the hotel for the damages. Because California is a community property state, his lawyer said that Riva might be more amicable in the divorce if Rock turned the other cheek about this incident."

"I don't believe any of that," Mac said.

They came to a halt in the corridor, outside the hotel suite.

"Neither do I," David said.

"Someone wanted Riva Sinclair released," Mac said in response to the stern expression on David's face.

Hector extracted his master key card from his breast pocket. "While you two are cleaning up this mess, I'll go check on the status of our number one suspect, Riva Sinclair. If we're lucky, we'll find her in her room."

"And not halfway back to Hollywood," David said.

"I've already got my people pulling the security recordings from last night," Hector said. "We'll concentrate on the elevator and this floor. Maybe we'll get lucky."

Mac laid his hand on the security manager's elbow before he turned to leave. "Are you sure Gnarly is going to be okay down in your office? He's been on a thieving spree lately."

"Mac," Hector chuckled, "everyone on my staff is a highly trained security specialist. They'll be able to keep that kleptomaniac in line. They may even rehabilitate him by the time you're through here."

The security manager trotted back down the corridor to the elevator. When the doors opened, he held the doors open for Bogie and Jeff Ingles to step off before getting on and pressing the button to descend to the floor where Riva Sinclair's room was located.

"Do you know what the media is going to do to us when they get hold of this?" David whispered to Mac.

"The media is more focused on Lindsey York dying during the Diablo Ball at the Spencer Inn than they are on you," Mac said. "We'll just keep it that way until we get this sorted out."

"Do you believe this?" Bogie asked them when they approached from the elevators.

"As you can imagine," Jeff said, "Mr. Sinclair is insisting on speaking to you two ASAP."

"I can imagine." David went into the suite.

"Jeff," Mac asked as casually as possible, "did you call the police department to tell them that you weren't pressing charges against Mrs. Sinclair?"

A glare came to the hotel manager's eyes at the very suggestion. "Mac, do you know how much that china costs? It's special order." His face growing red, the veins on his neck popped. "Yes, we have insurance, but no way would I even entertain the thought of letting these bunch of gutter snipes leave this mountaintop without someone handing over a credit card—"

David laid a hand on Jeff's shoulder. "Take a breath, Jeff. Mac was just asking."

Taking several deep breaths, Jeff took a moist handkerchief from his pocket and mopped the beads of sweat from his brow.

Glancing in David's direction, Mac saw that the police chief was having the same thought. Someone *had* arranged for Riva Sinclair's release. The question remained, was Riva Sinclair in on it or not?

In the sitting room, Rock Sinclair was on his cell phone when David entered the suite. Upon seeing them, he said into the phone, "The police chief is here now. I'll call you back." After tossing the phone onto the coffee table, he stood up to his full height. "That was Jasmine's mother. Just so you know, my attorneys are already filing papers to sue not only the Spencer Inn but the police department for letting this happen."

"Then I guess we have nothing further to discuss," Mac said before David could respond. "Jeff, call security to remove Mr. Sinclair and his crew from the Inn. I want all of his people off the premises within the next thirty minutes." With an eye on Rock Sinclair, he added, "But we'll be keeping any footage they've shot here at the hotel, because I don't recall signing any release giving them permission to film on the premises, do you, Jeff?"

"No, sir." Jeff gulped. "We did not."

"You can leave all copies of your recordings with Chief O'Callaghan on your way out," Mac told Rock. "My lawyers will file an injunction preventing you from using any footage filmed on the premises, including interviews shot in the suites. As the producer, how much lost time and money do you think you'll lose on your investigative report when that happens?"

Rock was sputtering at the unexpected reaction. Fighting to regroup, he said, "My attorneys—"

"In light of our current circumstances," Mac stepped into the producer's face, "I'm not warning you, I'm promising you—" He lowered his voice. "I hate lawyers. I hate people who use them like pitt bulls to intimidate people into allowing them free rein under the threat of lawsuit. No one bullies me. You want to break out measuring sticks to see who's got the biggest lawyers? Bring it on. In the meantime, you and your crew are permanently banned from the Spencer Inn. My staff will have you and your crew out on the curb within the hour; at which time, no hotel on Deep Creek Lake will take you because I will text each manager that you are a litigious so-called documentary producer living off lawsuits. How long is your crew going to stick with you living in the back of a van?

How is your production going to look with no place to film your interviews?"

"A.J. Wagner and Corey Haim's lawyer already called saying that they want out of their contract after Lindsey York's murder," Samuel Nash announced from behind them.

The color drained from Rock's face. Backing away from Mac, he glanced around the room at Mac, Bogie, and David. Jeff was holding his breath. "You have to understand, finding Jasmine that way ..."

"Chief O'Callaghan ..." A member of the hotel security staff came out of the bathroom. "Mr. Faraday. You'll want to see this. She's in here."

While David stepped into the bathroom, Mac kept his eyes on Rock Sinclair, who swallowed.

"Mac," Jeff asked in a quiet voice, "do you want me to call security to remove Mr. Sinclair and his crew?"

"That depends on Mr. Sinclair."

With a growl, Rock said, "Just find Jasmine's killer." Even though he was relenting, it sounded like a threat.

Tearing his glare from Rock Sinclair's face, Mac went into the bathroom adjoining the suite's master bedroom. David and Bogie were examining Jasmine Simpson's naked body laying in a sunken tub filled with cold water. Except for her bathrobe draped across a chair and her cosmetics and toiletries on the counter, the bathroom showed little evidence of being occupied or used.

Bogie had sent the security officer into the corridor to lead in the crime scene investigators and medical examiner.

Not wanting to see the dead guest himself, Jeff waited in the bathroom's doorway. "Mr. Sinclair said he found her when he got up this morning. It could be an accident, right?"

"Depends on how much fun she had last night," Bogie replied. "I don't see any recreational party favors in here, do you, Chief?"

At the counter, David was reading the labels on the two prescription pill bottles. "Standard antibiotics and a migraine medicine."

Kneeling next to the whirlpool tub, Mac peered at the dead woman while struggling to pull an evidence glove onto his injured right hand. Jasmine's once pink flesh was now bluish, though he noticed welts and dark blue bruises on her shoulders and across her neck. "I have a feeling that if she was partying last night, she was not alone."

David joined him at the edge of the tub to observe the marks on her body. "Doesn't look like an accidental drowning to me."

"Nope." Mac noted that the bathwater had a reddish hue. "It looks like she was bleeding from some place." After asking David for the flashlight he wore on his utility belt, he leaned over the edge of the tub while shining the beam into the water.

Bogie extracted his flashlight to shine into the water until Mac's beam reflected off a shard of glass sticking out of Jasmine's naked thigh, near her rump.

"I see it." Not wanting to disturb possible evidence, David leaned further over the tub to peer through the pink water to examine her wound and the object that had punctured her leg. It was round and possibly as thick as his little finger. He could see sharp jagged breaks on the end which was visible.

"It's a piece of broken glass." Mac cocked his head while trying to distinguish where the glass had come from.

"Broken glass?" Glancing around the bathroom, David said, "I don't see anything broken in here."

Mac sat back on his haunches. "I think it's a stem broken off of a wine glass."

David picked up the trash can and peered inside. "No glass or wine bottle."

"Someone cleaned up and I don't think it was housekeeping." His knees cracking, Mac rose to his feet.

Doc Washington and the forensics crew were entering the bathroom while David and Mac were going out to question Rock Sinclair, who was sitting at the kitchenette counter with his director, Samuel.

After stepping out of the bathroom, David turned around to tell Mac, "I'll question Sinclair. Considering that he's anxious to sue you, he might be more cooperative with me."

"Hey," Mac said, "when I was working homicide in D.C., I was threatened with being sued on a daily basis. I was also threatened with getting fired, not to mention being killed."

"I never noticed that about you before," the police chief said. "You don't play well with others, do you, Mac?"

"You're just now finding that out? I thought you were more perceptive than that."

With Mac chuckling behind his back, David went over to the counter where Samuel was in the midst of telling the producer, "We've gone too far into this project to stop now, Rock. Jasmine would want us to find Ashton's killer ... and hers."

The producer was nodding his head. "Now, this isn't a simple film project, now it's personal—my own personal quest to uncover the identity of who took away the woman I loved." He tapped Samuel on the arm. "Get marketing working on a press release."

"Great idea."

With his good hand, Mac caught Samuel by the arm to stop him when he slipped off the bar stool. "No one is going to be writing any press releases yet."

"What do you mean?" Samuel asked.

While Mac went about explaining the need to keep information close to the vest during a police investigation, David led Rock Sinclair to the other side of the living room, out of ear shot. "Mr. Sinclair, when did you last see Jasmine alive?"

"Last night," Rock said. "You must have figured out that we were lovers. She was staying here ... in this suite ... with me. We came upstairs after that fiasco downstairs with Riva. We were having a production meeting with Samuel when you and your people arrived with the news about Lindsey York."

"I remember that," David said. "Samuel Nash was still here when I left shortly before ten."

"He left not long after you did," Rock said.

"No one else was here after ten o'clock?" David asked.

"It was only Jasmine and me."

"Do you know what time Jasmine went in to take her bath?"

Rock chewed on his bottom lip before answering. "No. She must have gotten in the tub after I had fallen asleep."

"You didn't notice her get out of bed?" David was doubtful. "You didn't hear the water running?"

Rock grumbled a curse before saying, "I'm a very sound sleeper. I sleep like a log. The whole place could go up and I wouldn't hear it."

David eyed him. A long stretch of silence filled the space around them, during which Rock tried to avoid the police chief's gaze.

Rock wiped beads of sweat from his brow. "I snore—horribly. So, Jasmine insists that I sleep in the other bedroom, okay?" With a firm set of his jaw, he added, "We made love in her bed," he gestured at the master bedroom, "and then I went to bed in the other bedroom."

"What time did you leave her bedroom?"

"A little after midnight."

Doc Washington stepped into the doorway leading to the bathroom and gestured for David and Mac that she was ready with a preliminary report of her findings.

Before excusing himself, David told Rock, "We're going to need a sample of your DNA to eliminate you as a suspect."

"Of course," Rock Sinclair agreed surprisingly easily.

When David joined Mac across the room, Samuel was telling him, "I know she was really scared about Riva tracking her and Rock down the way she did. You saw her last night. That bitch is crazy."

"You seemed pretty amused by the whole scene." Mac turned to David. "If I recall, you said something about what goes around … What did you mean by that?"

A wide smirk crossed Samuel's face. With his dark hair and goatee, he resembled a cartoon villain. "You noticed that, huh?"

"Yeah," Mac replied.

"I guess I might as well tell you before someone else does."

"That would look better for you," David said.

"Jasmine and I used to date," Samuel said.

"I recall you mentioning that last night," Mac said. "You were her escort at the Diablo Ball five years ago. The year that she and Lindsey York got into that fight. A table was overturned. Both Lindsey and Jasmine were banned."

"Obviously not since Jasmine was invited back this year," Samuel said while checking a text on his cell phone.

Noting that Samuel was holding the phone in his right hand while texting with his left, Mac nudged David quickly with his injured arm. When the pain shot from his wrist up to his elbow, he flinched.

"Speaking of that night," Mac said, "How well did you know Ashton Piedmont?"

"What does she have to do with this?" Samuel asked.

"Isn't that what this film project is about?" David asked. "Finding Ashton's killer?"

"Maybe Ashton's murderer killed Jasmine because she was getting too close to finding out the truth," Mac said. "Last night, I heard you arguing with her because she was planning a huge twist at the end of the film that viewers would never expect. I can't think of a bigger twist than to point the finger at the very director of the investigate report searching of her killer."

"That's ridiculous," Samuel said.

"You didn't answer my question," Mac said. "How well did you know Ashton?"

"We were acquaintances," the director said. "The same for Jasmine, who was in her dorm at college. Not much more. She saw Ashton here on the lake during the summer and they all socialized, but that was about it. When Ashton disappeared and her body wasn't found, I thought it would make a good film project."

"An idea that Jasmine stole," Mac said.

"True," the director answered. "We were both in communications in college. We were going to be a team. She would be the on air personality and I was going to be the producer and director." He gestured at his computer tablet. "This whole show, the in-depth investigative report into Ashton Piedmont's disappearance, was my idea and she stole it. That's the way Jasmine was."

"Must have made you pretty mad when she sold it to Rock Sinclair as her own," Mac said.

"That's why I'm the director," Samuel said. "Jasmine wasn't a complete idiot. She knew after she sold the show to him that she couldn't pull it off without me."

"And now that she's dead," Mac noted, "it's completely yours."

To Mac's surprise, the corner of Samuel's mouth curled upwards. "Yes, it is."

"What time was it when you saw Jasmine last?" Mac asked him.

"We rode up together in the elevator," Samuel said. "Me and her and Rock. We came upstairs after that fiasco downstairs with Riva. We were having a production meeting when the police came up with the news about Lindsey York."

Before Mac could respond with his next question, he saw David cock his head at the director. David's eye's narrowed to blue slits before he asked, "Where were you five years ago when Ashton Piedmont was killed?"

Samuel chuckled. "Seriously?" When he saw by their expressions that the police chief was indeed serious, his smile fell. "I don't know exactly where I was, but I do know that neither Jasmine nor I were in Deep Creek Lake. We left Spencer the day after the ball. If I remember correctly, we were staying with friends in the Hamptons."

"Chief," Doc Washington called to them from the bathroom. "You may want to see this before we move her."

As soon as they had stepped away, Mac whispered to David, "What was with the look? Did you catch him in a lie?"

"How often do you hear people use the word 'fiasco'?'" David asked.

"Not often," Mac replied.

"I've heard that word used twice today already," David said. "Samuel used exactly the same words Rock did to recount what they did last night."

"They compared notes before we got up here," Mac chuckled. "Makes me wonder what they're hiding."

In the bathroom, Doc Washington led Mac and David over to the tub where Bogie stood over Jasmine's lifeless body, which they had extracted from the tub and laid out in a body bag on a gurney to be taken down to the morgue.

"I can only give you a preliminary report right now," the medical examiner said, "but I think it is entirely possible that this young lady did not drown."

Mac nodded his head. "We saw the bruises on her shoulders and neck. Like someone fought her to force her down under the water to drown her."

"I'll need to check her lungs back at the lab for that," she said. "What I'm talking about is what I found when we took her out of the tub."

Bogie rolled Jasmine over onto her side and moved Jasmine's hair to the side to expose the back of her neck. Moving in closer, they could see that the entire back of her neck was covered with a nasty bluish black bruise from the base of her skull to the top of her shoulders.

"She was most likely dead before she was forced under the water," the medical examiner said.

"She put up such a fight that they slammed her back against the rim of the tub and broke her neck," Bogie said.

"Even if she didn't drown," David said while extracting his vibrating phone from its case, "it's still murder."

"I think we need to have another talk with Sinclair," Mac said.

"What about the wife he cheated on?" Bogie asked. "She's got motive coming out of her ears."

"But Sinclair and Nash were on the scene," Mac argued. "Langford will get us a report on the security lock for the suite. If anyone else used their keycard to come into the suite, we'll know. Between that and the hotel security cameras, we'll know if someone besides Sinclair and Nash had access to the victim at the time of the murder."

"Unless the killer knocked on the door and someone who was already here let him or her in," Bogie said.

"Why does every case have to be so difficult?" Mac asked the deputy chief.

"It's not me," he answered, "it's you."

David turned around from where he had finished talking on his cell phone. "Airport security at Dulles has Rachel Breckenridge in custody. Maryland State police are bringing her back to Spencer."

Mac's cell phone buzzed to indicate a text from Hector.

```
Found Riva Sinclair in room. Ready for
questioning. Bring coffee & speak softly.
```

CHAPTER SEVENTEEN

"She killed the mini-bar," Hector whispered to Mac and David when they arrived two floors below Rock Sinclair's suite. After meeting them at the door, the security chief led them down the short entrance hallway to where Riva lay motionless on her back across the king-sized bed. The lights were dim and the heavy curtains drawn.

Thinking Riva had passed out, David crossed over to the window to yank open the curtains.

As soon as he touched the shade, she snapped, "Don't!" Grabbing her head in both hands, she uttered a loud groan. Unable to sit upright, she flopped back onto the bed.

Hector opened the door for the mini bar to show them that every shelf was empty. "She's been busy since getting out of the slammer."

Mac knelt down to pick up one of the many empty single serve bottles of liquor that littered the floor. Taking note of the empty bottles thrown across the desk and bedside table, David asked, "How much does it cost to drink a whole mini bar?"

"Doesn't really matter," Hector answered. "It's automatically added to the room bill. The mini bar is computerized so that every time a bottle is taken out—" He uttered a ka-ching noise to mimic a cash register— "the drink is charged to the room."

"Do you have to be so loud?" Riva asked in a pitifully raspy choice.

Struck with a thought, Mac said, "Doesn't the charge appear on the bill with both what she took out and the time she bought it?"

A grin on his lips, Hector nodded his bald head. "I love it when a guest argues the mini bar charge and we show him the time stamp. Between that and the time recorded by the use of the key card to enter the room, then they have no ammunition. I mean, we can prove they were in the room when the bottle was taken out. So who else was doing the drinking?"

Mac and David exchanged knowing glances.

"Not only do the time stamps establish what and how much she drank, but when," Mac said, "which also establishes her movements after she returned to the Inn. Once we establish the time of death, all we have to do is compare that to Riva's emptying of the mini bar."

Raising his voice, Hector tapped Riva's leg. "Congratulations, Ms. Sinclair. Your binge may clear you of murder."

"Murder?" With great effort, she pulled herself up into a sitting up position.

"Murder," David repeated.

"Who was murdered?" A smile came to her face. "Is Rock dead? Did that little witch kill him? He deserved whatever he got."

"Sorry to disappoint you," Mac said, "but it was Jasmine. Someone killed her."

"How?" She looked from Mac to David to Hector and then back to Mac again. Clasping both hands to her chest, she gasped. "You don't think I did it, do you? I was in jail."

"You aren't now," David pointed out.

"Because the hotel manager called the police station and said Rock didn't want to press charges."

"That call wasn't made by the hotel," Mac said.

"I know," she sobbed.

"You know?" David asked.

"I thought that Rock had a change of heart since the police officer at the station said he had said he wasn't pressing charges." Her hair spilled down into her face while she hung her head. "That witch Jasmine made a fool of me. She had left a note for me in Rock's name to meet him in the lounge to talk and not to call the room because he didn't want Jasmine to know we were talking. So I sat waiting for him like a fool. Then he sent a note saying that Jasmine was asleep and to come on up to their suite."

"What time was that?" Mac asked.

"I don't know," Riva said with a shrug. "Close to midnight. The note said not to knock—that he was leaving the door open for me."

"What happened up in the room?" David asked.

Riva sniffed. "The door was open. The lock was swung around to keep the door from latching. I went in and found all these clothes on the floor and heard them."

"Heard who?" Mac asked.

"Them," she bit out. "Jasmine and Rock ... in the whirlpool tub—making love like a couple of horny rabbits." She let out a shuddering breath. "I know she did it on purpose. She wanted me to watch them—to see what that impotent bastard could do for her that he never gave a damn to do for me—because he didn't want me, but because he wanted to please her…"

"Wait a minute." David held up his hands to signal a time out. "Are you telling us that Rock is impotent?"

"He was while I was married to him," Riva said. "He's already begging for a secrecy agreement on the divorce."

"If he's impotent—" David started to say.

214

"There are pills," Riva said, "but Rock didn't like how they made his heart race. He was afraid of having a heart attack … or so he said." She broke down. "He obviously wasn't afraid of having a heart attack with her."

"Did you say anything to Jasmine about seeing the two of them?" Mac asked her.

"No, I didn't want to give her the satisfaction."

"Did you go into the bathroom at all?"

She shook her head. "I turned around and ran back down here and spent the rest of the night drowning my sorrows." With a gasp, she said, "Maybe it was Rock who sent me that note to go up to the suite so that he could set me up to kill Jasmine."

"Why would Rock want to kill Jasmine?" Mac asked.

"She was a manipulative conniving little witch," she said.

"But did Rock know that?" Mac asked.

"No!" She broke down into uncontrollable weeping.

Careful not to jostle her, Mac sat on the edge of the bed. "Riva?" he said in a soft voice. "He's not worth this."

Letting out a loud guttural sob, Riva covered her face with her hands. "Oh, Rock! How could you leave me like this?" A waterfall of tears flowed freely from her eyes.

His eyes widening in dismay, Hector hurried for the door. "I better get to checking out the hotel security videos for clues to solving these murders, Mac." The door slammed in his rush to leave.

Her sobs turned into wailing. Rolling over onto her side, Riva threw her arms around Mac's midsection and buried her tear soaked faced into his chest.

Staring at him, David cleared his throat. "Uh, Mac, do you …"

Seeing that David was begging to be dismissed, Mac sighed. "I've got this covered."

Not giving him a chance to change his mind, David ran for the door.

Once they were alone, Mac patted Riva on the back while saying in a soothing voice, "Riva, you need to get ahold of yourself."

With her face buried in his chest, he was uncertain of her reply. It sounded like, "I can't."

"Yes, you can." He continued patting her on the back. "I know it's hard, but if you set your mind to it …"

"I have nothing more to live for!"

As best he could with his one good arm, he pried her away from him to loosen her grip. "Riva, listen to me." Lifting her head by the chin, he forced her red and swollen eyes to meet his. "Do you really want to give Rock that much power?"

She sniffed. "I don't understand."

Grossed out by the discharge flowing from her nose, Mac went into the bathroom to get a tissue. "Think of what a bolster it must be to Rock's already huge ego seeing you like this—completely broken—all because he took away his love." Returning into the room, he held out the tissue to her. "No one person should have that much power over another person."

Taking the offered tissue, she blew her nose noisily. After wiping off the excess snot, she offered the soiled tissue back to Mac, who declined it with a shake of his head. "Keep it."

"You don't understand," she mumbled, "I love Rock."

"I do understand." Mac's tone was hard. "I was in your shoes not too long ago." He sat down next to her. "I loved my first wife and gave her twenty years of my life."

She hiccupped. "Twenty years?" She gazed at him with her eyes wide. "That's a lo-ong time."

"Yes, it is," Mac said in a soft voice. "After two decades, working long hours and double shifts to get enough money together to build a house in a nice neighborhood, having two children together, she decided to trade up for a district attorney."

"She left *you?* But you're a multi-millionaire."

"I wasn't then," Mac said. "I didn't inherit my money until after our divorce was final." He steered her back onto his point. "I was just as much in love with her as you are with Rock," he said. "I did everything for her but nothing I had done, none of the sacrifices I made, were good enough for her. While the wounds were fresh, I felt like curling up and dying. But then one night, after getting good and drunk, I woke up completely hung over, like you are now, and went into the bathroom and looked into the mirror and it hit me."

She was breathless. "What?"

Mac wiped the tears from her face with the corner of the white sheet. "I was a mess. My face was pale. I had huge bags under my eyes. I had a headache and my stomach hurt from all the booze I had drunk on an empty stomach. When I looked in the mirror, it hit me. Christine did this to me—me. After all I did—for her—she had vowed to love, honor, and cherish me—until death do us part. I was the father of her children and she could just trade me in like an old car for a faster model."

With his hand under her chin, his eyes met hers. "The thing that really sucked was that I gave her the power to do that to me."

"So what did you do?"

"I took it back," he said. "No one has the power to destroy you unless you give it to them. She didn't deserve my love … She wasn't worthy of my destroying myself over her. Once I made that decision, she lost all her power and then I was able to survive."

She gathered up the sheet into both of her hands. "How do I do that?"

"You start by telling Rock to hit the road," Mac said, "to get up and get out of your life." He pointed toward the bathroom. "But first, go take a shower, get dressed, and move on."

❧ ❧ ❧

When Mac stepped off the elevator into the lobby, he caught sight of Savannah giving Brian Gallagher a kiss on the cheek. A grin crossed the young man's face before he wrapped an arm around her waist to pull her in for another kiss on the lips. In soft voices, they spoke to each other while he escorted her to the service elevator to go downstairs to the kitchen to begin her afternoon shift.

"I'm still trying to wrap my head around it," Mac heard Betty Cosgrove, Savannah's mother, say to him from her post behind the registration counter. When he turned to her, she explained, "If that maniac was stupid enough to believe Brian, he would have killed him as soon as he found out he was a poor college student with barely a penny to his name."

"But Savannah would have been safe," Mac said. "That was more important to Brian than his safety."

Betty's eyes were moist. "Like I said, I'm still trying to wrap my head around it. I would have done anything to save her, but I'm her mother. Brian has only known her a few weeks and he—" She stopped to swallow before saying in a husky voice, "I'm sorry, Mac."

"Don't you believe in love, Betty?"

"Used to," she said. "But after getting your heart ripped out so many times, you lose hope." She smiled at Brian Gallagher when he trotted past them on his way to Jeff Fleming's office. The bounce in his step was unmistakable.

"Never lose hope, Betty," Mac told her.

"I'm a middle-aged grandmother," she replied, "living in a small condo with a daughter, granddaughter, and two cats."

"Only grandmother I know who has legs that could stop traffic," a distinguished male voice announced from behind Mac.

Betty's face turned a bright red. After clearing her throat, she said in a formal tone, "Well, hello, Mr. York. I see you've returned for the summer season."

"Have I missed one yet?" The tall, slender man with dark hair and gray at the temples reached across the reception desk to take Betty's hand and kiss her fingertips.

Her mouth dropped open.

Seeing a dreamy look come to her eyes, Randolph York took her other hand and kissed that as well. His eyes met hers.

Slowly, she took in a deep breath.

When Mac saw Randolph York was clutching a small bouquet containing three white roses to his chest, he joked, "Oh, Randolph, I didn't know you cared," while reaching for the flowers.

"I don't." Randolph York snatched the flowers out of Mac's reach and handed them across the reception desk to Betty. "It's sad really—I'll bet you a million dollars that within a matter of days, these poor flowers are going to die of an inferiority complex because, next to your beauty, they just can't compete."

While Mac tried not to mutter at the cheesy compliment, Betty gushed. "Oh, Mr. York, I bet you say that to all the grandmothers with great legs."

"No, I don't."

The seriousness in his tone caused Betty to turn away from where she was admiring the bouquet of roses.

The billionaire's sunny demeanor almost made Mac forget that he was Lindsey York's father. Reminding himself, Mac shook his hand in a firm grasp. "Randolph, I'm sorry about your loss."

Mac's condolence prompted a gasp from across the desk. "Oh, my! That's right! I forgot all about that." Dropping the flowers, Betty rushed out from behind the desk to go through the office leading into the lobby.

"Thank you." The billionaire sucked in a deep breath, which he let out. "Lindsey and I had been estranged for years. I knew the last time she walked out of rehab that this was how she was going to end up."

Arriving out from behind the desk, Betty threw her arms around Randolph York. "I am so sorry, Mr. York!" She buried her face in his chest while holding him tight. "I can only imagine how terrible you feel about losing Lindsey. Would you believe I almost lost Savannah last night? Why, if anything had happened to her ..." She let out a sob into his chest.

Randolph York wrapped his arms tightly around Betty while laying his head on top of hers. He was so tall that her head rested perfectly at his shoulder. "I really needed this hug."

"If there is anything that I can do ..." She started to pull away.

The expression on his face softening, Randolph York pulled her in and tightened his arms around her again. "Hold me," he murmured.

"Of course." She pressed her head against his shoulder.

The hug continuing beyond that of casual friends, Mac found himself feeling like a third wheel. Seeing no sign that they were going to part soon, he finally said in a soft voice, "I think he's comforted now."

Reminded of Mac's presence, they parted as if hit by an electrical jolt. Flustered, Betty brushed her hand down Randolph York's arm while offering one last expression of condolence before returning behind the registration desk to tend to the roses.

"I'm sure you have questions, Mac." Randolph York forced a business-like tone to his voice. "So do I. Are you working with Chief O'Callaghan on the investigation?"

"Yes, I am," Mac said. "Lindsey died here at my hotel—during the Diablo Ball."

"Which she wrecked five years ago, too." Randolph shook his head. "I am so sorry about that. If there's anything—"

"Mr. York!" Jeff Ingles called out while rushing out of his office. He trotted down the length of the registration counter to clasp the distinguished guest's hand into both of his. During the hotel manager's offer of condolences on his loss, Mac noticed Brian Gallagher slip out of the office wing. Upon seeing Randolph York, the intern slipped past the group to head across the lobby. Casting a quick glance over his shoulder, he rushed out the front door.

Turning back to Jeff and Randolph York, Mac saw that the billionaire had also caught sight of the young intern hurrying away.

"Mr. York, if there is anything that we here at the Spencer Inn can do to help you through this difficult time," Jeff offered.

"Well," Randolph glanced across the reception desk. "It would really help if there was someone that I could talk to."

"Why, of course." Jeff gestured toward the restaurant. "I was about to go to lunch."

Seeing Randolph York eying Betty, who was returning his grin, Mac cleared his throat. "I think it would be more beneficial for Mr. York if he talked to another parent. Since Betty has a daughter the same age as Lindsey, she may be better suited to sympathize with what Mr. York is going through."

"But I just came back from lunch," Betty said, "and Frank is on break ..." She gazed pleadingly at Jeff.

Feeling all three pairs of eyes on him, Jeff finally offered to man the desk while Betty went on a second lunch break with their most influential hotel customer.

With a wide charming grin, Randolph York grasped Betty's hand when she came out from behind the counter. "To think that it has only taken me a dozen years or so to finally get a lunch date with the most beautiful woman in Deep Creek Lake."

Betty blushed.

Randolph York swallowed. "I'm sorry, Betty, if I'm embarrassing you. I've been so looking forward to—"

She slipped her hand into his. "No, Mr. York—"

"Call me Randolph."

"Randolph." Her smile filled her face. "It will be a pleasure to have lunch with you."

While they walked away, Mac let his gaze drop to Betty's famous legs—proudly displayed in four inch heels. Noting their long slender curves, he cocked his head to one side. The corner of his lips curled. *Nice, but no way are they in the same league as Archie's.*

As if he had read Mac's thoughts, Jeff said, "She should insure those."

Mac leaned across the desk to ask Jeff in a low voice, "It's taken him how many years to ask her out?"

"Believe it or not," Jeff replied. "A blind man can see their hormones screaming at each other. I wouldn't be surprised if Betty wasn't really the prime reason Mr. York comes back to Deep Creek Lake every season."

"I noticed Brian hurrying out of here like he had a bus to catch," Mac said.

"I sent him out to run an errand for me," Jeff said quickly. "Why? Did you or David need him to answer any more questions? I thought he already gave his statement."

Mac caught a glimpse of something he had never seen in Jeff's demeanor before. It took a full moment for him to interpret the stern expression on the hotel manager's face.

Defense. Jeff Ingles was ready to do battle in his intern's defense. While Jeff considered the employees at the Spencer Inn to be one big family, Mac had never known the hotel manager willing to go up against him to defend one.

"No," Mac replied. "I was curious because he seemed to be in such a hurry to get out of here as soon as Lindsey York's father showed up. It was almost as if he didn't want Randolph to see him here."

"Brian left because I sent him. He has no reason to be avoiding Mr. York." Jeff shook his head with a laugh.

"A witness told us that Brian and Lindsey had an argument last night, shortly before she ended up dead," Mac said, "an argument which ended with you sending Brian home after Lindsey demanded that he be fired. Yet, when she went over that railing, Brian was standing right there at the top of the stairs."

"Ah, the camera operator who was shooting up with Lindsey in the bathroom," Jeff said. "Yes, that did happen as he said. I saw him recording the whole thing. What he didn't record was what happened here at the desk after I left there."

"What did happen here?"

"I caught up with Brian before he could leave and told him that I needed him here," Jeff said. "I assured him that he was not fired and to continue working—just stay out of sight of Lindsey York." He continued, "A couple minutes after that, a woman came up to the desk to report that there was a man in the ladies restroom. *I* sent Brian in to shoo him out. If I had known it was Lindsey in there, I would have gone in myself and it would have been me at the top of those stairs instead of Brian."

"Lindsey seemed very determined to ruin Brian's career here at the Inn," Mac said. "Maybe you did send him into the ladies room, but once he got in there and had a couple of minutes alone with her—"

"You're wrong this time, Mac."

CHAPTER EIGHTEEN

Like a couple of twins, David and Hector stood with their arms folded across their chests. In front of them, one of Hector's security officers was examining footage captured from one of the many cameras placed around the Inn on a wide-screen computer monitor.

"You texted?" Mac called out to them when he hurried in.

His eyes on the computer screen, David nodded his head. "You have snot on your shirt."

Snatching a tissue from a nearby desk, Mac said, "Rock Sinclair turned Riva's whole world upside down." As best he could, he wiped the nasal discharge from the front of his shirt. "You should have seen me when Christine decided to end it for another man. It was not my finest moment."

"She wouldn't be the first discarded first wife to kill off the competition in hopes of getting her husband back," Hector said.

"I'm starting to bet on Rock for killing Jasmine," David said. "He and Samuel Nash went over their statements before we got up to the room for a reason. Those two are hiding something. Maybe they both decided to get rid of Jasmine together. Samuel called the jail to get Riva released. Rock lured her up to the room—"

"Am I the only one thinking Jasmine's murder is connected to Lindsey's high dive off the top of the stair case," Mac asked, "and that both of their murders trace back to Ashton's murder and the phony invitations?"

Glancing around the resort's security office, Mac took note of the officers monitoring the feeds from the multitude of security cameras placed around the resort. Some were running background checks. Since Mac had inherited the Spencer Inn, he had increased the security teams into what resembled a full fledge police force in an effort to ensure the safety of the hundreds, sometimes thousands, of well-heeled guests who visited the resort every day.

"What's wrong?" Hector asked about the puzzled expression on his face.

"I feel like I'm missing something."

"It'll come to you," Hector assured him. "It always does."

David told Mac, "Doc gave us a time of death for Jasmine. She died between quarter to and quarter after one o'clock. COD is blunt force trauma at the base of the skull and a broken neck. There's very little water in the lungs. She didn't drown."

Hector unfolded his arms to point over the officer's shoulder. "Looks like Riva Sinclair is in the clear for killing Jasmine. She used her keycard to enter her room at twelve twenty-two and took a bottle of white wine from the mini bar at twelve twenty-five."

"Twenty minutes before the kill zone." David turned to Mac. "There's more."

"More?"

"The crime scene investigators found a listening device in Sinclair's suite," David said. "It was in the sitting room."

"Have they been able to run a trace on it?" Mac asked.

"It was disabled when they found it," David said. "It was a cheapo that you can pick up at any gadget store or order anywhere on the Internet. They're running a trace for the serial number. If we're lucky, whoever is behind it used a credit card—"

"I don't think our guy is that sloppy," Mac interjected. "We have phony invitations sent out to bring together all of the suspects in Ashton's murder, notes luring bitter ex-wives to potential murder scenes, and now bugs in in the rooms of journalists digging into said murder."

David nodded his head. "Something is really fishy here."

"The common denominator is Ashton Piedmont's murder," Mac said.

"Don't you think it's weird," Hector asked, "Riva says Rock Sinclair is impotent and refused to do anything about it, yet he's cheating on her? Doesn't add up if you ask me. Someone is lying. My vote is for the wife."

"Sex is not always the primary motivation for cheating," Mac said. "Most of the time, couples come together because they fulfill each other's primary needs or desires. Granted, very often it is sex. But if you take sex out of the equation with Jasmine and Rock, then they both have other needs, which may or may not be more important to them than sex."

"What's more important than sex?" David muttered under his breath. In response to Mac's glare, he asked, "Did I just say that out loud?"

With a shake of his head, Mac continued, "Jasmine was looking for someone with the power to advance her career and—"

"Rock Sinclair, with his huge ego, was looking for a beautiful trophy to have on his arm," David concluded with a grin. "He wasn't really trying very hard to hide his affair. He was flaunting it."

"That kind of reminds me of something Robin used to say," Hector said with a low laugh. "It's the people who brag the loudest about their sex lives who usually have the biggest problems."

"There might be some truth to that," Mac said. "Riva claims Rock is already making deals for her to keep his impotency a secret in the divorce settlement. Now, he may have wanted Jasmine enough to bite the bullet and take medication, or maybe it's a sexless affair. He makes her a star in exchange for her making him look like a big man with the ladies."

Considering the possibilities, David mused, "If they're having a sex-less affair, then who did Riva hear Jasmine having sex with in the tub? And if Jasmine was having sex with someone other than Rock ... would he or would he not be jealous?"

"That's something we need to ask him," Mac said. "I have investigated murders where the husband was impotent and the wife was having sexual relations outside the marriage. The husband did not mind as long as the wife was discrete—so that no one would know about his problem."

"The Inn has a few wives who regularly check in with their lovers exactly for that reason," Hector told David in a low voice. "They actually put the charges for the resort on their husband's credit cards. Everything is cool as long as no one knows."

"So I need to ask Rock for more information about his equipment failure," David grumbled.

"And the exclusivity agreement he had with Jasmine," Mac said. "Riva went up to their room shortly *after* midnight— after someone sent her a note telling her to come up and she found the door open. I think that note was sent to get her on that floor and on the security video to put her at the scene at the time of Jasmine's murder, which tells me this murder was planned—it was premeditated."

Hector said, "Rock may have wanted Jasmine enough to bite the bullet and take the drugs, in which case he was the one who Riva heard in the tub with Jasmine."

Slowly, Mac shook his head. "If he did, then it's highly unlikely that he would have been slept through Jasmine's murder—depending on when he took the drugs." Seeing questioning glances from both David and Hector, he asked, "Do either of you read? The basic principle of all those drugs is the same. They increase the heart rate to pump blood to the extremities to cause the erection. That's why they have strict warnings about taking them if you have a heart condition. Those pills don't turn on and off like a switch. If Rock took one of those drugs after they got back to the room, he would have been up for hours—in more ways than one. He would have been awake to hear Jasmine get into the tub and hear her murder."

David said, "So he must have been in the tub with Jasmine when Riva walked in. He could have killed her."

"Why send that note to Riva to come up to their suite?" Mac asked.

"Like you just suggested," Hector said, "to set her up. Everyone saw her attack and threaten them. Makes her the perfect patsy."

"Nah," Mac said.

"Nah what?" David asked.

"Nah," Mac said, "something is really fishy about all of these murders." He gestured at David. "You need to question Rock Sinclair again."

The police chief cringed. "I'll confront Rock Sinclair about his impotency and ..." The vibration of his cell phone on his hip was a welcomed interruption. "It's Chelsea."

"We're investigating three murders." Mac turned to Hector when David pressed a finger to his ear and turned away to listen to his fiancée. "This is no time to be sensitive about the cheating liar's feelings about his equipment failure."

"Tell us how you really feel about Rock Sinclair," Hector said with a grin. "You really don't like cheaters, do you, Mac?"

"Nope."

David hung up the phone. "Chelsea found a wedding gown."

"Great," Mac said.

"It's only going to cost an arm and a leg and a kidney."

"How about if we take your mind off your upcoming nuptials by looking for the poison that killed Lindsey York?" Mac suggested.

"I told the cleaning staff not to touch anything in the ballroom or the special events kitchen," Hector said. "So we can start there."

❦ ❦ ❦

With David O'Callaghan leading the way, Mac and Hector followed him down the hotel hallway to the upper entrance into the ballroom. The doors were blocked off with yellow crime scene tape. Spencer Police Officer Fletcher greeted them before removing the tape on one side of the doorway to allow them into the ballroom, which was now an active crime scene.

Stepping to the railing over which Lindsey had plunged, they stopped upon seeing Rudy Crowe, the Inn's public relations officer, at the bar down below. With his back to them, he was zipping up a camera case.

"Crowe!" Mac yelled down at him.

Rudy Crowe's feet appeared to leave the floor when he jumped and turned around to look up at the police chief, head of hotel security, and the Inn's owner. He clutched the camera he wore at the end of a neck strap looped around his neck.

Mac's outburst brought Officer Fletcher running in. Upon seeing the intruder, he called out, "How did you get in here?"

Hector was already running down the stairs.

With wide eyes, Rudy resembled prey that was being pursued from all sides by predators. "I—"

Hector grabbed the camera, which was still attached to the neck strap. "You're a leak. You were taking pictures of the crime scene to sell to the media, weren't you?"

"How did you get in here?" David demanded to know.

"Through the loading dock," Rudy said. "I showed my Spencer Inn ID to the sheriff's deputy guarding the door and told him that I needed to pick up a couple of vases for the florist. He allowed me to come in."

"Give me your ID," Mac ordered.

Rudy stared at his outstretched hand.

"This is an active murder investigation," Mac said. "You potentially contaminated the crime scene, and jeopardized our investigation all to make a few bucks sensationalizing a young woman's tragedy." He snatched the employee identification from where it hung on Rudy's blazer. "You're fired. Hector will take you to your desk to collect your stuff and security will escort you out of the hotel."

Rudy picked up the camera case and tucked it under his arm. "Can I have my camera back?"

Hector ejected the memory card, which he handed to David. After grabbing the camera out of Hector's hand, Rudy slung it over his shoulder by the strap. When Hector reached to take him by the arm, he jerked away and stepped up to Mac. "Do you really want to know what I think about you and this five-star dump, Mr. Faraday?"

"Not really." Mac folded his arms across his chest. "Your opinion doesn't matter to me, Mr. Crowe, but if you want to get something off your chest, go ahead. Give it your best shot."

"People think that just because you come from a middle class background that you're like the rest of us, but you're not. You're just as hypocritical, two-faced, and fickled as—"

"That's enough, Crowe!" Grabbing Rudy by the arm, Hector pulled him toward the stairs. Clutching the camera case tighter under his arm, Rudy jogged up to the steps where Officer Fletcher ushered him and Hector out of the ballroom.

"That young man has a big chip on his shoulder," David said.

"That he does," Mac said.

The door at the top of the stairs flew open again. Jeff practically went over the railing before yelling down to Mac, "What's going on? I just saw Hector escorting Rudy Crowe out."

"We caught him red handed taking pictures of the crime scene to leak to the media." David patted the memory card he had slipped into his breast pocket.

"The fool!" Jeff said. "Something about him hasn't seemed quite right ever since Rock Sinclair and Jasmine Simpson came breezing into town. I suspected he was sucking up to them for a job." He snapped his fingers. "I'll bet you that was who he was trying to get pictures for."

"That certainly sounds like Rock Sinclair," David said. "Think about it. Lindsey York's murder, during the course of his investigation into Ashton Piedmont's murder, will certainly up the publicity of his film project."

"If he was involved in Lindsey's murder, he'd be looking for an inside source to get information about the progress of our investigation," Mac said. "And who better than an ambitious young man who had access to practically every place in this hotel to spy for him?"

"We only assumed Rudy was looking for information to slip to the media." David tapped the button on his radio. "I'll contact Bogie to keep a man on Rudy to see who he contacts as soon as he's out of here."

"Not only that," Mac said, "but with his job in public relations, Rudy also had access to the invitation list and the invitations for the Diablo Ball. If he was sucking up to Sinclair and Simpson, he very easily could have gotten copies of the invitations for them." Delighted with himself for solving that part of the mystery, Mac bumped fists with David. "Can't wait to tell Archie that we solved that piece of the puzzle for her."

While David was on the radio with Bogie, Mac saw that Jeff was examining the damage to the white grand piano that had broken Lindsey fall—as if there was hope in restoring it. With the broken legs, top, and keyboard, the consensus was that it was a loss to be submitted to the hotel's insurance company.

"Jeff," Mac interrupted his assessment, "about Brian Gallagher—"

"Mac," the hotel manager said, "I told you before, Brian Gallagher has nothing to do with any of this." He gestured at the demolished piano.

In spite of the manager's assurance, Mac asked, "Could Brian have thought he was in danger of being fired? If so, that may have given him cause to do something to her."

Jeff answered, "Brian would never have thought that. He knew he was safe."

Mac sucked in a breath. He wondered what the Inn's manager had meant by use of the word "safe." He recalled a police lieutenant named Harris who had been promoted to head of the burglary division when Mac was a detective in Washington. During Mac's police career, he saw Harris moved from one department to another, always in a supervisory position, in spite of his reputation as a screw up.

Before Mac had been assigned to the homicide division, Harris' department was dealing with a string of robberies in a particular neighborhood. The media was making his unit look like a bunch of bumbling fools. One day, Harris asked Mac if he could join him for lunch in the cafeteria and asked for the young detective's opinion about how to solve the crimes. Later, after the gang was captured, Mac was surprised to discover that the case was solved in exactly the way he had suggested to Harris, who took full credit for the bust.

Mac never trusted him again.

Mac and other detectives marveled at how Harris was transferred time and again, but never reprimanded for his ineffectiveness or even fired. Eventually, Mac learned that it was because a close friend with political clout in the upper echelons within the department protected him.

"Who's protecting Gallagher?" Mac asked Jeff Ingle.

"Someone with a lot more influence than Lindsey York had."

Before Mac could ask further questions about Brian Gallagher's protector, David O'Callaghan turned away from the police radio to the Inn's manager. "Our crime scene investigators are on their way back to pick up all of the glasses and utensils to process them to look for the poison that killed Lindsey York."

"Good luck with that," Jeff said. "I know for a fact that Lindsey was all over this hotel. Right out in the lobby, I saw her grab a glass off a passing serving tray that was meant for someone else. The server had to go back to the bar to get another drink for the guest who had ordered the drink."

"That was in the recording." Mac let out a small gasp. "I also saw her do that shortly after she arrived. A server brought over a red velvet champagne cocktail for Carlisle Green. The server said the drink was sent to her from a young man, but when they turned to look for him, he was gone. Carlisle turned down the drink and before the server could take the drink back to the bar, Lindsey swept in and took it."

"What time was that?" David asked.

"It was before seven o'clock," Mac said, "and Lindsey took the swan dive before nine o'clock. Time wise it would work."

"Then the poison could have been meant for Carlisle Green," David said.

"Or someone else," Mac said. "We now know for a fact that Lindsey stole two drinks. The poison could have been in another drink." Slipping an arm across the police chief's shoulders, he explained in a low voice, "Think about it, David. Carlisle Green was there the night Ashton Piedmont was murdered. Yes, she blacked out and has no memory of what happened, but she *is* a witness. Now that Ashton's body has been found and everyone knows she was murdered—"

"And the whole case has been reopened," David added.

"The killer could be very afraid that Carlisle will remember something," Mac said. "He or she may not want to take that risk."

"She's a liability." David grasped his radio. "I need to get people over to her place to protect her."

"Mr. Faraday!"

Mac turned around to find one of the Inn's chef's leading Gnarly by the collar in from the patio. Hitting the palm of his hand against his forehead, he swore. "Gnarly! You're what I was forgetting!" He growled at the dog, "You were supposed to be in Hector's office getting rehabilitated."

"Rehabilitated? I'll give you some rehabilitation! Do you know what this thieving canine did?"

His ears laid back flat on top of his head, the German shepherd slinked behind Mac's legs to hide and lick his snout.

"I can only imagine," Mac replied.

"The Red Hatters' lunch! Twelve plates! Each one filled with lemon tarragon salmon with Greek salad! Beautifully

235

set up on the deck overlooking Deep Creek Lake! And this—this—demon dog! He ate it all! Twelve salmon filets, salad and all! Plus every slice of bread in the three bread baskets, including the whipped butter!"

"Oh, dear," Jeff uttered.

"Mr. Faraday!" the chef continued to rant. "What do you have to say about this mess?"

Mac looked down at Gnarly. Sensing his trouble, the German shepherd laid down and buried his snout under his front paws. He gazed up at his master with his big brown eyes.

"I guess it's a good thing you hadn't put out the yellow bird cocktails yet," Mac finally said.

CHAPTER NINETEEN

Outdoor water sports came to an abrupt halt when an afternoon downpour drove Deep Creek Lake residents indoors. Some chose to amuse themselves with electronic games. Others sought companionship at the local watering holes.

David and Mac took the opportunity to question Rachel Breckenridge who had been returned to Spencer by the Maryland state police.

First, they allowed her time in the interrogation room to think about her situation while they kept an eye on her from the observation room. Mac watched her confidence evaporate through the two way mirror. The longer she sat alone, the more rapid her manicured fingertips tapped the tabletop. She chewed her bottom lip like it was chewing gum.

David was finishing up a phone call to Bogie when he joined Mac. "Let me know if she thinks of something. Mac and I will come over as soon as we're done with Rachel Breckenridge." He hung up the phone. "Carlisle is wracking her brain trying to think if she can remember seeing anyone last night who jogged her memory about the night Ashton was killed. She's coming up with nothing."

"I wouldn't hold out much hope for that," Mac said. "If she hasn't remembered anything yet ..."

The phone on David's hip vibrated.

"I feel like I got more done before we got cell phones," Mac said.

Checking the caller ID, David said, "It's Doc. Back in the old days, you would have had to wait until you got back to your desk to find a message that she called and then call her and hope she is near a phone …" With a wink, David pressed the button to put the phone on speaker. "Tell me you have good news, Doc."

"We got DNA from under Ashton Piedmont's fingernails," she replied. "Not just from one contributor, but from two. A woman and a man. How's that for good news?"

"That's great news," Mac said. "Did you run it through the database?"

"Yes, but so far no hits."

"Then what good are you?" Mac joked.

"Hey," Doc shot back, "I just collect the minute pieces of the puzzle. It's your job to put them together to make sense of them. You find me someone to compare with the DNA I found and then I can tell you if that someone got scratched by our victim."

"That sounds fair enough, Doc," David disconnected the call before saying, "Ashton scratched both a man and a woman. It could have been a couple. It's not Carlisle. We've been over the report taken at the time of the disappearance. Carlisle had bruises on her knees and hands, but no fingernail scratches."

"I'm thinking Elizabeth Breckenridge." Mac gestured at the dark haired young woman fidgeting at the table in the interview room. "Does she know we picked up her daughter yet?"

"I told the state police to confiscate her cell phone," David said. "But I guarantee you that she'll be screaming for a lawyer as soon as we go in there."

"Corey Haim told me that Rachel can't stand her mother," Mac said. "If that's true, we can use that to our advantage."

Squinting at him, David cocked his head. "Are you thinking of making Rachel roll over on her mother to implicate her in Ashton's murder?"

"Carlisle does remember hearing two women screaming at each other the night Ashton disappeared. One had a deep voice."

"Rachel's mother has a low voice," David said. "She almost sounds like a man."

"A.J. says Ashton was the one who left that note that sent Lindsey over the edge at the ball five years ago. The one saying that she knew her secret. A.J. swore Ashton said she did find proof that Breckenridge stole Dr. Piedmont's research, and that proof disappeared when she did. Elizabeth Breckenridge had a whole lot to lose if Ashton had made that proof public."

"Motive," David said. "But is that enough to get a warrant for her DNA? Dr. Breckenridge will not give it up freely."

"Did anyone question them about where they were at the time of Ashton's disappearance?" Mac asked him.

"It was treated as an accidental drowning," David said. "No one was interviewed as a suspect except Carlisle. Since Ashton's body was found, I've had Tonya running background checks on everyone involved. So far, nothing has popped."

Mac's eyes narrowed to blue slits. "Do you remember when we first talked to Dr. Breckenridge. She said something about Carlisle being so drunk on her knees that she couldn't get up to help Ashton while she was being killed. You just said Carlisle's knees were bruised."

David's eyes lit up. "Why didn't I catch that?"

"Maybe because we talked to Breckenridge before you had a chance to go over the evidence again."

"Carlisle's bruises were never released to the media," David said. "It wasn't necessary at the time because everyone thought it was just an accident."

"How would Elizabeth Breckenridge know about Carlisle being too drunk to get up off her knees unless she was there when Ashton was killed?" Mac tapped David on the chest. "We've got her." He went to the door and laid his hand on the knob. "Follow my lead."

❧ ❧ ❧

"Hey, Bogie!" Carlisle yelled over her shoulder to the deputy chief who she thought was downstairs, only to be startled to find the tall, muscular silver-haired deputy chief standing almost directly behind her in the guest room of her home. Seeing him peering down at her from his height, she jumped so high that she almost fell into the closet that she was cleaning out.

"Anything I can do for you, Ms. Green?"

"Call me Carlisle, for one." She turned back around and tried unsuccessfully to reach up onto the top shelf. "And then, you can put that Incredible Hulk build to good use and take everything down off the shelf to help me sort through it."

Bogie looked at the stack of moving boxes that littered the guest room, as well as in every other room in the round house. "I take it you aren't staying here in Deep Creek Lake."

"No, I don't belong here anymore." She moved out of his way to allow him to reach up to the top shelf in the closet. "My place is in Africa. That's where I can do the most good and where I get what I need."

Bogie pulled an armload of sweaters and sweatshirts down off the shelf. When he handed them to her, he paused with his hand on the pile. His bushy mustache twitched and his eyes softened. "You know, when I heard that you were back in town, I have to admit that I was not too happy. I remember all the trouble you used to cause every summer when you blew in here."

"Kind of like a tornado, only worse, huh?"

"Exactly." The corners of his mustache curled up. "From what I can see, you're living proof that a leopard can change its spots."

"It is true, you know," she said. "Leopards can and do change their spots based on their environment in order to blend in with their surroundings—as camouflage. I guess that's why I belong in the bush, away from the sex, drugs, materialism, and cut throat lifestyle here. Too much temptation to get involved in it. Life is simpler in the jungle."

"All you have to worry about there is getting eaten by a lion." Bogie reached up into the top shelf and ran his hand along the wall in search for anything else that may have slipped out of sight.

"Lions only kill what they need to in order to survive," she said. "Humans stab each other in the back for much more senseless reasons, which begs the question—who really is more civilized?"

Clutching a cubed shaped device in his hand, Bogie stepped back out of the closet.

"What's that?" Carlisle asked.

Bogie read the wording imprinted on the side of the black device which he recognized as a data storage device. The police station had many on which to locally back up case files. "It's an external hard drive."

"Where did it come from?"

Bogie jerked his thumb over his shoulder in the direction of the closet. "Up there."

"I never saw that before."

"Must've belonged to your grandpa," he said.

"Grandpa had a laptop that he brought out here to the lake that he used to work on." She took the external hard drive and turned it over in her hand. "I don't remember him using one of these …"

"Maybe he left some really juicy stock tips on it," Bogie said with a grin.

"He died almost ten years ago," she replied.

"If you want, I'll hook it up to your laptop to see what's on it for you."

With possibilities of what secret information the hard drive might contain racing through their minds, they giggled at each other. Their fantasies of found treasure were cut short by the ringing of the doorbell.

Instinctively, Bogie clutched the weapon he wore in on his utility belt before going downstairs to the front door. Through the windows, he saw Parker Lander waiting on the deck. Recognizing the neighbor, a regular summer resident of Spencer, Bogie opened the door.

"Deputy Chief Bogart." Standing up straight, his eyes wide, Parker swallowed. "I'm surprised to see you here."

"My cruiser is in the driveway," Bogie said.

"I came over through the old path along the water," Parker explained. "Is everything okay?"

"Everything is fine," Bogie said. "Anything I can do for you?"

The older man hesitated before a smile came to his lips. "I was worried about Carlisle. You know I had come over that night because I heard Carlisle and Ashton arguing. Now, with Ashton's body being found, I've been going over what must have happened and I know I said that the last I saw Ashton, she was diving into the water off the dock. But then, afterwards, later on that night, I woke up hearing what I thought was a screech owl. Now, I wonder if maybe that wasn't an owl, but Ashton screaming while being killed after Carlisle had passed out."

Bogie's mustache twitched while he digested Parker's information. "That could be. Do you remember how much later this was?"

"I'm afraid not," Parker said. "If that was the killer I heard, he's probably still around. I don't know if my imagination was playing tricks on me, but just now, I could have sworn I saw someone lurking in the woods watching the house."

"Really?" Stepping out, Bogie peered into the trees and bushes lining the lake and surrounding the houses along the shore. Rainwater from the downpour an hour earlier dripped from the leaves. Steam rose up from the planking on the dock and walkway.

"We might want to check it out," Parker said. "We can't be too safe."

Chapter Twenty

"I want my lawyer," Rachel Breckenridge announced as soon as Mac and David entered the interrogation room. "You have no right to hold me here."

"You'll get to call your lawyer after we talk." Mac sat down across from her while David leaned up against the wall.

"I didn't do anything wrong," Rachel said.

"You're at least a material witness to a murder," Mac said, "who was caught trying to leave the country under an assumed identity, which ups you from material witness to suspect."

"What murder?" Rachel said innocently.

With a chuckle, Mac kept his eyes on Rachel while asking David behind him, "Like mother, like daughter. Did your mother teach you how to lie like that?" He sat back. "What would you say if I told you that we have copies of the texts between you and your mother discussing Lindsey York's murder and you telling your mother that was why you had to get out of the country?"

"But I didn't mean I had to leave because I killed her," she said. "I meant that I had to get away from that whole outfit—that whole gambit that they were all running was ruining my life."

Mac pounced. "What gambit?"

"It was like that saying," she said, "'Oh, what a mighty web you weave when first you practice to deceive.'"

"Tell us about it and set yourself free of the web," David said.

She looked from Mac to David and then back again. "I want immunity and protection."

"Immunity from what and protection from whom?" Mac asked.

She narrowed her eyes while peering across the table at Mac. "You give me immunity from everything that I got roped into, and get me into the witness protection program and I'll hand you my mother and Lindsey York's partners on a silver platter."

Without a word, David left the room.

Mac fought the smile working its way to his lips. "We can't offer you anything until we know what you have for us."

In silence, Rachel stared at Mac from across the table. Her expression became more pleading with the passage of time. Knowing that he had the upper hand, Mac gave her nothing by way of encouragement. His face was void of emotion. He could see her trying to read his thoughts.

She swallowed. "Mom made a deal with the devil."

"Is that devil Lindsey York?"

Rachel nodded her head. "We knew Lindsey was trouble, but my mother was already in trouble and thought Lindsey could get her out."

"What type of trouble?"

"My mother was Ross Piedmont's protégé," Rachel said. "He was researching 3D printing for prosthetics and organ transplants. He'd been working on it for years. As luck would have it, he had just completed his research and his book to publish the results when he died. My mother found his body. Ashton was in Europe doing a summer internship, so …"

"No one would be the wiser," Mac said. "Your mother took advantage of the opportunity to put her name on everything."

"Since she was his assistant and protégé, she knew where everything was in the house," she said. "Of course, Ashton knew what her grandfather had been researching, but she was just a student. Mom thought that if she offered her a free ride through medical school that she would keep her mouth shut. Even if she didn't, who would take a little girl's word against Mom—a distinguished researcher and doctor by the time Ashton realized what she'd done." She laughed. "My mother thought she had it all planned out."

"Thought?" Mac asked.

"There were a couple of loose ends that she wasn't counting on," Rachel said. "One being A.J.'s father. Dr. Piedmont had been keeping him apprised of all the research. When he found out that Mom had sold it to a publisher as her own, he threatened to blow the whistle." She shrugged her shoulders. "Suddenly, he was dead of a heart attack. Then, A.J. and Ashton got together. The year after Mom's book came out and she became the toast of the medical community, Ashton told her that she had proof positive that it was her grandfather's research. She had found the stack of printed hard copies of her grandfather's book that she had mailed special delivery to him. Turns out that, with every draft he completed, she was printing them, packing them up, and then mailing them to him. He put them straight in his safe. They were all unopened and date stamped. Proof that he had been working on it years before Mom claimed she had written it."

"Sounds like Ashton had your mother over a barrel," Mac said.

"It would have worked, too," Rachel said. "But Ashton was such a little fool that she got herself killed."

"How was that?"

"She gave Mom a choice," Rachel said with a shake of her head. "Very bad idea. Mom could confess to everything herself or be exposed for the fraud she was."

"Then Ashton disappeared and your mother's problems were over," Mac said. "What happened to the copies of the book?"

"She found them right where she figured they would be," Rachel said. "Mom had the security code for the Piedmont place from back when she worked for Dr. Piedmont. So, after she made Ashton disappear, she went in and found a whole drawer of them. She shredded them and burned them all in our fireplace."

"Was this before or after your mother brought Lindsey into your web?"

"Same time," Rachel said. "Mom needed some dirt on A.J. to keep him in line. Lindsey is—was very good at that. Since she couldn't *find* anything, she decided to seduce him."

"Why Lindsey and not you?" Mac asked. "I mean, you were a med student like him. You were friends—"

Rachel laughed. Upon seeing the confusion on Mac's face, she said, "You haven't figured it out yet, have you?"

"No, enlighten me."

She leaned across the table. In a stage whisper she said, "I'm a lesbian. But don't tell anyone. Mother would be horrified if the world found out." With a wicked grin, she sat back in her seat. "A.J., Corey, Ashton, they all knew. So if I went to A.J. and tried to seduce him, he would have laughed me out of Maryland."

Sitting back in his seat, Mac studied her to determine if she was telling him the truth or not. He decided to dig a little further. "A witness told me that you and Ashton used to be friends, but that ended when A.J. came into the picture ..."

247

"That was about the time I realized I was in love with Ashton," Rachel said with a note of sadness in her tone.

Could she be Greaser? Mac stared at her. *Ashton may have kept the fact that Greaser was a woman from Carlisle.*

It was almost as if she wanted to fill the silence in the room when Rachel plunged on. "I knew Ashton was hetero-sexual, but I thought ... hoped that maybe if she knew how I felt. All it did was put a wedge between us."

"The jealousy over A.J. wasn't because you wanted him," Mac said, "but because you wanted Ashton."

A hint of tenderness filled her face and she shrugged her shoulders. "I didn't realize until after she was gone what a good friend she was. She had told A.J. and he told Corey, but they kept it to themselves—even when Mom blackmailed A.J., he never once threatened to out me. He said his war was with my mother, not me."

"Since you couldn't seduce A.J., your mother brought in Lindsey York to," Mac said. "She drugged him and then took advantage of him." He ordered her to continue.

"Mom was going to use that tape to keep A.J. in line and get him to convince Ashton not to expose her," she said. "But it didn't work. Ashton didn't care what she had on whom. She called Mom that night and told her time was up. She was sending those manuscripts to her lawyers and they were suing Mom for all she was worth. Mom went to go have it out with her. When she came back, she had scratches on her arms and across her face ... and her problem was gone."

Mac glanced over his shoulder at the two-way mirror. He sensed David was watching from the other side.

"I take it that was not the end of it," he said.

"Lindsey York had recorded every conversation she had with my mother and me, asking her to seduce A.J., and why," Rachel said. "She knew that my mother had stolen the research, which was why she became head of the medical school. Suddenly, out of the blue, Lindsey was calling the shots. As head of the medical school, Mom had access to drug supplies. All she had to do was some juggling with the numbers in the inventory. Since she was head, no one would question her. If they did ... well, my mother can be pretty intimidating in case you haven't figured that out yet. Within a couple of years, Lindsey had us supplying illegal prescription drugs to dealers connected to major South American cartels operating in California."

"We?" Mac asked. "If this was your mother's mess—"

"She was giving me orders because she couldn't get caught with her hand in the cookie jar," she said. "Do you think I wanted to be forced into a shotgun wedding with A.J.? Do you think it's fun living in a closet pretending to be someone that you're not?"

"Why the shotgun wedding?"

"Two reasons," Rachel said while holding up her fingers. "One, A.J. Wagner is Dr. Howard Wagner's son. Everyone at the university remembers Dr. Howard. If A.J. and I got married, it would be like the merging of two dynasties, at least, that is the way Mom likes to see it. Two, she wanted A.J. to be my cover—" She whispered harshly, "so no one would know that I'm a lesbian."

"You didn't want to marry him anymore than he wanted to marry you."

"Nope," she replied. "Now that I'm a hair's breathe from getting my medical license, I wanted out from under my mother's thumb. We're talking about my future. I told both of them that I was getting out. Mom said that she was going to take care of it, but then Lindsey showed up at the ball with that thug. Her message was loud and clear. Don't mess with them. As soon as I saw Raul, I was out of there."

"Do you think your mother took care of the situation by killing Lindsey?"

Rachel sat back in her seat. "She's now in the running to be university president. Mom had too much to lose. What do you think?"

"Do you have proof to back up any of this?" Mac asked her.

"Lindsey isn't the only one who knows how to make incriminating recordings."

❧ ❧ ❧

Mac waited until he was out in the hallway before he allowed himself to smile.

David came out of the observation room to join him. "I'll call the DEA about Dr. Elizabeth Breckenridge. I think it's safe to say she's going down for everything from fraud to drug dealing to murder. If her DNA is a match for the women's skin found under Ashton's fingernails, we'll have her for her murder."

Mac's chuckle fell abruptly. "Then who was the man?"

"What?"

"Doc said there was a *man* and a woman's DNA found under Ashton's fingernails," Mac said.

"Well …" David scratched his ear. "Parker Lander went over to break up the fight …"

Biting off each word, Mac asked, "Why would he say Carlisle scratched him when it was Ashton who did it?"

David paused before asking, "Are you now saying Dr. Breckenridge *didn't* kill Ashton? Rachel just said she did."

"Dr. Breckenridge is right handed. Ashton's skull was bashed in on the right side towards the front. Her killer is left handed."

"Maybe—"

"Let me think about this." In deep thought, Mac adjusted the sling around his arm while pacing up and down the corridor. "If Parker Lander went to break up the fight, he would have seen Dr. Breckenridge on the scene. Rachel says her mother admitted to Ashton scratching her. *She* was the one that Parker and his wife heard fighting with Ashton, not Carlisle. After he went to break up the fight, he returned home with scratches on him."

David was nodding his head. "Gloria Lander said that in her statement."

"Which means Ashton Piedmont was alive *after* Dr. Breckenridge left." Mac stopped pacing and turned to David. "She didn't kill Ashton. Parker Lander did."

"But Rachel just said her mother got the copies of the book that proved she had stolen it and she shredded and burned them," David said.

"Imagine you were Dr. Breckenridge," Mac said. "You just had a big fight with Ashton in which she's given you a deadline to confess or be exposed. Drunk, Ashton jumps back into the lake to resume skinny dipping. You may want to kill her, but you don't have to. The house where she is hiding the evidence to expose you is right there on your way home and you know the security code from all the years you worked there."

David concluded, "While Ashton was being murdered by someone else, Dr. Breckenridge went into the Piedmont place, found the proof that Ashton was holding over her head, and destroyed it."

"She didn't kill Ashton because she didn't have to," Mac said.

"Chief!" Tonya hollered from the end of the hallway. "I've got a detective on the phone who wants to talk to you real bad."

When they reached the squad room, the desk sergeant handed the phone to David while telling him in a hushed voice. "Detective Susan Williams from the Lancaster County sheriff's department in Pennsylvania. She's calling in response to my background check on the Landers for the Piedmont case."

"Detective Williams, this is Police Chief David O'Callaghan," David said into the phone. "My desk sergeant said you wanted to talk to me."

The feminine voice on the other end of the phone line oozed with excitement. "May I ask why you're running a check on Parker Lander?"

"He's a witness in the disappearance of a young woman here at Deep Creek Lake." David wrote down Parker Lander's name on a notepad for Mac to read. "Her body was recently found and the case was reopened."

"Was she murdered?" Detective Williams asked.

"Yes."

"How?"

"Her head was bashed in," David said. "Why are you interested?"

"Parker Lander is a person of interest in the disappearance of two young women in our area," the detective said. "One of them was his son's girlfriend. Neither of their bodies have been found. His own son is convinced his father had something to do with it, but he has nothing to offer us in the way of evidence against him. We were working on Lander's wife and thought we were about to break through with her when, conveniently, she broke her neck falling down a flight of stairs."

"What about the young women?"

"Both college-age girls," she said. "Very pretty. From well-to-do families. Liked to party. Is that your victim?"

"Very much so."

❧ ❧ ❧

The woods surrounding the lakeshore seemed to be filled with movement. While Bogie had grown up on the lake, he had trouble discerning what threats were real and what was simply a squirrel scurrying from one bush to another. Behind him, Parker Lander was thrashing about like a real city slicker while they searched the woods between the Piedmont estate and the Green home.

Finding no tell-tale footprints in the rain soaked woods surrounding the Green estate, Bogie concluded that he was wasting his time. Parker Landers' active imagination had drawn him away from Carlisle Green, who he had left in the house with instructions to lock the door. With a curse, Bogie turned around on the path. "I'm going inside to call for a couple officers to come out to search these woods. Most likely you scared whoever it was you saw away, or it was simply a deer."

"Whatever you think is best, officer," Parker said.

Bogie's radio cackled when he passed Parker on his way back down the path to the round house. "Bogie, pick up," Tonya's voice came through the speaker. "We got an important lead on the Piedmont murder. Green's neighbor, Parker Lander is suspected—"

Hearing the name, Bogie reached for his gun while turning around in time to see the blur of a thick branch connect with his face.

❦ ❦ ❦

Mac's mind was speeding as fast as David's cruiser which was racing along the lakeshore's tight twists and turns. "Parker must have freaked when Ashton's body was found." He held onto his seat. In the side view mirror he saw a Spencer police cruiser and a sheriff's deputy car fall in behind David's cruiser. All of their lights and sirens were going. "If Carlisle can remember him killing Ashton—"

"He probably bashed her head in after raping her," David said. "Since Carlisle was so stoned, he let her live so that he could pin the blame on her for Ashton's disappearance."

"The male DNA under her fingernails has to belong to him."

Pulling into the driveway, David cursed when he saw Bogie, his head bloody, staggering out of the woods to his cruiser. The muscle bound man collapsed to his knees.

While taking his gun out of its holster, David rushed to Bogie's side.

"Weapon," Bogie gasped while tapping his empty holster.

His gun drawn, Mac raced ahead of the other officers around the circular outside wall of the house. As they neared the front door, they heard a scream followed immediately by a crash.

Mac banged on the door with his fist. "Lander! Police! It's over! Come out with your hands up!" After a long silence, he pounded on the door again. "Lander!"

Carlisle's voice replied, "He can't talk right now!"

Mac glanced over at David who came running up to move ahead of the deputies and officers positioned to storm the house with their weapons drawn.

"I could use some help in here!" Carlisle called out again. "Can someone bring me some handcuffs, please!"

Mac opened the door. Leading with his gun, he stepped through the foyer into the center of the circular living room. Furniture and packing boxes had been overturned and dumped over in the fight. Unused, Bogie's gun rested next to a collapsed coffee table.

In the center of the mess, Carlisle and Parker Lander lay on their backs on the floor. Carlisle's legs were tightly wrapped around Parker Lander's neck. She had him pinned between her thighs in a choke hold. She had both arms wrapped around his head.

With only a minimal amount of air to breath, Parker Lander's face was red. Pleading for help, he wheezed, "She's crazy." With one hand, he reached out for help, while trying to pry her legs loose from their strangle hold.

"I guess rehab saved my life in more ways than one," Carlisle said. "I was required to take a fitness class and really got into mixed martial arts. Best thing a woman can ever learn."

"She wasn't supposed to fight back," Parker panted. "They never fight back."

"Everyone should go through rehab," Carlisle said with a grin. "I've taken down a wild pig, crocodile, and now a psychopath using the life skills they've taught me."

Stunned, the officers surrounding them stared down at the woman who had singlehandedly taken down a suspected murderer—possibly a serial killer.

Carlisle broke through their collective thoughts. "Well, don't just stand there, guys. I can't hold him for you all day."

Chapter Twenty-One

Sitting at a bank of computer monitors set up in the study at Spencer Manor, Mac, Archie, David, and Chelsea were up to their eyeballs in candid shots taken by guests of the Diablo Ball.

While they had caught Parker Lander in the act of trying to kill Carlisle Green in her home, the server at the Diablo Ball was unable to identify Lander as the man who had sent the possibly poisoned drink to Carlisle Green, which Lindsey York had taken. Not surprisingly, Parker Lander claimed he was not at the Spencer Inn that night. Without any witnesses, they had no way of pinning Lindsey York's or Jasmine Simpson's murders on him.

So, Archie had sent out a request to the gala's attendees requesting their help by sending all of their candid shots in hopes of catching the killer on the scene on the night of the murders. They now had hundreds of selfies and other pictures to search the faces and action taking place in the background to find one shot of the killer handing the poisoned cocktail to the server.

While their humans searched the multitude of images on the computer monitors, Gnarly and Molly were sacked out on the leather sofa taking a long nap. Molly rested her head across Gnarly's front legs, while he rested his head on top of hers.

Lindsey York's murder was only one more charge they hoped to pin on Parker Lander, who was already being held for assault on a police officer and attempted murder of Carlisle Green. Suffering from a concussion as a result of the blow to his head, Bogie was taking a well-deserved week of sick leave with his favorite lady, Doc Washington, who was giving him some tender loving care at her farm in the Maryland countryside.

Garrett County prosecutor Ben Fleming believed they had a strong case against Parker Lander for the murder of Ashton Piedmont. Lander's DNA was a match for the male skin left under Ashton's fingernails.

"When his wife sent Parker over to break up the fight, he decided to take advantage of the situation by raping and killing Ashton Piedmont," Archie said.

"There's no proof of rape," Chelsea pointed out while scouring the pictures on one monitor.

"Unfortunately, the body was too badly decomposed to prove rape." Squinting, Mac zoomed in on a picture of Vincent Van Dyke and his daughter on the red carpet. "At least we have more than the sheriff's department in Lancaster. They have nothing solid. If they could at least find the bodies of these young women …"

"One being his son's girlfriend," Chelsea said with disgust. "Now that is a monster."

"What about Dr. Breckenridge?" Archie said. "She stole an old man's research, probably killed a university president, and dragged her daughter into dealing drugs to cover up her original theft. Talk about dysfunctional families."

"Having grown up here on Deep Creek Lake with the rich snowbirds who fly in during the summer season," Chelsea said, "you'd be surprised how dysfunctional many of these families can be."

"I've seen enough to get a sense of it," Archie said. "Personally, I think you're wasting your time trying to pin any of these murders on Dr. Breckenridge. As soon as the DEA weighs through all the evidence that Rachel gave them, they can arrest her mother for her involvement in the drug dealing at the medical school. Her lawyer will no doubt cut a deal in exchange for her testifying against Lindsey York's partners and both mother and daughter will go into the program. You'll never be able to touch Dr. Breckenridge for anything. You and David don't even know where Rachel is since the U.S. Marshals already swept her up to take into the program."

"You wouldn't believe all the evidence Rachel had been collecting against Lindsey and those drug dealers over the months," David said. "She really wanted to get away from her mother."

"Still," Mac said, "No harm in trying to get to the truth."

"Dr. Breckenridge told her daughter that she would get them out from under Lindsey York's control. She certainly had motive to kill her." David pointed at the monitor in front of him. "And I've got a picture of the two of them over by the piano. The doctor looks like she's about to blow."

The four of them crowded around the monitor while David zoomed in on the image, pixelating it in the process. After taking the mouse from him, Archie cleared up the picture for them to see that Lindsey had a wicked grin on her face while Dr. Breckenridge's face was contorted in fury. On the piano between the two of them was a champagne flute half filled with a red liquid. The red drink in the champagne flute was easy to spot at the event in which every other champagne flute contained a clear sparkling drink.

"She had that drink for a little while." Archie checked the time stamp on the picture. It read 6: 54 pm. "We're looking for pictures before this time if we want to get a picture of Lander giving the drink to the server."

"That's assuming the drink sent to Carlisle was the one with the poison." Mac squinted at the picture while zooming in on the glass closer. "We have yet to be able to place Lander at the Inn on the night of the murder. Maybe Dr. Breckenridge slipped the poison into Lindsey's drink while talking to her."

"Do you see something, Mac?" David asked.

"That champagne flute."

David moved in closer to the monitor. "What do you see?"

"It's what I don't see," Mac said. "The Spencer Inn logo. All of our dinnerware, china, glasses, including the champagne flutes, have the Spencer Inn logo stamped on them. The crystal pieces have the logo cut into them. This champagne flute does not."

Taking the mouse out of Mac's hand. Archie zoom in on the image even closer. "He's right. This isn't one of the Inn's glasses. As a matter of fact, I'm willing to bet this isn't even crystal."

"Why would the killer bring his own glass?" Chelsea asked.

"Because he had the poison coating the inside of it," Archie suggested.

Chelsea shook her head. "But why bring his own glass? All he had to do was order the drink, drop the poison into it, and then give it to the server to take over to Carlisle."

"Chelsea's right," David said. "It doesn't make sense. The server stated that the man gave the drink to him to take over to Carlisle."

A slow grin came to Mac's face. "The killer *gave* the drink to the server, who didn't notice him enough in the sea of faces to be able to identify him. Think about it. If the killer was wearing gloves when he gave the drink to the server, I'm willing to bet money he would've noticed him."

"The killer had to be able to identify the glass in order to get it back so that we would not find his fingerprints on it," Archie said. "So he brought his own glass, without the logo on it."

"Still doesn't work," David said with a shake of his head. "When you order a drink, the bartender uses a fresh clean glass from behind the bar. Health department regs. Even when you request a refill, they use a fresh glass."

"So the killer mixed his drink elsewhere and carried the glass in," Mac said. "It's easy enough to do. The resort is huge. It was Saturday night of a big gala. No one would have noticed a man carrying a drink around."

Archie and Chelsea sucked in deep breaths. "We have a lot of work to do," Archie said. "Instead of 'Where's Waldo,' we're playing 'where's the killer cocktail?'"

"Speaking as the lawyer of this group," Chelsea said slowly, "even if we find a picture of Lander, or whoever, carrying in that glass, you still won't have a case for murder because you won't have the glass itself. All you'll have is a picture of a suspect carrying a champagne flute without the Spencer Inn logo with a red velvet cocktail in it. Without the glass itself with the poison in it, and real evidence connecting the killer to that glass, you won't have enough evidence for an indictment, let alone a conviction."

Archie looked from Chelsea to Mac and David, who regarded her with the distaste that comes from a dose of unpleasant reality.

"Just saying," Chelsea said to break the silence.

"Even so," Mac said after a long pause, "with that picture, we'll be getting a step closer to the evidence we do need for an indictment and a conviction."

❧ ❧ ❧

"Just to be clear," the federal agent in charge of the surveillance on Dr. Elizabeth Breckenridge reminded the Spencer police chief and Mac, "you're here as a professional courtesy. This is a DEA operation and bust." The hard core, older agent allowed a smirk to come to his lips. "To tell you the truth, we have all we need to make an arrest now without getting the doc to incriminate herself, but you seem to think that the daughter can get her to admit to killing the university president ..." With a shrug, he turned back to his agents who were monitoring the listening devices they had managed to plant around the Breckenridge home.

"Hey," Mac told his back, "you know as well as I do that if you can nail her for murder in addition to all the other charges you have against her, then you'll have a lot more ammunition to have her put away where she belongs instead of living a comfy life of leisure in witness protection."

"That's why we agreed to this, Faraday."

To the federal agency, immunity was worth it to arrest the cartel who Lindsey York had brought in from South America. Agents in California were sweeping in to arrest Lindsey's partners while the agents in Deep Creek Lake prepared to pick up Dr. Elizabeth Breckenridge.

In a matter of days, the Drug Enforcement Administration and Department of Justice had struck a deal with Rachel Breckenridge. The U.S. Marshals had taken her into custody. While getting their sting operation in place, the agents had Dr. Elizabeth Breckenridge under surveillance. Periodic texts were sent to her from Rachel's burner phone to tell her that she was moving about in the Cayman Islands until she got some place safe to contact her.

Upon learning the good news of a possible break in his father's death, A.J. Wagner did not hesitate to exhume Howard Wagner's body in hopes of investigators finding proof of his murder. However, Mac was painfully aware that even if they did find evidence that his father had been murdered, there was little hope of finding real evidence to connect Dr. Elizabeth to the deed.

Now, from a secured location which even Mac and David were not aware of, Rachel was set up to contact her mother in a video call in hopes of extracting an admission to murder from her.

Carlisle Green was kind enough to allow the agents to use her home, which was directly across the cove from the Breckenridge home. The wall to wall, floor to ceiling windows provided a perfect view into the doctor's home.

As the lead agent had reminded Mac and David, they were only along for the ride. While curious about their progress, Carlisle Green kept out of the way by cleaning out her kitchen cupboards. This was not an easy task with Gnarly's help in the form of ripping up the newspapers she was using for packing material for the aged dinnerware, cups, and mismatched glasses.

After accepting her offer for a bottled water, David told her, "Bogie told me that you were planning to move back to Africa."

"At least for now." Giving up on getting a weathered box back from Gnarly, who appeared to be trying to turn it into a den, she decided to put together a fresh box. "I guess Gnarly doesn't want me to move."

Taking the box from her, David proceeded to tape the bottom together for her. "Your family has summered here for how many generations …"

"And that's okay," she said. "But their way is not mine. I've found my place and Deep Creek Lake is not it. These—" she gestured across the cove at the Breckenridge mansion "—are not my people."

"Have you been tempted to go back to your old ways?" David asked. "Is that why you're leaving?"

Squinting, she held up her fingers and thumb pressed together. "I am human. I admit, I do have some fond memories of the past, but I also have a lot of memories that make me want to bury my head in shame." She took the offered box from him. "I'm sure you know what I'm talking about." Her eyes met his.

"Yeah." David tried to hold her gaze. "About that?"

She laid her hand on his. "Listen, I really am sorry for how I used to treat you."

"It wasn't exactly a one way street." Looking her up and down, David saw that since that night, she had filled out, become healthier. He pushed away the desire to find out how she would look in a red thong now. He bet she would be sexier.

"I was disrespectful to you, David," she said. "To me, you were a piece of meat and that was how I treated you and, as a human being and an officer of the law, you deserved a lot more than that. I had no right pawing at you the way I used to when you would pull me over."

A moment of confusion turned to clarity when David recalled the time when he had pulled Carlisle over for speeding in her red sports car. While he was giving her a breathalyzer test, she grabbed his crotch. When he pulled away and chastised her, she responded with a laugh.

Her face turning red at the memory, she looked down at the floor where Gnarly had shredded so many newspapers that they could not see the hardwood floor.

"I did forget about that," David said softly. "I meant a different time."

"There was another time?"

"The summer before Ashton disappeared," David said. "You showed up at Benny's while I was there and they refused to serve you …"

Her face was blank.

"I drove you home …"

263

Still her face was blank.

"You came into the kitchen to get me a beer and came out wearing nothing but your panties …"

Her eyebrows came together to meet between her eyes. "Sounds …" She swallowed. "I seem to recall a fantasy that went like that."

"It was real," David said. "Listen—"

"Did we have sex?"

"No but we came very close."

"Damn!" she said loud enough to make the agents heads turn in the living room. After David shushed her, she continued, "Blackouts can be both a blessing and a curse. You can forget the things that can leave you paralyzed with embarrassment, but you can also forget some really juicy stuff too." She looked David up and down. "You have no idea how many fantasies I had about getting you in between the sheets since I was twelve years old and to think I came that close and—did we kiss?"

David sighed. "Yes."

"Damn," she said with a shake of her head. "Did I enjoy it?"

"You don't remember that night at all?"

"I'm sure it had nothing to do with your kissing," she said. "Now that you're engaged I guess it's too late for a do-over?"

"Very much so," he said. "Which is why I brought it up in the first place." He sucked in a deep breath. "I would really appreciate it if you didn't mention that night to Chelsea."

She grinned. "How can I bring up what I can't remember?"

"Which is what makes this blackout a blessing." He smiled back at her.

When she moved in closer to him, he was uncertain if she was seeking the do-over of a kiss that she had mentioned. Instead, her eyes searched his in silence—long enough to make him look for a graceful retreat out of the kitchen.

"David," she said in a soft tone, "do you know why the past is called the past?"

"Because it has already passed?"

"Exactly," she said. "It is in the past. It is behind us. Have you ever tried to move forward while looking behind you? It's very difficult to do. Sometimes, you end up falling on your face because you are so busy looking into the past that you fail to see the wonderful offerings right in front of you." She moved in to whisper into his ear. "You have a beautiful bride-to-be who is madly in love with you and your life spread out ahead of you. Embrace the future and don't look back."

"What are you two so serious about?" Mac's abrupt tone caused David to almost trip over Gnarly who was cleaning up the floor under the refrigerator.

Sensing a fossilized dog treat, Gnarly was sprawled out on his stomach with his legs spread eagle while reaching with his snout under the kitchen appliance. Failing to capture the treat, he cried out for help in pulling out the refrigerator.

"Gnarly," Mac chastised the dog, "what are you doing? Clean up this mess." He grabbed David's arm and pulled him out of the kitchen. "Rachel is calling her mother via Skype. They're about ready to start."

Once they were out of Carlisle's earshot, Mac squeezed David's elbow. "Are you behaving yourself?"

"Yes," David hissed. "Carlisle and I were just talking. I'm not a kid."

"I know you're not a kid," Mac said, "but it is my job as your best man to get you to the altar and flirting with a passing ship is very dangerous when it comes to you." He poked David in the chest with his finger. "Considering your past relationship with her, keep your distance."

"Our past relationship is in the past, Mac," David said. "That's where we intend to keep it."

"Breckenridge has just picked up," the agent called over to them.

Mac and David rushed over to the laptops and computer monitors that littered the dining room table. The lights in the room were dimmed and the shades pulled to prevent Dr. Breckenridge from seeing inside the house.

On one monitor, Dr. Breckenridge's image appeared as she spoke into the web cam. In the one next to it was Rachel's face with a sun filled image behind her.

"Hey, Mom," Rachel said with forced brightness in her tone. "I'm here … finally."

"Where are you?" Dr. Breckenridge demanded to know. "I expected you to call me two days ago when you got settled."

"It took me this long to get settled," Rachel replied. "I felt like I was being followed. What was that you texted about Lindsey York being murdered?"

Mac could see that the young woman's face was tight with nerves. Her grin was forced. Since Dr. Breckenridge was her mother, he worried that she would notice the nerves and sense that something was up.

"She must have OD'd," Elizabeth said with a roll of her eyes. Her tone sounded bored. "What's the weather like there?"

"It's fine," Rachel said. "What's the media saying? Have the police questioned you?"

"Why would they be questioning me?" Dr. Breckenridge's eyes narrowed. "I saw on the weather channel that a storm was coming in from the east. It's been chilly the last couple of days."

Mac could see Rachel's mind working. Finally, she responded, "Yes, it has. I've been staying inside because I don't know if Lindsey's goons had seen me leave or not. Mom, did you take care of everything like you said you would?"

"Yes, I did," Elizabeth answered. "I told you I'd take care of everything. Now that Lindsey is gone, you can come back home."

"I thought you said she OD'd," Rachel said.

The expression on Elizabeth's face betrayed her growing impatience. "She did ... at least, that's what I assumed. The police aren't talking. But you know Lindsey. She was downing everything she could get her hands on."

"So you didn't ... "

"No! I didn't kill her," Dr. Breckenridge said.

David and Mac exchanged looks of disappointment.

Rachel said, "But you said you took care of—"

"I hired a private investigator to break into her house in Los Angeles. He found everything she had against us, that's what I meant."

"So you didn't take care of Lindsey the same way you took care of A.J.'s dad?" Rachel asked.

Sparks of anger came to Dr. Breckenridge's eyes. "Why did you bring that up?"

"Just, when you said you'd take care of Lindsey," Rachel rattled on, while wiping sweat from her brow, "I had assumed—that's why I thought you were the one who poisoned her."

"No one said anything about Lindsey being poisoned," Dr. Breckenridge said. "You little bitch! Are you putting words into my mouth?"

"Considering everything that Lindsey was into, and then how conveniently Dr. Wagner died after he threatened to expose you."

"Dr. Wagner had the same problem that his son has," Dr. Breckenridge said in a low voice. "He underestimated me. He thought that he could defy me, pass me over for key slots in the university. He thought I would roll over and allow him to kill my reputation and career. He was wrong. Unfortunately, he discovered that too late. When the digitalis hit his heart, I could see him trying to rethink his position about making me confess and walk away from all this."

"We got her!" Mac yelled, but the chief agent was already giving the order for his people to move in.

"Digitalis," Mac breathed to David. "That's what she used. Let's hope when A.J. exhumes the body they can find it to pin his murder on her."

"You little bitch!" Elizabeth Breckenridge was screaming from the monitor in front of her while two agents grabbed her arms and pinned them behind her back. "Let go of me!" Fighting the men holding her, she screamed at her daughter. "You set me up! Don't think I'm ever going to forget this!"

"I'm sorry, Mommy," Rachel Breckenridge sobbed.

Both monitors went black.

Chapter Twenty-Two

Spencer Inn Restaurant

Dr. Elizabeth Breckenridge's arrest for dealing drugs at the medical school in Maryland made all of the major news stations—overshadowing the capture of Ashton Piedmont's murderer.

By the morning after the noted doctor's arrest, Lindsey York's and Jasmine Simpson's murders in the Spencer Inn seemed to have been forgotten by everyone—except by the Inn's owner, Mac Faraday.

During breakfast, the reminder of the two murdered women was sitting directly across the restaurant in the form of Rock Sinclair and Vincent Van Dyke having a heated discussion—probably some sort of production meeting. Smirking at the bickering, Samuel Nash sat at the table along with Kassandra Van Dyke. Dressed in a summer dress with flat shoes and her lush hair pulled back into a ponytail, Kassandra appeared as bored as Samuel was amused.

Recounting the details of each murder in his mind, Mac didn't realize he was staring while holding a slice of toast in mid-air until David sat down across from him.

"I thought you'd be happy," David broke through his thoughts. "You solved a murder case that wasn't even ours and I see that your arm is no longer in a sling."

Mac blinked to the present. "I was supposed to wear the brace and sling for another week, but they kept getting in the way."

After dropping the slice of toast onto his plate of scrambled eggs and hash browns, he flexed his right hand. The pain shot all the way up to his shoulder, which was still tender. Through sheer force of determination, he refused to allow it to show on his face.

Steering David's attention back to the case, Mac said, "Hector says they have had no luck of finding Parker Lander on any of the security videos for the night of the ball. It's starting to look to me like he didn't do it."

"Ben gave me more bad news when I dropped Chelsea off at his office just now," David said.

"What's that?"

"Even though Dr. Elizabeth Breckenridge admitted to Rachel last night that she slipped digitalis to A.J.'s father, who did not have a heart condition, they may not be able to make the murder charge stick," David said.

"Digitalis will kill you if you take it when you don't have a heart condition," Mac said. "It will *cause* you to have a heart attack."

"And Howard Wagner did die of a heart attack," David said. "But Breckenridge's lawyer is already looking to have the statement thrown out because in her conversation with Rachel she said nothing about stealing Piedmont's research and book. Her PI destroyed everything that he stole from Lindsey York's home. Since the feds have no proof of her stealing Piedmont's research and book, then they can't prove motive. If the judge throws out Breckenridge's statement, then they won't have a case to indict her for killing Dr. Howard Wagner."

"I've lost my appetite." Mac pushed his plate away.

While shaking his head, David saw Carlisle Green, carrying a valise under her arm, enter the restaurant with Corey Haim and A.J. Wagner. The three of them were seated at a table near the windows with a view of the lake down below.

Mac saw Kassandra Van Dyke sit up at attention upon seeing them.

Corey and A.J. ordered coffee and Carlisle ordered tea. After the server hurried away, Carlisle took a thick folder out of her valise and opened it on the table. The three of them huddled in close together.

Her eyes filled with longing, Kassandra openly stared at the group.

"What's that about?" David asked Mac.

"A.J. and Corey seem to be working with Carlisle on something," Mac said. "Corey Haim had said he wanted to build a clinic in the rural area where he came from in West Virginia. Maybe he convinced Carlisle to donate towards that."

"Kassandra, pay attention," they heard Vincent Van Dyke snap at his daughter. "This is important."

"Lindsey's death has left your show wanting," Rock said.

"But you already signed a contract with us," Vincent reminded him. "Just because Lindsey died, doesn't mean you can back out of the show now. My lawyers have looked over the contracts. Nowhere is there a provision that you can cancel because Lindsey York passed away."

Samuel Nash chuckled. "Guess Lindsey's death worked out well for you, huh, Van Dyke. She was squeezing you out as star of the show and now you're back in the lead."

"And since Jasmine is dead, I noticed you've taken over as producer and director," Vincent Van Dyke said.

"You're absolutely right," Rock said to Vincent Van Dyke. "There was no provision for Lindsey's death. So we are obligated *for now*. Problem with your show is that Lindsey's death left a void. She was the catalyst for conflict—she was the live wire. People aren't going to want to watch a happy loving father-daughter team. Can Kassandra do anything else besides flash her breasts?"

Seeing Kassandra's attention diverted at the table across the way, Vincent snapped his fingers. "Kassandra, pay attention. Tell the man what you can do."

Kassandra turned to the men sitting at the table. "I can quit."

Vincent Van Dyke laughed loudly. Seeing Rock's stunned expression, he insisted, "She's joking."

"Mr. Sinclair really doesn't want to do the show with Lindsey gone and I don't really want to do it anymore," Kassandra said. "So why not drop the whole thing? Then everyone will be happy."

Samuel Nash was chuckling.

Vincent Van Dyke's rage reminded Mac of one of his strong arm tough cop performances on his old police show. "Do you have any idea what I've done for you to get you this far? The sacrifices I've made? The risks I took?"

Anyone who wasn't watching the men at the table before now diverted their full attention to it. Kassandra cowered in her seat. David stood up, but Mac was already on his way across the restaurant to the table.

"Do we have a problem here?" he asked.

Vincent turned on Mac. "This is none of your business."

Mac's low tone contrasted that of the aged actor. "My joint. My business." He turned to Kassandra. "I think your friends are waiting for you over there, Kassie. Why don't you join them?"

"Sit down, Kassandra," Vincent ordered. "We have business to discuss."

With wide eyes, Kassandra looked from her father, who dared her to move, to the table across the way where Carlisle was in the process of pulling up an extra chair. With a wave of her arm, Carlisle invited the young woman to join them.

"They're waiting for you, Kassie," Mac said.

The young woman tossed her napkin onto the table. "I'm sorry, Daddy, but I just can't do it anymore." Like a frightened rabbit who had suddenly been set free, she scurried across the restaurant to sit with Carlisle, A.J., and Corey.

"You're going to regret this, Faraday!" Vincent Van Dyke said.

Mac said, "You're going to regret it if you keep pushing that young woman into a life that she doesn't want. I've only seen her a handful of times and I can see that she doesn't want any of this." He swung his arm to indicate the men seated at the table. "She doesn't want to be a star. She wants to do that." He gestured across at the table where Kassandra was giggling and smiling while talking with Carlisle over the papers that she had spread across the tabletop.

"I think our business here is over." Rock Sinclair stood up.

"No, it's not!" Vincent raged. "We have a contract."

"One of our stars is dead, the other doesn't want to do it, and you're a has-been, Van Dyke," Rock said. "Have your lawyers call mine and we'll work out a settlement, but there's no show." He gestured at Samuel. "Come on, Nash, our work here in Deep Creek Lake is done."

"Actually, it's not," David said. "We still have the matter of two murders to solve and both of you are witnesses. I'd like to ask you a few questions."

When Mac tried to follow them, Vincent Van Dyke grabbed him by his injured arm. "We're not through yet, Faraday. You can't just ruin a man's life and then walk away."

Refusing to let Vincent see him cringe at the pain shooting up to his shoulder, Mac told him through gritted teeth. "I didn't ruin your life, you did. Now get your hand off me."

"You owe me," Vincent hissed in his ear.

"You're right. I do owe you." Mac whirled around and grabbed Vincent's arm that had grasped his arm. Spinning the unprepared actor around on his heels, Mac pinned his arm behind his back and shoved him face down onto the table.

"Give it up, Van Dyke," Mac snarled. "It's over. Time for you to follow your daughter's lead and walk away from Hollywood and their sick games to find a real life—not just a pretend one on TV… while you can still do it with a shred of dignity."

Releasing Vincent Van Dyke, Mac stood up and straightened his shirt. Seeing that every guest was focused on him with wide frightened eyes, he said, "He didn't leave a tip for his server."

As Mac made his way through the tables, there was a flurry of activity as customers slammed tip money down onto their tables.

❧ ❧ ❧

David had escorted Rock Sinclair and Samuel Nash over to the lounge, which had yet to open for the day.

"I was beginning to think that you forgot about Jasmine," Rock Sinclair was telling David when Mac joined them.

"No," David said, "we don't forget about murders that happen here in Spencer." He glanced over his shoulder at Mac. "We also don't like it when witnesses lie to us while we're trying to solve those murders."

"I didn't lie to you," Rock Sinclair said.

"We spoke to your wife." Mac made a point of making eye contact with Rock Sinclair. "She told us *everything* about your marriage."

Rock cast a quick glance in Samuel Nash's direction.

"We're going to go over this again, Mr. Sinclair," David said. "You're going to have a word with Mac while I talk to Samuel Nash out in the lobby. Then, maybe we'll make some headway in this case—unless you two want to lie to us again."

Mac watched Rock Sinclair squirm while David ushered Samuel Nash out of the lounge, leaving the two of them alone. He waited for the door to close before folding his arms across his chest. "Now, the truth; are you really impotent, or did you just tell your wife that because you were cheating on her?"

"Yes, I lied to Riva," Rock said. "I was trying to spare her feelings."

"We spoke to your doctor."

"There are laws about that," Rock countered.

"Okay." Mac uncrossed his arms and stepped up to Rock Sinclair. "You do have a problem. Maybe not sexually, but you do have one. You're a cheating liar. You didn't have sex with Jasmine the night she died. Your DNA was not on or in her."

"We used condoms."

Mac shook his head. "There would have been evidence of it in the autopsy. So what was your relationship with Jasmine Simpson? You weren't having sex with her. You left your wife for her. Explain."

"What Jasmine and I did or did not do had nothing to do with her murder," Rock said.

"That's for us to decide," Mac said. "Maybe you came to suspect that she was using you and that was why you decided to bug the suite—to catch her in the act … maybe with Samuel Nash, the director she had recommended for the job."

He watched Rock's face for his reaction to the mention of the listening device found in their suite.

Rock's eyes grew wide. "Listening device? Bug? Someone was listening to us?" His face grew red. His eyes darted around the lounge before his face turned white. "Oh, Lord." He gasped out. "Had to be Riva. Wanting proof about ... that witch." Breathing heavily, the producer slumped in his seat.

Convinced that Rock Sinclair had not planted the listening device, Mac eased down into the seat across from him. "You and Samuel Nash compared notes to get your stories straight before calling the police after you had found Jasmine's body. Why?"

"Why not?" Rock replied.

"It's been my experience that only people who are lying about something need to get their stories straight."

After uttering a deep sigh, Rock said in a low voice, "Samuel Nash knows about my condition. He and Jasmine were sexually compatible. He, and only he, satisfied her sexual needs, but she was with me. Before we called the police, we came to an agreement that Nash would keep our agreement to himself so no one would know my problem."

"In exchange for his silence, Nash would take over the film project," Mac finished. "Did you love Jasmine?"

"Yes!" The producer clenched his fists and pressed them against his temples. His face contorted in frustration. "And I wanted to please her so much, but I just couldn't. So, I took those pills but they would only work so much. I loved her so much, but I could only satisfy her in one way."

Mac waited in silence for him to continue.

"I opened the doors for her to become a producer," Rock said. "For that, she loved me ... and because I loved her and wanted to make her happy, I allowed her to be with Samuel." He sank down into a chair. "You must think I'm a pathetic excuse for a man doing what he has to do to have a beautiful young woman on his arm."

"So you knew all about Samuel Nash and Jasmine?"

"The three of us had an agreement," Rock said. "That cocky twerp flaunted his sexual prowess every chance he got."

"Did you see him in the suite that night?"

"I didn't see him," Rock said. "I heard them. He came up a little before midnight. I was in the guest room. I had drifted off the sleep. Then, I heard him leave shortly after one o'clock. I went back to sleep and found Jasmine the next morning."

"Could Samuel have killed Jasmine to take over as producer and director?" Mac asked him.

"Sure," Rock said without hesitation. "He was using her the same way she was using me."

"You heard him come in and you heard him leave," Mac said. "Did you see him?"

Rock shook his head.

"Did you hear them arguing?"

"Not over the jets," Rock said with a shake of his head. "That's how I knew he had left. The jets turned off and then I heard the door open and shut. I looked at the clock and it was five minutes after one o'clock."

※ ※ ※

"That wasn't Samuel Nash that Rock Sinclair heard," David told Mac after he reported on the revision to the producer's statement when they met in Hector's security office. "According to Samuel Nash's room keycard, he used it to enter his room at twelve forty-seven in the morning. Now that is within the kill zone, but there was someone else."

David turned around in his chair to show Mac the monitor displaying the security recording for the hallway outside the Sinclair suite. "Nash told me that he and Jasmine drank a whole bottle of champagne while hooking up in the Jacuzzi."

"There was that broken stem of a wine glass in the tub," Mac recalled.

"I remembered that when Nash told me about the champagne." David pointed at the monitor.

A man in a Spencer Inn service staff could be seen walking down the hallway carrying a tray with an ice bucket and two wine glasses. Keeping his face from the camera, he knocked on the door to the suite. The door opened and he stepped inside. The time on the recording was eleven-fifty-eight.

Mac waited.

"He doesn't come out until much later, which is weird. Why wouldn't she show him out?"

"Maybe he only pretended to leave," Mac said. "Easy enough to do. The closet door is right there in the entrance hall. He opens the door. She turns her back for just a second. He jumps into the closet and closes the door."

David fast forwarded the recording to show Samuel Nash knocking on the door. Jasmine answered the door and invited him inside. Few minutes later, the door opened, but they were unable to see who was on the other side. Then, Riva Sinclair arrived several minutes later, and hurried out. A half hour after she departed, Samuel Nash left the suite.

Twenty minutes after Samuel Nash left, the server stepped out into the hallway carrying the ice bucket with an empty champagne bottle and one wine glass on the tray. Keeping his face adverted from the camera, the server strolled down the hallway.

David froze the image. "Look at his sleeves. They're wet."

"Like he just killed a woman in a bathtub," Mac said. "He must have been hiding in the suite the whole time waiting for the opportunity to kill Jasmine Simpson."

David nodded his head. "Wearing a Spencer Inn server uniform."

"No." Reaching over David's shoulder, Mac paused the video. "Take a closer look at his suit. That's not a Spencer Inn server uniform. There's no logo on the breast pocket. It's close. It's the same color and it's a suit, but it's not the same."

Squinting, David peered at the blurry image on the security video. Mac was right. There was no logo on the suit jacket's breast pocket. "Jasmine probably did the same things I just did. Noticed that his suit was the same color and didn't look any closer. She assumed he was the server bringing up the champagne and let him in."

"And she did order champagne?" Mac asked.

David checked his notes. "At eleven-forty."

"Then what happened to the server who was ordered to deliver the champagne to their suite?"

"Good question," David said.

"If you like that one, I have a few more," Mac replied. "Who is this man? Why did he kill Jasmine? And did he murder Lindsey York, too?"

CHAPTER TWENTY-THREE

As the chief of police, David considered it his duty to keep the father of the victim informed about the status of their investigation, especially when that man was as rich and powerful as Randolph York. Since the murder occurred at his resort, Mac felt obligated to ride along to the York estate located down the road from the Spencer Inn.

With its stone and log front and a panoramic view of the lake at the bottom of the mountain and the valley behind it, the York summer home resembled a European ski chalet.

After David drove his cruiser through the stone pillars and wrought iron gate entrance to La Maison de York, they noticed an old, blue sedan with Illinois license plates parked in front of the stone walkway leading to the front door.

"Not what you would expect a billionaire to drive," Mac noted.

"Randolph York is pretty down to earth," David said.

"That car is at least ten years old," Mac said. "That's very down to earth." He noticed a University of Chicago student parking decal on it. "I wonder if that belongs to Brian Gallagher."

"Why Brian Gallagher?" David asked.

"He's going to college at the University of Chicago."

After being made to wait in the foyer, Mac and David were escorted by a casually dressed housekeeper into a rustic library. In contrast to his high-style daughter and luxurious surroundings, Randolph York was dressed in jeans and wore loafers on his sockless feet. He sported a fishing cap on top of his head. While they spoke to him, he practiced making fishing lures from diagrams displayed on a computer tablet.

"Have either of you ever fished?" he asked them with the enthusiasm of a child.

"I used to go fishing all the time with my father," David said, while Mac shook his head.

"So did I," Randolph said. "Haven't fished in decades since he passed away. Decided recently to take it up again." He held up a shiny new fishing rod. "Take a look at this baby. What do you think?"

With the eye of experience, David admired the fishing rod. "That's a nice one all right."

Peering out the window onto the patio, Mac asked in a casual tone, "Are you going fishing alone?"

"I'm taking a friend," Randolph replied without offering any further information.

"Would that friend be Brian Gallagher?" In response to the fall of Randolph's grin, Mac said, "What would you say if I recognized Brian's car out front?" He cocked his head in the direction of the doorway leading out onto the patio. "I see your shadow out there, Brian."

Clad in jeans, a polo shirt, and dock shoes, Brian Gallagher stepped through the doors to come inside.

David handed the fishing reel back to Randolph York. "Why were you hiding from us, Brian?"

"I told him to," Randolph said. "It was foolish of me, I know. But my lawyers had advised that we try to keep his name out of this investigation as much as possible."

"Hiding the truth in a murder investigation is never a good idea," Mac said.

David agreed. "It makes you look guiltier when the truth comes out."

"It also makes it harder to find out who the real killer is," Mac said.

David asked, "Mr. York, are you aware that your daughter accused Brian of stalking her moments before she died?"

"Are you aware that my daughter had many issues, one being a pathological liar?" the businessman countered. "Brian did not kill Lindsey."

"I didn't even know she was there until the night of the Diablo Ball," Brian said. "I heard Senator Fleming announce her and I went hiding in the kitchen. I knew that if she saw me that she'd make a scene, which she did, so I spent most of the night avoiding her."

"You told me that she was poisoned," Randolph reminded Mac and David. "I thought that Lander guy was supposed to have killed her by accident while trying to poison Carlisle Green."

"We can't find any evidence placing Lander at the hotel," David said. "It very well could have been someone else—maybe even someone targeting Lindsey, who was mixed up with some major drug dealers."

"Which means they all have more reason than Brian to want Lindsey dead," Randolph said.

"Why are you protecting him?" David asked while looking from one of them to the other. "Lindsey was your daughter."

"And Brian is your son," Mac said. "That's why you're protecting him."

Randolph York set the tablet aside. "How did you figure it out?"

"I made a few phone calls. Your lawyer's wife and my lawyer's wife have the same hair dresser." Mac stepped over to Brian to study his reaction when he said, "You didn't want us to know because then we would know that Brian had motive to kill Lindsey. With her dead, he's your *only* heir."

Randolph chuckled. "I disinherited Lindsey years ago. That's why she threw a fit when she saw Brian. She blamed him because she was never able to take responsibility for her screw ups. She was just like her mother."

Brian said, "She tried to make me out to be a fraud and got caught."

Randolph sucked in a deep breath. "Brian's mother was my executive assistant. Lindsey's mother was a model looking for a rich husband. I was naive, but I caught on eventually to her being manipulative and conniving. I was ready to leave her when I realized that I was in love with Eve, Brian's mother. Lindsey's mother caught wind of it and got me drunk one night. She got pregnant—on purpose. She knew I was too much of a gentleman to leave a pregnant wife. When I told Eve, it broke her heart. She quit and I never saw her again until a few years ago." He swallowed. "She never told me that she was pregnant. I didn't find out until Brian contacted me that she was dying."

Brian said, "She didn't tell me until then. She admitted that he never knew."

Randolph looked up at his son with affection in his eyes. "Brian and Lindsey were born three weeks apart, but there was a world of difference between the two of them. Brian inherited his mother's work ethic. He works hard and gives his all to whatever he sets his mind to. All Lindsey ever learned was to take-take-take."

Mac concluded, "So you started grooming Brian to take over SuperMart and Lindsey didn't take it very well."

"She hired a lawyer to sue him for fraud. She wanted a DNA test to prove that Brian was my son," Randolph told him. "The test came back saying that he wasn't."

Mac and David shot suspicious glances in Brian's direction.

Randolph said, "Then my private investigator found the lab technician whom she had paid fifty-thousand dollars to switch Brian's DNA sample with another. That was the last straw. I cut her off. All she had left to live off of was her mother's trust fund."

Brian added, "She swore to get even with me."

"In addition to dealing drugs," Mac said, "Lindsey told some of her friends that she had gone into banking. I think she meant blackmail."

"Sounds like my daughter," Randolph grumbled.

"Any thoughts on who she was blackmailing?"

Brian confessed, "She tried to blackmail me. Didn't work though. She found out that I had been pulled over when I was in high school with marijuana in the car. It belonged to one of my friends, but since I was driving and it was my car, I was charged and got probation. The record was supposed to be sealed, but she found out somehow. She said that unless I paid her five thousand dollars a month, she would tell our father. Thing is," he grinned. "I had already told him. She went ballistic."

David asked, "Do either of you have any idea who else she could have been blackmailing?"

"We really had no contact with her in the last few years," Randolph said.

"I did see her fighting with a man," Brian said. "It was not long after she'd been introduced. I was hiding in the kitchen." His cheeks flushed. "That was how I ended up being there when Savannah was taken hostage. I had to get upstairs to check in with Senator Fleming, and was looking through the door to see if the coast was clear. That was when I saw Lindsey going ape at some guy who tried to take her drink."

"Tried to take her drink?" David tapped Mac on the arm. "Someone else told me about an incident like that."

"I saw the whole thing," Brian said. "Lindsey was going toe to toe with Vincent Van Dyke. He accused her of screwing him over on this deal he had with Sinclair. He said she was squeezing him out and she wasn't going to get away with it. She put her drink on that table next to where they were arguing and I saw some guy come up and take the drink. Lindsey was in the middle of a sentence when she whirled around and went off on the guy. He said he thought it was his and she just about hit him."

"What type of drink was this?" David asked him.

"It was in a champagne flute."

"What color?" Mac asked.

"Red. Sparkling."

Mac's mind was working. "If Lindsey wasn't the target— then whoever put the poison in the drink may have been trying to retrieve the glass before she finished it to keep from killing her." He grinned. "In which case, Archie and Chelsea might be able to find him lurking in the background in pictures of Lindsey."

"The guy works at the Inn," Brian said.

"He isn't a guest?" Mac asked.

"I don't know his name," Brian said with a shake of his head, "but I know I've seen him around."

CHAPTER TWENTY-FOUR

At the Inn's security office, David and Mac found Hector standing watch behind a server who was going through identification photos from the Inn's employee database.

Upon seeing the database, Brian Gallagher stepped up to the monitor to study each photograph along with the server.

"Meet Gary," Hector introduced the young man who, when he saw Mac, practically knocked over his chair jumping up to shake his hand. "He was assigned to take the champagne up to the Sinclair suite the night Jasmine ordered it." He ordered Gary back to the computer monitor. "He says he was intercepted at the elevator by one of the suits from the business wing who said he'd take the champagne up to the Sinclairs because he was on his way up for a meeting."

"At midnight?" Mac asked.

"They were from Hollywood," Gary said with a broad shrug of his shoulders. "A suit tells me that he's got a meeting and offers to take up the champagne, who am I to question?"

"Suit?" Mac replied.

"I've seen him around the business offices in a suit and wearing an employee badge," Gary said.

"Then our killer is an Inn employee," David said.

"Or maybe he just makes people think he's an employee because he wears a suit similar to the Inn's blazers and hangs around the business offices," Mac suggested with hope in his tone.

"We are so screwed if he is." Nodding his head, Hector turned back to join Gary and Brian at the computer monitor.

"Remember the listening device found in the Sinclair suite?" Mac asked David.

Keeping his attention focused on the employee pictures flashing across the computer screen, David answered, "The serial number was traced to a local store. It was purchased a couple of weeks ago and the customer paid cash. So we can't trace it."

"That's how he knew Jasmine had ordered champagne and intercepted it," Mac said. "He heard her order it through the bug and the timing coincided with the note that he sent to Riva in the lounge to go up to the Sinclair suite. He wanted her to go up so that she could be placed at the scene at the time of the murder."

"That's all well and good, Mac," David said. "But we still don't know who he is or why he killed Jasmine. Nor do we know if her murder is connected to Lindsey's murder or if Lindsey was the target or someone else whose drink she stole." He tore his focus from the computer monitor. "In other words, we've got squat right now."

"We're getting close," Mac said. "Forensics didn't find the flute used to send the drink to Carlisle. That tells me the poison was meant for her. The connection between Carlisle and Jasmine is Ashton Piedmont."

"But we know Parker Lander killed Ashton and we can't place him here at the Inn," David said. "Why would he kill Jasmine? He wasn't even on her radar as far as the show."

Across from the computer where the two Inn employees were going through the photo ID, Mac saw a young security officer with a camera bag slung from his shoulder arrive at his desk.

"Is that your new camera?" another officer asked him. "Let me see."

Proud of his recent purchase, the young man unzipped the case, and carefully extracted the camera from it to hand his friend. In doing so, the case slipped off the desk and fell to the floor. Enthralled with the new camera, they ignored the fallen case.

"The case," Mac murmured.

Hearing him, David asked, "Which case is that?"

"The camera case." Mac was still piecing together his memory of the scene in the ballroom. "He was holding the camera. So the case should have been empty. But he was clutching it like—" Turning to the computer monitor, Mac ordered Hector, "Show them Rudy Crowe's picture." While the security chief went to work in bringing up the requested picture, Mac asked David, "Did you look at the pictures Rudy took of the ballroom when we caught him there?"

With a nod of his head, David said he had. "The flash card was empty. I assumed we caught him before he had a chance to take any pictures."

"That's him," Brian and the server said almost in unison upon seeing the picture of the terminated public relations employee.

Hector rubbed his chin. "Why would Rudy—"

"Bring up his resume," Mac ordered. "I'm willing to bet he went to the University of Maryland and graduated in communications with Jasmine Simpson."

While Hector went through the employee record, Mac said, "When we walked in on Rudy in the ballroom, we jumped to the conclusion that he was there to take pictures of the crime scene to leak to the media. He went along with us because he couldn't let us know the real reason he was there."

"To retrieve the glass that he had used to poison Carlisle," David said. "But why try to kill her?"

"You're right on the money, Mac," Hector said. "University of Maryland. Graduated with a degree in communications."

"Print up Crowe's picture and let's take it to Samuel Nash," Mac said. "He went to school with Jasmine, too."

While Hector rushed to the printer, Mac told David, "Jeff said that as soon as Sinclair's group arrived here to do this investigative report on Ashton Piedmont that Rudy started hanging around them. Jeff assumed he was angling for a job. Suppose he wasn't. Suppose he was really stalking them."

"But Parker Lander killed Ashton," David objected.

"*They* didn't know that." Mac grabbed the picture from Hector. "They were working on the same assumption that everyone else had—that Carlisle Green killed Ashton. We need to find Samuel Nash. I'm willing to bet he can fill in the blanks."

David took his radio out of his security belt. "I'll put out a BOLO on Rudy Crowe to have him brought in."

❧ ❧ ❧

They intercepted Samuel Nash, dressed for the fitness center, coming out of his room. Upon seeing Mac, the police chief, and security manager, he froze. "What is this?"

Mac handed the picture to the director. "Do you recognize this man?"

Samuel Nash studied Rudy Crowe's image. "Oh, yeah. That's the hotel public relations guy I was telling you about."

"Is this the same public relations guy in the bad tux that you saw arguing with Lindsey York?" David asked.

"Yep," Samuel said, "he tried to take her champagne and she went ape on him. Strange dude."

"That's two witnesses who saw him try to retrieve that drink," Mac said. "The poison had to have been in that flute."

"He's the one who got Jasmine and Rock the invites we needed to the Diablo Ball," Samuel said.

"That's right," Mac said. "Since Rudy worked in public relations, he worked closely with the event coordinator, who had the guest list and arranged the printing of the invitations. It would have been a cinch for him to get copies of the invitations."

"I thought he helped us because he wanted to come work for us," Samuel said. "That's why we let him hang around. He told us that he was writing a blog about our investigative report. Was that a lie? Did he really do all that so that he could get close enough to kill Lindsey and Jasmine? Why? Why would he want to kill either of them?"

"Since you guys let him hang around, then Jasmine would have no problem letting him in the suite that night when he brought up the champagne that she'd ordered," Mac said.

Samuel let out a gasp. "She did say that he had stopped by that night. I forgot all about it."

"What did he want?" David asked.

"I wasn't there," Samuel said, "and I wasn't in the mood to discuss some loser looking for a job." He nodded his head quickly. "That's what I thought he wanted. A job with the production company. He wanted us to take him with us. Jasmine was put out about him stopping by because it was late."

He paused to look at each of them. His eyes fell on Mac. "Do you think he killed her because she turned him down for a job?"

"No, I think the request for a job was just an excuse for her to let him into the room, and then he pretended to leave," Mac said. "What he really wanted was to kill her. You said you went to school with Jasmine."

"I did."

"Take another look at this guy," Mac said. "Think back over five years. Picture him with different colored hair … more casual…"

"Goth," Samuel said. "Yeah, that's right! Back then he had black, greasy hair and always wore black and—"

"Greaser," Mac said.

"Who?" Samuel said.

"Ashton Piedmont and Carlisle Green's codename for him. Greaser."

"I didn't know that," Samuel said. "If he's the guy I'm thinking of, this guy hung out on the fringes of our group. He changed so much—I didn't recognize him."

"Did you see him have any conversations with Jasmine?" David asked.

"He interviewed her," the director said.

"The twist that she was going to have at the end of the investigative report," Mac asked, "did that include someone so obsessed with Ashton that he killed her because he couldn't have her?"

Samuel's mouth dropped open. "Maybe. She refused to tell me what it was, but she was practically giddy about it."

"I saw you two arguing about that twist at the gala," Mac reminded him of walking in on them in the closet. "I heard you say you were afraid of getting sued."

"She refused to tell me anything specific. I'm the director. I need to be kept in the loop."

Mac pressed him. "Did she come up with this twist after her interview with Rudy Crowe?"

Looking at the photograph, Samuel tapped the image of Rudy Crowe's face. "He had interviewed Jasmine at lunch that day. It was after lunch that she started talking about this new angle in the investigation. I remember her using the word 'stalker' at one point."

291

"That's our guy," Mac muttered. "It was Greaser all along."

"You mean this nut killed Jasmine over our investigative report?" Samuel Nash asked.

"How would you like to be publicly accused of a murder you didn't commit all in the name of ratings?" David asked him.

"The way I remember this guy, he wasn't wrapped too tight to begin with," the director replied. "Can I go workout now?" Without waiting to be dismissed, he hurried down the hallway to catch the elevator.

"Jasmine must have noticed Crowe's obsession with Ashton," Mac told David. "He had planted a bug in the suite to keep tabs on their investigation. Like everyone else, they assumed Carlisle had killed Ashton, so he targeted her for revenge at the gala. But Lindsey took the poison meant for Carlisle. Then, Crowe overheard Jasmine discussing with Rock Sinclair her plan for the twist. He must have realized she was going to implicate him as Ashton's killer. When he overheard her order the champagne, he sent a note to Riva to lure her up to the room to frame her because she was the logical suspect after that fight they had only hours before. Then, he intercepted the champagne and delivered it himself. Since Jasmine knew him, she let him in the room and he used the excuse of looking for a job for being there."

"Then," David picked up the story, "he pretended to leave. When Jasmine turned her back, he hid in the room and waited for the opportunity to kill her when she was alone."

"Chief," Officer Fletcher's voice came through David's radio.

David pressed the button. "Yes, Fletcher."

"I've got good news and bad news for you."

David let out a groan. "What is it, Fletcher?"

"Bad news," Officer Fletcher said, "Crowe ditched our tail on him a little over an hour ago."

With a heavy sigh, David pressed the button on his radio to ask, "What's the good news?"

"We found his car," the officer reported before adding, "Only now we've got some more bad news."

"Is the bad news that you found his car at the airport?"

"No, he's not at the airport."

"Then where is he?"

"His car is in the Spencer Inn parking lot," Officer Fletcher said. "He's at the Spencer Inn."

❦ ❦ ❦

"Why would he come back here?" Hector asked after dispatching his whole security staff out in search of Rudy Crowe. "Returning to the scene of the crime?"

In the Spencer Inn lobby, Mac turned around in circles while searching the faces of everyone coming and going in the busy summer resort. It was the first official week of the summer season and the resort was packed with guests.

Spotting Jeff Ingles manning the busy reception desk, Mac asked, "Jeff, have you seen Rudy Crowe?"

In the midst of programming key cards for a family checking in, Jeff shook his head. "Not since we fired his butt."

"Where's Betty?"

"Randolph York," Jeff said with a growl while handing the key cards to the guests. "To tell you the truth, I'm starting to doubt this father in mourning act of his. He's been taking Betty on two hour lunches every day to talk about how lost he's been feeling since Lindsey's death. Then, she's been coming in late in the morning because he's been taking her out dancing every night."

The capture of Rudy Crowe foremost on his mind, Mac hurried away. Behind him, Jeff was still venting. "Who goes dancing with leggy brunettes when they're in mourning?"

Hector was worried. "Mac, this is a huge resort. He could be anywhere."

"We need to think about this."

"We need to find him before he kills someone else," Hector said. "He's killed two people."

"Rudy, why did you come back here?" In deep thought, Mac murmured. "We can assume you got the glass that you had put the poison in to kill Carlisle." He turned to Hector. "Carlisle! She was the target when Lindsey was poisoned. He must blame her for Ashton's murder because she was there but too stoned to save Ashton! Is Carlisle still here at the Inn?"

"I saw Carlisle Green and Kassandra Van Dyke go out running on the mountain trail," Hector said.

"He must be following her to finish what he started." Mac headed across the lobby to tell David.

"I'll go get Gnarly." Hector went in the opposite direction to his office.

Mac stopped and asked Hector from over his shoulder, "Gnarly's here?"

"Archie put him in my office while she was getting her stone massage," Hector explained. "Remember he's been banned from the spa ever since he decided to take a mud bath without an appointment, and they had to close the place down for a week to get all the dog hair out of the mud."

With no regard for decorum, Mac yelled across the lobby to where David was briefing a team of his officers. "He's going after Carlisle on the running path."

Gnarly had caught up with Mac by the time he reached the beginning of the running path. Hard core runners who enjoyed challenging trails with a nature view made good use of the path which snaked through the woods and across the ski runs down to the bottom of the mountain.

Sensing an adventure, Gnarly jumped on Mac and then Hector before attempting to take off down the path. "First, we have to let him know what he's chasing." Mac held him back by his collar.

Officer Fletcher took a towel out of a plastic bag. "I took this out of Crowe's car. Hopefully, it has his scent on it." He rubbed Gnarly's nose with the towel. "Go find him, big guy."

The German shepherd sneezed. With his nose twitching, he stuck his snout up in the air. Then, catching the scent, he took off down the running path.

"Follow that dog!" Hector yelled.

With Gnarly leading the way, David, Hector, and more than a half dozen police and security officers raced down the running path in pursuit of a killer.

Strictly on a hunch, Mac commandeered a dirt bike from the vendor working the recreational vehicle booth and zig-zagged down the ski slope until he caught up to where David was running ahead of the mob.

"Want a ride?" Mac offered. "I've got an idea of where we'll find Crowe." He patted the seat behind him. "Hop on. If I'm right, we don't have much time."

David climbed onto the back of the bike and wrapped his arms around Mac's middle. "You better be right."

Mac spun out while making his way down the mountain.

CHAPTER TWENTY-FIVE

At the bottom of the ski slopes, Spencer Inn had a lakeside café. In the winter months, skiers could sip coffee or cocoa or eat a quick snack before hitting the slopes again. In the summer season, the café offered snacks or quick lunches on the lakeside deck which joined the docks for boaters. It also offered kayak and waterski rentals.

At one of the tables, Kassandra Van Dyke's mouth watered at the sight of the huge hot fudge sundae nestled on top of two brownies with a cherry on top. "I'm eating every calorie we just burnt off." She dug in.

Carlisle took a bite of her vanilla frozen yogurt. "Life's too short to deny yourself innocent pleasures once in a while. How much joy does starving yourself to be thin give you?"

Kassandra stopped with the spoon filled with vanilla ice cream and hot fudge poised in front of her mouth.

Crossing her arms in front of her, Carlisle leaned onto the table. "Are you happy, Kassie?"

In silence, Kassandra took a mouthful of the sundae. "I don't like who I am."

"Then change who you are."

"Truth is, I know I'm not who my father wants me to be." Tears came to her eyes. "But if I'm not her, then he'll be disappointed and maybe not love me when he finds out who I really am."

"If he doesn't love who you really are," Carlisle said, "then he doesn't really love you."

The roar of the dirt bike interrupted their conversation, along with the conversations of the other hotel guests in the café.

David jumped off the bike and ran across the outdoor café. "Carlisle! Kassandra! We need to get you inside!"

Seeing the uniformed police chief, guests scattered. They didn't know what was happening, but they sensed that they didn't want to be outside if the chief of police was saying to go indoors.

Not wanting to waste any precious time, Mac laid the bike down on its side and directed the patrons into the café. Off in the distance, he could hear Gnarly barking and several officers yelling. "I hear him! He went that way!"

Carlisle sprung out of her seat at the same time that a shot rang out from the tree line up the mountain. With a shriek, Kassandra grabbed her left arm and fell out of her chair.

"Kassie!" Carlisle dropped down to the deck and covered her friend with her body.

"What happened?" Kassandra cried.

"Stay down!" David ordered them while pulling the table over onto its side to provide them with cover. His gun drawn, he scoured the tree line for Rudy Crowe while radioing for EMTs and back-up.

Near the edge of the deck, Mac took cover behind a Jeep and gripped his injured shoulder. His teeth chattered from the pain brought on by the jarring ride down the mountain on the dirt bike. The pain from his sprained right wrist shot all the way up to his shoulder and then from his shoulder down to his wrist.

Firing his gun with his right hand would be impossible. Hoping the situation would not come down to a shoot out, Mac transferred his gun to his left hand.

Gnarly's barking had stopped.

"Do you see him?" David called to Mac.

Mac shook his head. He couldn't see any movement in the trees and Gnarly was quiet. Experience had told him that when Gnarly was quiet, be afraid. Be very afraid.

"Chief," Fletcher called David on his radio. "We lost Gnarly."

Thinking the officer was telling them that Gnarly was a victim of the shooter, David responded with clinched jaws. "What do you mean you lost Gnarly?"

"We can't find him. He was right up ahead of us— barking all the way. Then, the barking stopped, and now we don't know where he is."

"Find the shooter," David said. "He's somewhere up in those woods. We have a woman down and as long as we don't know where he is, we can't move."

Behind him, Carlisle had taken off her top to make a bandage for Kassandra's arm. She displayed no modesty about wearing nothing more than a sports bra and a pair of running shorts.

"How is she?" David asked.

"She'll live," Carlisle said with a wink. "I'm getting control of the bleeding. You saved my life. If I hadn't moved, then that bullet would have gone through me. I owe you."

"You don't owe me anything."

The sound of sirens coming in from every direction prompted a gunshot from the woods that struck the Jeep behind which Mac was hiding.

Before Mac could return fire, a snarling bark came from the woods followed by a series of gunshots and a scream. Raising his head from where he was hiding, Mac watched the bushes and small trees tumble away while the two bodies rolled straight down the hillside. The viciousness of Gnarly's barks and growls was matched by the man's pleading cries for help.

The rolling bodies picked up speed down the steep hill until they became airborne over the last leg of the trail to land on the roadside next to the café. As luck would have it, Gnarly landed on top of Rudy. The dog's fangs were poised to finish him off.

David stood guard over Kassandra and Carlisle while Mac rushed out from behind the Jeep to take possession of Rudy Crowe's gun, which he had seen slide down the hillside before they were propelled over the embankment. Tucking it into his waistband, Mac ran over to where Gnarly had Rudy Crowe pinned on his back. Rudy was afraid to move for fear of his throat being punctured by one of the great dog's fangs.

Hector and the rest of the officers spilled in from the woods to join him.

"We found Gnarly," Officer Fletcher announced as if it was news.

"How about that?" Mac called Gnarly to his side. While he was released from holding the shooter, Gnarly refused to back down completely until Officer Fletcher had handcuffed him.

The Inn's medical Jeep, which was used to help skiers or hikers injured on the trail sped up to the dock. The hotel nurse jumped out to run over to where Carlisle and David were tending to Kassandra's wound.

"EMTs are on the way," Hector reported to Mac.

Upon seeing Carlisle, wearing David's shirt over her sports bra, coming toward them, Rudy raged while struggling against his handcuffs, "You're the one who should be dead! Ashton never did anything to anyone. All she wanted to do was become a doctor and save lives like her parents and grand-father and you killed her!"

"You're right," Carlisle replied. "I've been saying the same thing to myself every day for the last five years."

"Get him out of here," David ordered Officer Fletcher.

The security patrol's Jeep, loaded up with Rudy Crowe and three Spencer Police officers, left as the EMT van and ambulance arrived to tend to Kassandra Van Dyke.

Upon hearing the news of his daughter's shooting, Vincent Van Dyke rushed down with a camera crew to capture every moment for potential viewers of the reality show he still had hopes of selling.

"Told you that you took off your sling and wrist brace too soon." David stepped over to where Mac was clutching his arm close to his side, while examining a small cheeseburger in his left hand.

"Explain this to me." Mac held up the sandwich for David to see. "I solved the case and all I get is this piece of overcooked meat."

Down at his feet, David saw that Gnarly was attacking a foot long steak and cheese submarine sandwich that the café manager had prepared specifically for the hero of the moment for saving the day by capturing the bad guy.

Mac tossed the cheeseburger down onto Gnarly's plate. "It's not fair."

"I think it's because he's cuter than you," David said.

"I own this place," Mac pointed out.

"You're only cranky because your arm and shoulder hurts," David said. "Put the sling and brace back on and you'll feel better."

"I don't want to," Mac said, "and Gnarly is not cuter than I am."

"How's this being bull-headed working for you, Mac?" David asked.

As if to add his voice to the discussion, Gnarly uttered a bark.

"Keep it up and I'll dislocate your shoulder," Mac replied to Gnarly. "You're the one who did this to me."

With a whine, Gnarly picked up the overcooked cheeseburger in his mouth and held it up to Mac.

EPILOGUE

McHenry Airport: One Week Later

"You didn't have to come along," David told Mac when he pulled the police cruiser up in front of the small airport's terminal.

Glancing back at Gnarly in the back seat, Mac laughed. "What was I supposed to do? Jump out? The call came in while we were on our way to the lawyer's office."

"Well, this will only take a few minutes," David opened the driver's side door. In the rearview mirror, he saw a white stretch limousine pull up behind his police cruiser.

Mac took his cell phone out of the case. "I'll try to push the closing for your house back an hour."

"It isn't like you're going to back out on our deal if I don't sign over the deed today." After sliding out of his seat, David turned around to watch Randolph York get out of the back of the limousine. With pride, he reached out his hand to help Betty, the Spencer Inn's registration manager, climb out onto the curb. On the other side, Brian Gallagher took Betty's granddaughter Caleigh into one arm while reaching out a hand to help Savannah. All three ladies were dressed in stunning summer dresses.

Seeing Mac, Betty waved before rushing up to the cruiser the throw her arms around him in a warm hug. "Mac! I am so glad to see you. I wanted so much to say goodbye to you."

"Goodbye?" Mac asked, "Where are you going?"

"Hawaii!" she gushed. "Randolph popped the question! We're leaving right now!"

"I guess congratulations are in order." Mac shook Randolph's hand.

"Finding Brian made me take a long hard look at my life," Randolph York said. "I've been fearless when it comes to business but, ever since Lindsey's mother, I've been a coward when it comes to love. Seeing love bloom between him and Savannah gave me the shot of courage I needed." He smiled at where Brian was holding Caleigh who was alternating between petting Gnarly and shrieking with delight.

Mac asked Betty, "Does this mean we lost our registration desk manager right at the launch of our summer season?"

"Like I was going to give Randolph half-a-chance to change his mind?" Betty couldn't stop smiling.

Randolph took her into a bear hug. "No chance of that happening, Sweet Pea. If you had any idea how many years I have been waiting for the opportunity to kiss that face."

"Kiss away." With her arms around Randolph's neck, Betty told Mac, "Jeff was so happy when I put in my notice and told him Randolph and I were getting married. He cried."

"Cried?" David asked.

"Tears of joy ran down his face he was so happy for me."

"Did Savannah put in her notice, too?" Mac asked.

"Not yet," Savannah said. "We're just going away for a long weekend to see Randolph and Mom get married. Then we'll be back. I won't be leaving until the end of the summer when Brian is done with his internship."

"Then she and Caleigh will be going back to Chicago with me," Brian said. "With luck, we can get Savannah enrolled at the University of Chicago."

"And I will be a full time grandmother!" As if to enforce her role, Betty scooped up Caleigh from where she was hugging Gnarly, whose ears fell to the side with disappointment.

"Come along, family!" Randolph York called out like a drill sergeant to his platoon. "We have a plane to catch and a new life to begin."

With the chauffeur and Brian wheeling a cart filled with luggage, they hurried through the terminal and went out the other side to where Randolph York's private jet waited to whisk them all away.

"Jeff cried tears of joy, huh?" David muttered.

"I think we should change our plan for having lunch at the Spencer Inn," Mac said.

"Yeah, I'm feeling more like pizza and beer right now." David went up to the front door.

"Me, too."

A small airport with only one gate for charter flights, it was easy for them to find their suspects huddled together in the lounge drinking coffee.

"Nice day for flying out of the country," David told Carlisle Green, A.J. Wagner, Corey Haim, and Kassandra Van Dyke.

"Lovely day, David." Carlisle knelt down to pet Gnarly who greeted her with a kiss.

Mac took note of the bandage wrapped around Kassandra's arm. "How's your arm?"

"It's perfectly fine," Kassandra replied. "Thank you for asking." She had taken to her new life like a fish to water. The false eye lashes were gone, as was most of her makeup. The fancy blonde hairdo had been replaced with a ponytail.

Instead of a designer ensemble, she was clad in summer capris and a tank top. She had paired her coffee with a donut covered with a thick chocolate glaze.

"You came to see us off, Chief?" Corey Haim asked.

"Actually," David said with a chuckle, "I'm here on official business."' He turned to Kassandra. "Your father has reported you as being kidnapped."

Kassandra burst into a fit of giggles. Her new friends joined in.

"Since you're over eighteen," David said, "you're free to go wherever you want."

"And where I want to go is Africa." With a sense of purpose, she took a big bite from her donut. "I'm going to build a school and a clinic and pet a leopard." She held up her hand to show them four fingernails with chipped polish and one broken down to the quick. "Look, I broke my first fingernail yesterday. Isn't it great?" She was on a roll. "And I had chocolate cheesecake for dessert last night, plus I haven't done my sit ups in four days."

"I guess that means you're going voluntarily," David said.

"What do you want us to tell your father, Kassandra?" Mac asked her.

"That I love him the way he is," she said, "and if he loves me, then he'll love me for who I really am." With a shrug of her shoulders, she added, "Even if I went back, the reality show is dead anyway. Rock Sinclair signed over his production company to Riva and she has no interest in reality shows. She wants to do real hard hitting programs of substance geared toward helping middle-aged women living independent lives."

Blinking, Mac shook his head as if to clear his hearing. "Rock Sinclair signed over his production company?"

Kassandra nodded her head. "Yeah, Samuel Nash told me yesterday. I had run into him in the lobby at the Inn when he was checking out. Riva had Rock served with divorce papers and she had something on him … Nash said something about her getting her hands on a video or something—"

"Maybe a video of Rock cheating on his wife with Jasmine," Corey suggested.

Aware of Rock Sinclair's fear of his impotency being made public, Mac shot David a knowing glance.

"I don't know what she got," Kassandra said with a slight shake of her head, "but I'll bet anything Nash got it for her, because he seemed very pleased with himself—more pleased than usual when he was bragging to me about it. Whatever was on that video must have been bad because when Riva used the words 'YouTube,' Rock caved in and gave her everything she wanted." She giggled before adding, "And Samuel Nash has cushy job as producer working for her."

"Sounds like Riva decided to stop being mad," David said, "and to start getting even."

"My marriage is going to be nothing like theirs," Corey said.

"Corey's fiancée is joining us at Dulles," Carlisle said. "She's a teacher and she's going to help us to set up the school."

"In return, Carlisle is going to help fund a clinic in our hometown," Corey said.

"Who knows," A.J. said, "I might decide to stay on in Africa to run their clinic. It's a little warmer than Alaska but—" he cast a glance in Kassandra's direction, "I'm growing kind of fond of sunny weather."

"And I'm going to learn to drive a bobcat," Kassandra said.

"You're not talking about the animal, are you?" David asked.

"No, silly!" Kassandra said. "The big piece of construction equipment. Carlisle is going to teach me. She promised."

Seeing the pilot coming inside, the group gathered up their carry-on luggage.

"We got some great sending off news already," A.J. said while offering Kassandra her bag. "The medical examiner found the digitalis in my father's remains. Rachel has agreed to testify against her mother and Maryland is indicting Dr. Elizabeth Breckenridge for his murder."

"That is great news," Mac said.

Corey Haim wasn't so optimistic. "But the prosecutors warned us that Breckenridge's lawyers are already motioning to suppress the recording that the feds got of her admitting to killing Dr. Wagner. If the judge agrees, all the prosecutors will have is evidence that he was murdered and Rachel's testimony claiming it was her mother."

Mac could see how it would play out. "The defense will claim Rachel is lying because she has issues with her mother. Without any proof of Breckenridge stealing Dr. Piedmont's research, the jury won't see any reason for her to kill him."

The pilot announced in a loud voice, "All aboard."

"I only wish we could have found proof that Dr. Breckenridge had stolen Dr. Piedmont's research and book." A.J. picked up his backpack and slung it across his shoulders. "He was such a great man and to have his whole life's work stolen like that ..."

"The truth will come out." After giving Gnarly one final kiss on his snout, Carlisle stood up. "It always does. Look at Ashton's murder. Five years had passed, but with patience, the truth did come out after all."

"Not without a little push," Mac said. "If it wasn't for your phone call and note to pique my curiosity, I probably wouldn't have been intrigued enough to stick my nose into Ashton's disappearance."

"What phone call are you talking about?" Puzzled, Carlisle squinted at Mac with her head cocked. "I left a note at the Spencer Inn for you, but ..."

"To my cell phone," Mac chuckled. "Asking for Robin. You said you were Ashton."

"I didn't call your cell," she said. "I don't even know your number."

"Then who was it that called my phone asking for Robin?" Mac murmured.

"I don't believe it." David rubbed the back of his neck. "You let us get dragged into a whole murder case because of a wrong number?"

"I'll give you a thousand dollars not to tell Archie," Mac said.

❧ ❧ ❧

"Do you feel rich?" Mac held the front door open for David to pass through into the Spencer Manor's foyer. The smell of freshly baked cookies greeted his nostrils.

As if he feared losing his seat, Gnarly raced in ahead of them to jump up onto the loveseat, which was his chair.

"Only temporarily," David answered Mac. "All of that money you paid for my house will be gone as soon as Chelsea and I agree on a new home. But it will make a nice down payment."

"Be optimistic."

"Everything we like is out of our price range." In the living room, David paused to study a thick brown envelope with a certified mail receipt on it. It was addressed to him. "What's this?"

"I'm wondering the same thing." Chelsea had come in from the kitchen in time to hear David's question.

Carrying a plate of chocolate chip cookies, still hot from the oven, Archie came in behind them. "I told her to go ahead and open it, but she refused." In a mocking tone, she said, "It's a federal offense to open someone else's mail."

Unable to wait any longer, Chelsea picked up the package and thrust it out to David. As if he feared it was a bomb, David took it from her and studied the return address. It was from a lawyer's office located on Wall Street in New York City.

"What did you do?" Mac asked in an ominous tone.

Archie slapped Gnarly's snout when he moved in on the cookies. "We're dying here."

David ripped open the end of the envelope and extracted two envelopes from inside. One was an official looking letter with David's full name typed on the front. The other envelope resembled a greeting card. Seeing that it was addressed to both of them, Chelsea snatched the greeting card and ripped it open while David read the letter.

"What is this?" David asked Mac who was reading the letter over his shoulder. Unsure if he had skimmed the contents correctly, David blinked to read it again.

"This has to be a joke," Mac murmured.

Meanwhile, Chelsea let out a whoop that caused Molly to jump up onto the loveseat to hide behind Gnarly.

"What is it?" Archie grabbed the sheet of paper that Chelsea had found tucked inside the engagement card. Reading the top line, she gasped. "A deed to a *house?*"

"Then it is true?" David asked.

"But I just bought your house so that you could buy a house." Mac took the letter from David and read through it a third time.

"Who gives someone a house for an engagement gift?" Archie asked.

"Carlisle Green," Mac said. "She's been liquidating her estate of holdings that she has no use for to concentrate on her mission work and was planning to sell the Green house on the lake. When she heard about your engagement and for your kindness and for saving her life, she decided that rather than sell it, she would sign it over to you two as an engagement gift."

"So this deed is not a joke?" Archie waved the sheet of paper.

"I don't think so."

Chelsea threw her arms around David. "Our first wedding present." She trembled with excitement. "I have never been inside that house before. I've only driven past it."

"Her card says the keys are in the milk box next to the back door," Archie said. "We may have to fight the squirrels for them."

"But I just bought your house so …" Mac mumbled.

David kissed Chelsea on the lips. "Let's go see our new home."

"Actually, it's pretty old," Mac said. "Didn't you say it was about fifty years old, David?"

"Technicalities." Archie ushered Gnarly and Molly out the door.

❧ ❧ ❧

Chelsea squealed with delight when David pulled his police cruiser into the driveway. Before leaving, Carlisle had made short work of the gardening and trimming of the overgrown trees. Upon climbing out of the cruiser and rushing up to the front door, she gushed. "I love it! It's perfect." She threw open the milk box to extract the keys. Her hands shaking with excitement, she had trouble unlocking the door until David took the keys from her to work the decades old lock.

"We're going to need to do some updating," he said. "Luckily, we have the money that Mac paid for my old place. That will bring this place into the twenty-first century."

"I like the rustic décor." Chelsea took in a deep breath at the sight of circular layout of the interior. From every angle there was a view of the lake and woods surrounding the house.

"We're going to need to have it inspected," David said. "I don't know about the plumbing—"

"I love it!" Chelsea announced with a clap of her hands.

Like a guide giving a tour, Gnarly shepherded Molly around her new home. In her rush to get back to Africa, Carlisle had left the furniture and wall hangings.

"I always did love this house," David said, "but I never in my wildest dreams thought I would end up owning it."

"The lawyer's letter said you got the house and all of its contents." Mac took note of a box with a hodge podge of items resting in the middle of the dining room table.

"We can have a yard sale," Chelsea said. "It will be fun."

"Yay," David said sarcastically.

Mac rummaged through the box. An external hard drive rested on top of the rest of the items that looked like knick knacks. A yellow stickie was attached to the side of the hard drive.

"The Greens were billionaires," Archie said. "I would not sell anything without having it appraised first. There's no telling what Carlisle left behind."

Mac read the note written in Carlisle's hand writing: "Guest Room. Bogie said he could read this to see what was on it. Don't know whose it is or where it came from."

"Hey, Archie," Mac asked, "do you have your tablet?"

"Why?"

"Carlisle left a hard drive here that she says was in the guest room. She doesn't know where it came from or what's on it."

Archie took her tablet from her purse. "Are there any cords for me to hook it up?"

Saying that he had some cords in his cruiser, David hurried outside.

"What are you thinking?" Archie examined the hard drive.

"Rachel Breckenridge said that Ashton had hardcopies of her grandfather's book and his research," Mac said.

"She also said Dr. Breckenridge shredded and burned them," Archie said.

"But think about it," Mac said. "Ashton was a young woman. Younger than you."

"Your point?" Archie asked with a warning tone.

"Where did those hard copies originate?" Mac held up the external drive. "Digitally?"

"But why would that external hard drive be here at Carlisle's house instead of the Piedmont house?" Chelsea asked.

Having rushed back inside with a power cord and a USB cord, David answered, "If Ashton was smart, she'd hide that evidence where Dr. Breckenridge would never think of looking for it."

"Like her good friend's house which was right next door where she could easily access it." Archie attached the cords to the hard drive.

Mac plugged the power cord into the outlet while Archie attached the USB cord to her tablet. The hard drive powered on. Archie flipped though the folders until she located the drive. Upon opening the folder, she said, "These are old files that were created years ago in an old program."

"How old?" Mac asked.

"According to the date, created late 1990's."

"Can you convert them?" Chelsea asked.

"There's a notepad file here that I think I can open." Archie clicked on the file. While the tablet worked with the file, she held up both hands to show her fingers crossed.

"Watch it be a cookbook," David muttered.

"Let's be optimistic," Mac said.

"It's open!" Archie held out the table for them all to see. "It's a metadata file containing the front pages for what appears to be a book."

Mac read the information written in plain sans-serif text.

Quantitative Medical Research of Three-Dimensional Printing for Organ Transplant and Prosthetic Limb Replacement

By
Dr. Ross Piedmont, MD
April 11, 2003

"He wrote this years before Dr. Breckenridge published it," Archie said. "Once the medical community sees all this, she'll be revealed for the thief, fraud, and killer that she is. She'll be ruined."

"Which will prove motive for killing Dr. Howard Wagner, A.J.'s father," Chelsea said. "Between this and her daughter testifying against her, she'll be convicted for sure."

"Looks like your new home is lucky," Mac told David and Chelsea.

"I'm liking it so far." Chelsea wrapped her arms around David and kissed him on the lips.

"I love this kitchen." Setting the tablet aside, Archie went into the kitchen to examine the granite countertops.

"We should go take a look at the pipes to see exactly how bad the plumbing is," David told Mac.

"I wonder what else Carlisle left behind." Chelsea reached into the box and let out a high pitched laugh that caused everyone to turn around. Her pale face bright pink, she held up a red thong. "Look at this! Why on earth would she leave this for us?"

David felt his cheeks turn as red as the undergarment that Chelsea was waving about. *She lied. She did remember that night—right down to the red thong she was wearing.*

Joining in the laughter, Archie took the thong and held up to show them the broken strap. "Someone ripped this right off her body. No one was kidding when they said Carlisle was a bad girl."

"David, look at you," Chelsea giggled. "You're blushing."

With a glance over at Mac, David said, "Just trying not to look over my shoulder to the past while moving toward the future."

On their way out the door, Mac whispered into David's ear, "Pray that while you're looking forward to the future that your past doesn't come up to bite you in the butt."

The End

ABOUT THE AUTHOR

Lauren Carr

Lauren Carr is the international best-selling author of the Mac Faraday Mysteries, which takes place in Deep Creek Lake, Maryland. *Open Season for Murder* is the tenth installment in the Mac Faraday Mystery series.

In addition to her series set on Deep Creek Lake, Lauren Carr has also written the Lovers in Crime Mysteries, which features prosecutor Joshua Thornton with homicide detective Cameron Gates, who were introduced in *Shades of Murder*, the third book in the Mac Faraday Mysteries. They also make an appearance in *The Lady Who Cried Murder*.

Three Days to Forever introduced Lauren Carr's latest series detectives, Murphy Thornton and Jessica Faraday in the Thorny Rose Mysteries. Look for *Kill and Run*, the first installment in this series, to be reelased September 1, 2015.

The owner of Acorn Book Services, Lauren is also a publishing manager, consultant, editor, cover and layout designer, and marketing agent for independent authors. Visit Acorn Book Services' website for more information.

Lauren is a popular speaker who has made appearances at schools, youth groups, and on author panels at conventions. She also passes on what she has learned in her years of writing and publishing by conducting workshops and teaching in community education classes.

She lives with her husband, son, and three dogs on a mountain in Harpers Ferry, WV.

Visit Lauren Carr's website at www.mysterylady.net to learn more about Lauren and her upcoming mysteries.

Check Out
Lauren Carr's Mysteries!
Order! Order!

All of Lauren Carr's books are stand alone. However for those readers wanting to start at the beginning, here is the list of Lauren Carr's mysteries. The number next to the book title is the actual order in which the book was released.

Joshua Thornton Mysteries:

Fans of the *Lovers in Crime Mysteries* may wish to read these two books which feature Joshua Thornton years before meeting Detective Cameron Gates. Also in these mysteries, readers will meet Joshua Thornton's five children before they have flown the nest.

1) A Small Case of Murder
2) A Reunion to Die For

Mac Faraday Mysteries

3) It's Murder, My Son
4) Old Loves Die Hard
5) Shades of Murder (introduces the Lovers in Crime: Joshua Thornton & Cameron Gates)
7) Blast from the Past
8) The Murders at Astaire Castle
9) The Lady Who Cried Murder (The Lovers in Crime make a guest appearance in this Mac Faraday Mystery)
10) Twelve to Murder
12) A Wedding and a Killing
13) Three Days to Forever
14) Open Season for Murder (June 2015)

Lovers in Crime Mysteries

6) Dead on Ice
11) Real Murder

Thorny Rose Mystery

15) Pull Over for Murder (September 4, 2015) (featuring the Lovers in Crime in Lauren Carr's latest series)

KILL AND RUN

A Thorny Rose Mystery

Five women of various ages and backgrounds are found brutally murdered in a townhome outside Washington, DC. Among the many questions surrounding the massacre is what had brought these apparent strangers together to be killed.

Taking on his first official murder case, Lieutenant Murphy Thornton, USN, believes that if he can uncover the thread between the victims, then he can not only find out why they were killed, but who is behind their horrible deaths.

The investigation takes an unexpected turn when Murphy discovers that one of the victims has a connection to the late husband of his stepmother, Homicide Detective Cameron Gates.

When the FBI reveals that a recently arrested hit man has confessed to killing her husband, Cameron sets out for Washington to learn the truth about why someone would put out a contract on a Pennsylvania State trooper working a night shift on the turnpike.

In this first installment of the Thorny Rose Mysteries, the Lovers in Crime join newlyweds Murphy and Jessica Faraday to sift through the a web of lies and cover-ups. Together, can the Lovers in Crime and detectives of the Thorny Rose uncover the truth without falling victim to a ruthless killer bent on ambition?

Coming September 4, 2015!

(former working title *'Til Murder Do We Part*)